THE
DEADLY
KISS-OFF

THE
DEADLY
KISS-OFF

PAUL DI FILIPPO

**BLACK
STONE**
PUBLISHING

Copyright © 2019 by Paul Di Filippo

Published in 2019 by Blackstone Publishing

Cover design by Djamika Smith

Book design by Kathryn Galloway English

Printed in the United States of America

First edition: 2019

ISBN 978-1-5384-5029-1

Fiction / Thrillers / Suspense

1 3 5 7 9 10 8 6 4 2

CIP data for this book is available
from the Library of Congress

Blackstone Publishing

31 Mistletoe Rd.

Ashland, OR 97520

www.BlackstonePublishing.com

To Deborah, who inspires noirish thoughts.
And to my siblings, Cathy, Frank, and Bob,
who form a whole mob on their own.

PROLOGUE

The fake bills turned up in my wallet the morning after an extended debauch.

Counting with bleary eyes the contents of my nice Burberry leather bifold (a present from my girl), I immediately spotted the bogus bills, which were of a quality achievable, perhaps, by a couple of nine-year-olds using a process of Silly Putty color transfers. I spat out a few choice phrases, then replayed the previous evening in my head.

Feeling lonely with my woman away, I had decided to treat myself to a solo night on the town. With over five hundred thousand dollars to my name—not quite as much as I once dreamed of having, but not chicken feed, either—I could afford it.

To avoid leaving a potentially embarrassing credit card trail that I might have to explain later, I took out a wad of cash from the bank—mostly hundreds. So far, so legit. No fakes likely from that respectable source.

My first stop after the bank had been my favorite restaurant, Jerusalem & Galilee, a high-tone seafood place. There I disbursed only cash—slightly over three hundred with tip, for some Malpeque oysters, a bottle of Bollinger La Grande Année Brut, and a large trencher of jumbo lump crab cakes—and did not receive any bills back. Likewise for the strip club I visited next, Captains Curvaceous, where the interior decor resembled a Sponge Bob–themed stage set intended to background the Adult Video Awards. So it had to be my next and last stop where I was slipped the bad bills. And it made sense.

Around 2:00 a.m., after several expensive alcohol-abetted lap dances with two ladies named Perfidia and Celestina had left me feeling moderately degenerate but hormonally unsatisfied, I had been pretty woozy but not ready to call it an evening. So I headed to an exclusive shot house I knew from my days as a louche young lawyer.

The after-hours place was still there, behind the ordinary facade of a building that might have been a showroom for vinyl replacement windows. I gained entrance with a fifty-dollar solicitation to compensate for not being known to the doorman.

Inside, I discovered that the establishment had expanded from mere illegal bar service, adding gambling tables, complete with chips and croupiers. I bought a stack, got busy at the roulette wheel, and somehow came out a thousand dollars ahead. I cashed out and hailed a ride home.

The bad Benjamins had to be part of my winnings.

The night of the day I discovered my loss, I went back to the blind pig and buttonholed the manager, a slim young white guy with bad skin, dressed in a Gucci tracksuit. The shaved sides of his head contrasted with a shock of blond hair above that would have done credit to a North Korean dictator. About the time I was in prison, he was no doubt mourning the dissolution of the Beastie Boys while doodling heavy-metal insignia during study hall.

We conducted our conversation in a secluded anteroom, out of the customers' earshot.

"I need to see the owner."

The kid's voice was way too high and creaky to deliver the requisite tone of managerial competence and authority. "What for?"

"Last night, you guys paid me part of my winnings with a couple of fake hundreds."

His eyes narrowed. "Oh, yeah? Who says?"

This sort of stupid, mulish hostility was no way to run a customer-service window.

"If you had anything between those ears to stop my words from going unimpeded from one side to the other, you'd know *I* just said it. Now, let me see your boss."

"All right, smart-ass, you just wait here."

He left and returned with two guys in jeans and hoodies who could have been cast as Russian weightlifters from some future cyborg Olympics. They quickly bookended me, marched me into a back office notable for its drab utility, and took up positions on either side of the closed door.

Behind a beat-up gray-green Steelcase desk adorned with a condensation-flecked Big Gulp cup sat a figure I recognized: Vincent "Weeping Ear" Santo.

Santo, who looked like a dissolute, boozy Friar Tuck in a frowsy off-the-rack suit, was the acknowledged head mobster of our fair city. Hailed before judges and juries at least a score of times

during his career, he had always managed to beat all charges—
often thanks to the convenient disappearance or amnesia or stam-
mering recantation by key witnesses.

Suddenly, being compensated for my two-hundred-dollar
loss did not seem so vitally important to me. But it was too late
simply to back out.

Santo eyed me like a TSA worker who has spotted an ISIS
loyalty card in someone's plastic tray of surrendered possessions.
Then he said, "You know who I am?"

Luckily, I knew that Santo did not enjoy being addressed by
his abjured nickname (derived from a childhood ailment that had
fostered an attitude of brutal reprisal against all mockers, real or
imagined). Nor did he care for "Vincent" or "Vince" or "Vinny."

"You're Vin Santo."

"Very knowledgeable. Nice, very nice. And I know who you
are. You're Glen McClinton."

That surprised me. "Right. But how …?"

"How is easy. Your face was plastered everywhere, thanks to
your recent little crazy-ass dustup. But you should be asking *why*."

"Why you bothered to even remember my name?"

"Exactly. So I will tell you. It is because you took down
Barnaby Nancarrow, who was getting to be like a thorn, or even a
small, dirty, filed-down-toothbrush-handle shiv, in my side, tres-
passing on many of my trademark ventures."

Barnaby Nancarrow was the sleazy real estate guy who had
been the target of a scam that three coconspirators and I had
run—a deal we dubbed "the Big Get-Even." We came out of it
not with the premium prize we had aimed for, but with some
consolation dough of a million apiece—now reduced by taxes and
expenses to my current assets.

"That we did," I said. "I don't think he will see a parole board for about twenty years, minimum."

Santo canted his large butt to one side, to dig in the pant pocket of the upraised hip. He withdrew a roll of greenbacks that would have sent a lesser man to the chiropractor.

"You did me a real solid there, Glen, and I am going to show my appreciation. Now, my manager tells me you somehow left here yesterday with some bogus dough. I am truly sorry for that. We try not to burden our good local customers with such trash. The bad paper's supposed to be reserved strictly for obnoxious hicks from out of town. But nobody here knew your face. So, what was it? Two hundred?"

I nodded, and Santo peeled off two C-notes.

"Okay, here's what you won, fair and square. And just to show my thanks for the Nancarrow thing, here's a little more."

The lagniappe proved to be an additional *hundred* Benjamins, counted out with ceremonial panache.

I took the ten grand very tentatively, showing enough decorum not to recount or inspect it for authenticity before slipping it into my billfold, whose superior Burberry construction somehow accommodated the mass of currency without splitting apart. I managed to keep my voice from quavering excessively.

"Thank you … very much, Vin. Not necessary, but much appreciated all the same."

Santo had repocketed his roll, which seemed hardly diminished. "No problem. I like your moves. You were pretty ballsy barging in here. So anyhow, if you ever come up with any new scheme that you need a hand with, or which I might could maybe bankroll, keep me in mind."

"I certainly will, Vin. But I have to tell you now, I am pretty much done with that kind of thing."

Santo lifted his Big Gulp and slurped down about a pint before unlipping the large-bore straw.

"Kid, if I had a blow job for every time I heard that bullshit about going straight, my dick would be worn down to a pushpin."

PART ONE

1

Eight months after talking to Vin Santo, I finally came to the realization that the mobster had pegged me with complete accuracy. I missed the criminal life.

Not that I was planning to pursue any illegal schemes—I had too much invested in my current innocent, respectable lifestyle. But I knew myself well enough to recognize the yearning.

And besides, I was starting to need more money.

My financial advisor was a guy I knew from my old days as a lawyer, before I got disbarred and sent to prison. Leo Geneva. Worked for a firm called Lightyear Financial Investments. A snappy dresser, he reminded me of a young and skinny Walter Matthau, only more lugubrious. That was fine. I wouldn't really want a grinning, insouciant playboy handling my money.

In his office, I got ready to hear some bad news I already suspected.

Geneva tapped out a little fandango on the keyboard of

his laptop, then shifted his gaze from the screen to me, his eyes hound-dog mournful.

"Glen, just a little over a year ago, you entrusted half a million dollars with me."

My partner in the elaborate con that produced this money had been Stan Hasso, a burly lowbrow giant composed of two parts unbridled id, one part unabashed fuck-you, and three parts irreverent self-regard. We had been hoping to get revenge on his former employer and also score five million apiece. But we gratefully accepted a tenth of that, since the deal also included going scot-free despite our many crimes.

"Yes, this is accurate."

"And today, despite a decent return on your investments, you have a little over two hundred and fifty K in your account."

I knew where the money had gone. Buying a decent condo in the trendy neighborhood of Dashwell Corners. Moderate living expenses. And investment in the new enterprise of my girlfriend, Nellie Firmino, a small Cape Verdean cyclone of energy, smarts, and beauty, herself a collateral bonus derived from our failed scam.

Nellie's business, Tartaruga Verde Importing, exuberantly conceived when we got our windfall, specialized in bringing to this country Cape Verdean gourmet items. Liftoff, still in progress, had sucked up a lot of funds.

I said, "I can't quit bankrolling Nellie, Leo. I want to see her succeed. And after what she went through with Stan and me, half that money is rightfully hers."

"I totally agree. All I'm saying is that you are going to need to replenish the coffers somehow or else adopt a less extravagant lifestyle."

"I know. But I don't exactly have a lot of prospects lined up.

Not much call for a defrocked lawyer who also recently made headlines in a shady deal that brought down a corrupt but respected citizen."

What I didn't mention to Leo Geneva was that my mind just wasn't inclined toward legitimate pursuits. I found myself yearning for some larger-than-life excitement. Maybe some of my feelings had to do with approaching forty. But the larcenous impulses that had sent me to prison in the first place, rekindled by Stan and his Big Get-Even plans, had not been extinguished, but only banked as smoldering embers. I yearned for some kind of nose-thumbing antisocial activity. And if it happened to be a scheme that might net me a big profit, so much the better.

Geneva chewed meditatively on a pencil, presumably a relic of his trade from predigital days. "Maybe you could go with Nellie to Cape Verde. Help her out. Use your brains, get things moving faster, cut down on the burn rate."

I had wanted to do some traveling with Nellie, for both pleasure and business, but the restrictive terms of my parole still had some months to run.

I nodded. "Let me see what I can do about that."

But I quickly found, on a nonscheduled visit, that my parole officer, Anton Paget—also Stan's PO—wasn't inclined to cut either of us any slack. Not an unreasonable position, considering all the lies we had told him to promote our scam.

"McClinton," said the squat, hard-nosed arbiter of my freedom, his favorite gaudy Hawaiian shirt belying his flinty soul, "you and Hasso severely disillusioned me. I thought I knew all the bat-shit ways that a pair of criminal morons could fuck me and themselves over. But you two mooks invented at least half a dozen new ones."

"You always advised me not to settle for less than I'm capable of, Anton."

He regarded me stonily for a moment, then said, "So we just had diametrically opposed ideas for the proper vector of your ambitions—that's what you're telling me?"

"Exactly."

"Glen, please get your ass the hell out of my office right now, and don't ever again, during the rest of your parole, give me occasion to see your face on the wrong side of the mug-shot camera. You can travel all you want in a few months, when you depart my tender ministrations."

"Will do."

As I turned to leave, Paget said, "You still hanging out with your lunkhead-in-crime?"

That question made me sad. I had wanted to keep up my dodgy friendship with Stan Hasso—and, of course, with his Junoesque squeeze, Sandralene. Both of them still had a large claim on my affections and trust. And the feelings seemed mutual.

But although they had hung around companionably for a little while after we all returned to the city from the rural locale of our crimes, eventually the bonds of our shared exploits began to fade. We discovered we actually had little in common that would keep us together—at least, under current circumstances.

I pondered memories of one of my last get-togethers with Stan.

That night, the big galoot had seemed unwontedly antsy and ill-at-ease in his own skin, unable to turn his hand to anything he cared about—an attitude utterly foreign to the cocksure, competent guy I had known. With his revenge accomplished and cash in his pockets, he should have been on top of the world. But his long life of crime—he had worked as an arsonist for hire, along with many other illicit sidelines—had not remotely prepared him for his newfound semirespectability.

"Glen, amigo," he told me that night after much boutique bourbon in a hipster bar, "this motherfucking civic-righteousness gig is going to kill me. I feel all the time like fucking Han Solo frozen in that black plastic shit."

"You'll settle into it, Stan. It'll seem like second nature before long."

"Is that supposed to make me feel better? Because that's exactly the goddamn outcome I'm dreading."

We had parted with a mutual promise to stay in touch. But over half a year had flitted by with no further get-togethers. I couldn't even be sure where Stan and Sandy were living these days, and that made me feel mournful and guilty.

But I put those emotions aside to focus on the relationship I was still building with Nellie. She came first. I was chafing at not being able to go with her on the upcoming journey to her ancestral islands on another buying mission. (It was during one such separation that I'd had my meeting with Vin Santo.) We always parted with genuine sadness, temporarily alleviated by toe-curling predeparture sex.

This time was no different. I saw Nellie off at the airport that Saturday in May around 10:00 a.m. and started the drive home. Just to kill time, I took an alternate route through the city.

At a red light, my eye fell on a flea market–cum–rummage sale set up in the vast weedy parking lot of a defunct strip mall. On a whim, I pulled over, parked, and ambled into the sprawl of booths and fast-food trucks.

And that's how I found Stan again.

2

Most of the grim sellers at the flea market looked about two steps away from bankruptcy, eviction, suicide, or selling a spare kidney. Plainly, the economic growth enjoyed by so many in this city, state, and nation had not trickled down to their level. Their rickety folding tables boasted a raggle-taggle miscellany of domestic tchotchkes, oily used-car parts, lawn ornaments, distressed vinyl records by performers no one had ever heard of, barely worn Kmart clothing, chipped coffee mugs with office-humor mottoes, cheap socks bundled three pairs for five dollars, and the like. Here and there, jewelers and potters and metalsmiths appeared to be hawking the very creations that had gotten them expelled from their various amateur handicraft associations. And the clientele looked to be of much the same socioeconomic stratum as the vendors.

Nonetheless, a certain Dickensian vibe of life enduring—of suffering partly alleviated by its being shared, and a determination to clutch vigorously at any lifeline that chance might provide—

prevailed among the crowd, and I found myself somehow spiritually uplifted. The life on display here brought my own petty discontentments into perspective.

It was almost lunchtime. I bought a chili dog and a lemonade from a cart—they were surprisingly fresh and tasty—and continued strolling along the canopied aisles.

Ahead loomed a larger-than-average display of better-than-average stuff: a solid wooden table covered with an attractive colorful cloth, atop which were carefully arranged ranks of new designer handbags: Coach, Louis Vuitton, Hermès, Givenchy, Prada, Marc Jacobs. Befitting their classy allure, the table was surrounded by customers admiring the wares and obscuring the vendor.

Still a bit baffled at seeing these luxury items here, I stepped up to the spread, thinking I might spot something that would appeal to Nellie—a gift to celebrate her eventual return. I eased through the pack and up to the edge of the table. A dove-gray Marc Jacobs saddlebag looked like Nellie's style. The price tag on it read thirty-five dollars—about one-tenth of what such a bag generally sold for.

The obvious answer to the riddle of this impossible price came to me perhaps more easily than to some: these items had fallen off the back of a truck and were as hot as the sidewalks in Phoenix on a climate-change August day. Still, a bargain was a bargain.

I reached down to pick up the bag and suddenly found my wrist clamped in a grip that would have saved Gwen Stacy from a broken neck.

"I can spot a goddamn shoplifter from a mile off!"

Immediate recognition of the voice's owner stopped me from trying to jerk my hand away. I felt a wave of nostalgia, guilt, fondness, and melancholy wash over me.

Stan Hasso had lost a fair amount of weight. Any slight gut or distributed flab that he once carried had been pared away by lean times. His favored gaudy look of hip-hop overlord, replete with gold chains and styling streetwear, had been replaced by plain jeans, an off-brand polo shirt, and no-name athletic shoes. His face featured some new worry lines and raccoon patches under the eyes. Only his familiar leering grin evoked the Stan of old, the bold fellow who had been able to conceive, inspire, and guide our shared scam.

Reacting to what they assumed was a genuine accusation, the crowd had ebbed from the table, no doubt wanting to be elsewhere if the cops were called. This unanticipated outcome of his prank compelled Stan to reassure his customers.

"Hey, people, don't run off! Just playing a joke on my buddy. He's really too straight to take an extra penny from the register cup. Glen, you glorious bastard, get back here!"

Released, I walked around to Stan's side of the table and was instantly enveloped in a familiar bear hug. I could only be glad he didn't lift me off my feet, as he had been wont to do when his emotions demanded such a gesture. He still smelled like too much body spray, and I would probably reek of it myself once he let me go.

He eventually did, and only then did I notice that Stan had a fellow vendor with him behind the table: an older woman with frazzled red hair that was a shade too vibrant to be believable as natural and wearing a tatty beige sweater despite the balmy spring weather. She looked as if she were saving every cent she might earn today for her next bottle of Night Train Express.

"Stan—" I began, but he interrupted.

"Alice, can you watch the table for a few minutes? Glen and I have a lot of catching up to do."

Alice agreed in a tobacco-cured voice. "Sure thing, Stan. Take a good, long break."

He looked at her admonishingly, as if he expected her to pocket more than her share of any sales, but then said, "Thanks. We won't be super long."

Stan guided me out into the aisle. I noticed he had a slight limp still, from when Nancarrow's goons had shot him in the knee.

"What say we grab us a beer? My treat!"

"Okay, Stan, I'd like that."

He led us to a beer seller who actually had frosty kegs on ice, not bottled stuff. An umbrella-shaded plastic picnic table held a young couple who were making goo-goo eyes at each other and nursing an inch of warm beer in their plastic cups—until Stan glared effectively at them, inspiring them to down their drinks and move along. Stan sidled onto a bench, and I sat opposite him.

"You're looking good, Glen boy. Slick and spick-and-span, without a single mussed hair. Well fed, no worries, and neat as a department store mannequin or a castrated show dog."

I felt hurt at Stan's assessment, maybe because it had some truth in it. I started to frame some suitable sharp comeback, but he beat me to it with an apology of sorts.

"Oh, Christ, this is not how I wanted our reunion to happen, man. You just took me by surprise. And I'm feeling kinda lousy about everything. I wanted us to hook up again when I was riding high. I was planning to call you once I got myself sorted out. But having you see me now, like this—it just plain sucks. Can I take back the bogus shit I just spouted about you? I'll eat my words. Whadda ya say?"

I was vindictive enough to let him stew for just a few seconds before I answered. He nervously sipped his beer.

"Stan, I don't think even you could shovel horseshit high enough to bury what we've got between us. I'm your friend, and you don't have to keep up any pretenses with me. I know we've been out of touch for nearly a year, but it wasn't because I didn't want to see you and Sandralene. It was just that I felt ... I felt your path was different from mine, and we weren't really connecting anymore. That's all. Anyhow, I'm here for you now. You want to tell me what's up?"

Stan fussed with his Solo cup, rotating it back and forth like an improvised fidget spinner. I drank a little of my own beer for something to do in the awkward pause. Children ran and shrieked while their parents shopped. Finally, he knocked back his whole drink, tossed the cup over his shoulder in the general direction of the trash barrel, and looked me straight in the eye with a fierce wounded pride.

"I'm fucking busted, and Sandy's left me."

3

Stan's confession sent my mind racing down two parallel tracks—a sensation a bit like trying to play high-stakes poker while doing a jigsaw puzzle depicting polar bears frolicking in a blizzard.

The first track: he had managed to blow through five hundred thousand dollars!

The second track: he had let Sandralene slip out of his life!

I couldn't decide which was the greater disaster. The impact of both together was obviously enormous—a truth I could see written on Stan's hangdog face and slumped stance.

Trying to focus on whichever dilemma was more important and possibly subject to remedy, I decided to concentrate on the money angle. Maybe that said something about my own messed-up priorities—that I valued money above relationships. Or maybe I just wasn't eager to wrap my mind around the thought of never seeing Sandralene again.

Stan had planted both palms on the tabletop and squared his

shoulders. The gesture was simultaneously confrontational and submissive, as if he were a student expecting to get rapped on the knuckles, but also a desperate suspect under interrogation, who might lash out at his tormentors. I knew I had to offer just the right response or risk pissing him off, making him feel even lousier, and driving him away again.

"So," I said, "I'll bet the begging phone calls from relatives have tapered off lately."

Truth be told, I never knew whether Stan had any relatives or, having them, stayed in touch. Once, he had jokingly mentioned a sister, only to deny her existence later. So I was taking a risk in bringing up the potentially fraught topic of family.

Luckily, my instincts were good. Stan's wry laugh told me I had hit just the right note.

"Yeah, you got that right. You see the same people going down that you saw going up. But on the way down, don't nobody want to even know your name."

"Where'd it all go, Stan? That is, if you don't mind telling me." I had notions of several hazardous alleys down which Stan's funds might have wandered, never to emerge. Gambling, drugs, women—the usual culprits. But I never could have guessed the real story.

"I tried to be a fucking angel."

"An angel?"

"Yeah, you know, it's what they call suckers who decide to invest in something. A whatchamacallit—a venture capitalist."

"You decided to become a venture capitalist?"

"Well, why the hell not? You don't think I'm smart enough? Only the people in your scene can do such things?"

"No, no, it's not that at all. It's just that sinking your money into some nebulous new enterprise requires due diligence, real expertise …"

"Hell, I investigated the crap outta this project, and it seemed like a sure winner. And I was eager to parlay my money into a few million. The dough we got from MGM for our land was chump change. A million dollars! Half of that left after taxes! And I had to pay out nearly seventy-five grand for my hospital stay. How's a guy supposed to set himself up for life on that pitiful amount?"

Stan's complaints echoed my own dissatisfaction with the consolation-prize money we had earned for all our illegal dealings, so I could hardly fault him for wanting to grow his assets.

"And it's all your fault anyhow. You introduced me to the guys who took me for a ride. My only satisfaction is that they got burned even worse than me."

"I did? When?"

"The four of us were eating at that fancy steak house you like, and they came over to our table."

Instantly I recalled the night. Chris Tabak and Jess Inkley ran Burning Chrome Ventures. I knew them from my lawyering days. They seemed barely to acknowledge Stan at the time, but their money radar must have gone off.

Another couple stopped at our table as if to sit down with their drinks, until Stan's fierce glare sent them scurrying.

"So you handed over every penny to them?"

Stan scowled. "A few thousand at a time, but yeah. You woulda done the same thing, damn it! This was gonna be a major, major operation, with mega returns. The company we invested in even had a licensed theme song."

"*A theme song?*"

"Yeah, a famous one. 'The Wreck of the *Edmund Fitzgerald.*'"

"Shouldn't the fact that their theme song was about a major disaster have clued you in to the inherently iffy prospects of whatever they intended?"

Stan tossed his hands skyward in exasperation. "Dude, you know my personal tastes in music run toward the blues. But that song is golden, Glen, golden. Chicks especially dig it. Makes them all weepy and ready to put out, moneywise or nookiewise. And chicks were our market."

"What was this enterprise intending to sell, exactly?"

"Called themselves Lake Superior Bijoux. They were going to market jewelry made from the shipwreck."

"They were going to scavenge metal and other materials from the bottom of Lake Superior, from a ship that is a sacred sunken graveyard, and turn it into necklaces and earrings?"

"And bracelets and brooches, too. And those big-ass things chicks wear sometimes on their collarbones and above their boobs, like Cleopatra."

"Pectorals."

"Huh?"

"That style of necklace is called a pectoral."

"Oh, right. I remember that word now from the prospectus."

I considered Stan's sad story. "Well, it's not the dumbest idea for a business that I ever heard. Close, but doesn't take the prize. Who can tell? It might even have succeeded. What happened?"

"It was the goddamn Canucks. After the LSB guys blew through all my dough and a couple of million more just in the setup stages, they ran smack into something called the Ontario Heritage Act. Turns out they couldn't get the salvage licenses on the wreck that they thought they could get. End of story."

"You have just learned the sad truth that not all criminals rob banks or set fire to buildings, Stan."

"Yeah, right, tell me about it! I can't prove anything, but I think half the money ended up safe in the pockets of the LSB guys. I know a boatload of creditors went begging. But wherever it went, I don't have any of it anymore. That's why you found me peddling pocketbooks in this shit-hole. Just trying to squeak by."

I brought up the second, perhaps more sensitive topic.

"And is that why Sandralene left you? Because you blew through all the money?"

"Hell no! That's something else altogether!"

4

Sandralene Parmalee was perhaps the only woman fitted to be Stan Hasso's mate. At least, the only suitable candidate I had ever met. Amazonian in her eye-popping endowments, she exhibited an unflappable, taciturn, yet openhearted temperament that camouflaged a quick and canny mind. She struck me as something of a hybrid of Gaia, a Zen roshi, and Little Annie Fanny. Desirous of all the good and deep and simple sensual pleasures, she sailed a straight course through storms of drama that would have capsized someone of lesser mettle. Pondering Stan without her, or her without Stan, was like contemplating a sky from which either the sun or the moon had been removed, leaving the remaining orb unbalanced and lonely.

Once during our previous time together, I had been blessed by all the gods to have an amorous encounter with her, during a particularly charged moment when that unforgettable Olympian experience was just the elixir to fortify me in the midst of our dangerous machinations. Stan's implicit collusion with our hooking up had indicated both the depth of his faith in Sandralene and his confidence that no one could ever take her away from him—and maybe also some slight regard for me.

While I tried to integrate her absence into my conception of Stan, the big fellow got up wordlessly to buy us each another beer. Around our table, beneath the fresh blue spring heavens, the noisy, desperate, accepting life of the junk swap went on in its immemorial fashion. I had a brief fantasy of being present at some analogous Mesopotamian bazaar thousands of years in the past.

Stan returned with our drinks, and I took a long gulp of mine.

"What drove Sandralene off, if it wasn't money problems?"

"Glen, my man, you keep making the same boneheaded assumption. Nothing drove her *off*. Something *pulled* her away. A little thing like me losing all our hard-earned cabbage wouldn't knock the props out from under Sandralene and me. Our happy love nest was still rocketing along on all eight cylinders, right up until she hadda go. It's what happened after that's disturbing and leaves me up in the air, like."

I couldn't help myself. "What kind of cozy love nest features an internal-combustion engine?"

"Jesus H. Mohammed! I forgot what an annoying nitpicking jerk you can be! No wonder we ain't got together for so long. How does Nellie stand living with you, anyhow?"

"Nellie and I are doing just fine," I said, instantly regretting how smug and superior that sounded. Well, the hell with it. I *was* proud of the loving relationship that Nellie and I had developed and nurtured since we met nearly a year and a half earlier, especially after it survived some essential-at-the-time lies on my part. "My only complaint is that having a girlfriend fifteen years younger than me is tiring work—in every way."

Stan must have been reading my mind a minute or so ago, as I reminisced about that unforgettable night with Sandralene. "Yeah, sure enough. All the more reason you need me back in your life. Seems to me there is some little imbalance in our foursome that needs to be put right."

Now it was my turn to glare, which only made Stan bellow out a laugh. "Okay, pull your horns back in! That skinny little Portagee girl of yours don't appeal to me. She's too juvenile and hyper. It'd be like trying to screw a young bobcat on a merry-go-round."

"That is an image I will now never be able to erase from my mind."

"My work here on Earth is done."

"If we're past all the boasting about whose woman is the better lay, let's get to the reason why Sandy's not here."

"Simple. She had to go home to help her mama."

Somehow, I had never conceived of Sandralene as having parents. I had always assumed she sprang full-grown from the brow of some deity like Robert Crumb, à la Devil Girl.

Stan continued. "Sandy's mother is named Lura. She lives all alone on the ancestral homestead. Sandy got word she was ailing, and took off to play nurse."

"Whereabouts?"

"Hedgesville, West Virginia. Population three hundred and sixteen, on those days when the bearded hillbillies aren't out in the woods tending their stills."

"C'mon, now. You ever visited there?"

"Never. And I was hoping to maintain that stellar record for the rest of my days—until one Caleb Stinchcombe showed up."

"Nice. What's his real name? Where'd he come from? The neighboring town of Hooterville?"

"Ol' Caleb and Sandralene were an item back in high school. And now that Sandy's returned to town, Caleb, who never left, has come sniffing around."

"And you know all this how, exactly?"

"Sandy's told me as much when she calls me up. Totally up front, like always. She doesn't boast or tease or play games—just gives me the news like she was reporting the most natural thing in the world, like whether it rained that day or not. You know her way of saying things flat out. But the very fact that she's not dismissing this jerk out of hand is making me think maybe his charm offensive is having an effect. I mean, me and Sandralene have been together for a long time now, like old marrieds. Maybe she's yearning for a taste of something different. Maybe this Caleb guy, despite having a name like a puller of goat teats, is all slick and charming. Oh, how the hell do I know what's going on down there! It's driving me nuts."

"Okay, big guy," I said, "just take a long, slow breath. Any shenanigans are probably just in your head. When Sandy comes home, you'll see it was all in your imagination."

"But that's another thing. She was supposed to come home three or four times already, and she keeps putting it off, saying her mama's had a relapse or she's got to oversee some house repairs. It's awful suspicious."

"Awfully suspicious, or maybe just the plain truth. Listen, the only way you're gonna satisfy yourself that everything's all right is to go down there and see. I assume you can take a few days off from this high-pressure job of selling stolen handbags."

Stan jumped to his feet. "Christ! How long we been gone?

Alice has probably given away the store. I gotta get back to the table, Glen. Come with me for a while, will ya? We gotta talk this out some more."

"Okay," I said. "I've got nothing on tap." I explained about Nellie being off on a buying trip in Cape Verde.

"Okay, we'll hang out after the market closes, just like two single guys. You can be my wingman. And listen, this job of mine is not as small potatoes as it looks. It's gonna lead to something bigger. That merchandise is not stolen."

"No? How can you sell it so cheap, then?"

Stan leaned across the plastic table, his beer breath a pungent fog. "They're fakes," he whispered.

5

As we trotted back to Stan's table to check in on Alice, I pondered Stan's revelation. Aside from those bogus C-notes foisted on me at Vin Santo's speakeasy, I had not had much firsthand experience with counterfeit goods. I knew that knockoffs were generally available across a broad spectrum of products. I recalled recent headlines about local cops breaking up a ring that sold fake Oakley sunglasses. My only other encounter with such stuff had been to buy a football jersey once from a vendor hanging around the fringes of the stadium parking lot. When I got it home, I noticed that the team's hometown was misspelled on the back. And the thing fell apart after two wash cycles.

Stan's line of fake pocketbooks might be constructed better than that, but I wasn't going to buy one for Nellie. She deserved the real deal.

At the table, the dowdy, abstracted woman named Alice sat fervidly smoking. The array of handbags now had a gap or three.

Stan spoke sternly. "Alice, did you sell anything?"

"Nuh-uh, Stan. Nobody bought anything."

He did not bother to contest Alice's statement or upbraid her, as if he knew that such tactics would be fruitless. Instead, he kicked the table leg. "God damn it! There's definitely a few items gone since we left, and she's probably got the bills stuffed down her frigging bra. Which is territory I'm not exploring."

"What's the story?" I said.

"Alice is Gunther's wife. He's the guy I work for. She's half nuts. Early dementia. Part of my job description is to take her off Gunther's hands while I'm here at the flea market, so he gets a few hours' relief. He doesn't give her any money, because she just spends it crazy or gives it away or loses it. So she's always looking to scam some. By the time I drive us back to Gunther's, she will have hidden the money somewhere, and I'll be on the hook for it. She's like some kind of goddamn magician when it comes to making cash disappear. One time, Gunther lost fifty bucks from around the house, and he found it six months later inside a bag of dry cat food."

While Stan itemized her peculiarities, Alice continued to smoke with zealous contentment, simply ignoring us as if we were discussing someone not present.

"Let me make up for the loss."

"No way."

"C'mon, Stan, I want to. Just let me do it. Here's two hundred. Will that cover it?"

Stan looked genuinely embarrassed. "Yeah, that'll do." He took the cash. "You know this is just a loan, right? I'm in line to earn some decent dough once the right job comes up. There's an assignment from Gunther I can't handle yet, because of the travel limits that ballbuster Paget has laid on me. Same reason I can't go down to Hedgesville right now and straighten out this Sandralene mess. But that's all over with next month. I'll be a free man again! Hey, you must be suffering from the same thing, right? That's why you're not with Nellie."

"Exactly."

The fact that I chafed under the same curtailment of liberty, despite being much better off financially, seemed to lift Stan's spirits a bit. Misery loving company, and all that. He clapped me heartily on the back.

"Glen, my man, seeing you again has made me remember that I ain't dead yet. We did something wild and great in the past together, and I got a feeling that big things are waiting just around the corner for both of us again."

"Don't get any ideas about roping me into selling fake perfume or bras or golf clubs with you, Stan. Those penny-ante rackets are not my preferred line of work."

Deflating a tad, Stan said, "I know, I know; it's not mine, either. But it's all I got right now. No, I realize that what you and me need and want is a big score."

"Well, sure," I said. "I'll listen when you've got something, I guess. I mean, what could it hurt? I can always say no."

Stan slapped my back again with thumping force. "Sweet! That's all I ask. Now, let's grab a seat and shoot the shit while we fleece some rubes."

Stan borrowed a spare folding chair from a neighboring vendor, and we joined the imperturbable Alice behind the display of faux designer wares. For the next few hours, along with handling a steady flow of sales, Stan and I caught each other up with what had been going on in our lives during the past year,

as well as reminiscing about the improbable covert machinery
we had designed to serve justice unto Barnaby Nancarrow—the
thing that had first yoked us together.

Around four, the crowds started to thin, and Stan said, "I got
a feeling there's not many more sales left today. Guess it's time to
pack up."

I helped disassemble the setup. With the wares boxed and
the table legs folded, everything fitted neatly onto a dirty-carpet-
cushioned dolly that had been stashed under the table.

"Let's go, Alice."

"Where are we going?"

"Back home. To Gunther."

"That's my husband."

"Yes, true, such is the poor bastard's fate."

"Okay, then, I'll go."

I was struck by the genuine empathy—leavened with irrev-
erence, of course—that Stan showed toward Alice, despite all the
trouble she had caused him. Yet another peculiarity of his complicated personality.

Stan wheeled the dolly off, leaving Alice and me to follow.

In the vendors' vehicle lot, we stopped at a Dodge Ram cargo
van, vintage circa 2005. Its paint job might once have been forest
green but was now the color of wan celery. Stan unlocked the
doors and helped Alice into the passenger seat, making sure to
buckle her in. Then he opened the rear door and began offloading
the dolly.

"How's about you get your car and wait at the entrance here,
then follow me."

"Sure."

By the time I retrieved my car—no longer the ancient Impala

I had inherited from my uncle Ralph, but a handsome nebula-gray pearl Lexus IS—Stan was idling at the curb. He spotted me and took off slowly.

We ended up in that district of the city known as La Punta, the Point. Not the most savory part of town. Stan pulled up outside a warehouse. He got out, helped Alice debouch, and then unlocked the big padlock securing the building's garage-style doors.

"This is where I stash the truck, so nobody busts into it during the night. Then I walk Alice home—it's just a few blocks—and then I walk myself home."

"No wheels of your own?"

"Not precisely at this exact moment in time, no."

"Well, today anyhow, you and Alice ride in style."

"Much obliged."

Stan threw back the double doors and drove the truck in. I got a quick gander at neat ranks of industrial shelving, rising up to the ceiling and loaded with scores of cartons.

If those all contained fake handbags, they represented a considerable investment of capital.

After Stan had resecured the building, we all drove to Mercer Street, where elderly brownstones lined up on parallel dirty sidewalks and consorted with a botanica, a liquor store, a check-cashing operation, and a Dollar Store, among other fine mercantile establishments.

Alice's husband, Gunther, must have been watching from the first-floor window of their apartment in one of the better-maintained buildings, because he opened the door before we could ring the bell. He was a harried-looking middle-aged guy, pear-shaped and with thinning hair, dressed in corduroy pants, a flannel shirt, and a sweater that matched his wife's. But he did not exhibit Alice's befuddlement by any means as he cast a sharp and suspicious look my way.

Stan introduced me as an old pal, and Gunther lightened up some. Only then did he turn solicitously to his wife, ushering her gently inside. He returned to receive the sales proceeds Stan had collected, and paid Stan his cut. No W-2 forms necessary in this enterprise, I could see.

"Thanks for everything, Stanley," he said. "It does me a world of good to have a little time alone. You up for tomorrow and next weekend, too?"

"Sure."

"Okay. See you then."

Back in my car, I said, "'Stanley'?"

"Are you questioning my mother's taste in baby names, son?"

"Not at all. I just never thought of you as a Stanley. Kinda high-toned and delicate, isn't it?"

"And there, my friend, you underestimate me again."

6

I drove Stan the three or four shabby blocks of grimy La Punta to his place, a nondescript tenement building noticeably more rundown than Gunther's flat. I didn't express any reaction to the crappy lodgings, but Stan nonetheless felt the need to offer a mildly defensive comment, accompanied with a wry grin.

"It's still fucktons nicer than where I grew up in the Gulch."

"Always moving on up."

After leaving Stan at the door of his apartment, I drove to my place to change clothes for our night out. After I picked up Stan around seven, we tooled in leisurely fashion through town and out to a nice restaurant on the waterfront, just outside the city limits. A seafood place named Monte Cara, it was owned by Cape Verdean friends of Nellie's. Although our city did not boast the large immigrant population of Centerdale (Nellie's hometown upstate), we were seeing growing numbers of Caboverde folks as residents, providing a growing local market for Nellie's imports.

After he had tucked away enough delicious exotic food to bloat three college linebackers, Stan sat back with a groan of contentment.

"Man, I could get used to this lifestyle again. You know, I barely had six months of high living on that MGM payout dough before everything went kerflooey."

"I am truly sorry, Stan," I said. "I wish you had called me for some advice about that investment."

"Hell, I was too damn proud. I wanted to show you I could play your kinda game and win big."

This seemed a natural opening. "Stan, do you want to borrow some money to get back on your feet?"

"Fuck no! I did this to myself—and to Sandy, too, which is what really hurts—and I'm gonna get out of it myself."

"Okay," I said. "I understand completely."

"Never thought you wouldn't. But I appreciate the offer anyhow."

The rest of the evening passed in a pleasant, boozy succession of clubs, and when I left Stan at his place around 4:00 a.m., we sloppily vowed to do it again soon.

But I did not see Stan again for several weeks. When I gave him my phone number, he sheepishly confessed that he lacked a phone himself, being flat broke and a bad credit risk. Neither did he have a working credit card. Everything in his life was strictly cash-and-carry these days. For someone who had once been just as compulsively wired as the next social-media junkie, this deficit was shocking. But he just shrugged it off.

"I was relying on Sandy's cell, but she took it with her. Now I borrow Gunther's when I want to talk to her. I figured you'd understand, out of anyone. Once upon a time, you were all Mr.

Antismartphone Guy, with your antique flip phone and shit."

I recalled those old days with a twinge of chagrin at my self-righteousness. "Yes, that was pretty smarmy and stupid of me."

"Just keep reminding yourself. 'Every day, in every way, I'm getting better and better.'"

I laughed. "Where'd you hear that?"

Deadpan, Stan replied, "Somebody else said it first?"

"A Frenchman about a hundred years ago."

"A hundred fucking years ago? That's so outta copyright!"

Stan did not feel free handing out Gunther's number, so I was relying on him to call me, but he never did. And as the days ran into weeks, I just assumed that he was either too busy or too embarrassed to accept my convivial charity—or maybe even jealous and disgusted that I had managed to retain my relative wealth and my woman. Whatever the case, there was no use in forcing the relationship if he didn't feel like it, so I just let the silence build.

And besides, I had my own life to attend to.

Nellie returned from Cape Verde a few days after my surprise encounter with Stan. I picked her up at the airport and found her exhausted but elated. After a big hug and an enthusiastic wet kiss, she said, "*Oh, minha nossa!* Glen, you would not believe what I accomplished on this trip. I got a whole factory off the ground!"

When Nellie and I had first started this business, she trimmed her explosion of dark frizzy curls into a more businesslike cut, which complemented her sweet, heart-shaped face the color of crème brûlée even more than did the untamed mass of her immature days. I laid my hand against her cheek and said, "Let's get home and you can tell me all about it right away."

"Oh, yeah, I know you are so, like, very hot to listen to big, boring talk about zoning laws and bank loans before you jump my skinny bones!"

Such talk here by the baggage carousel was making me anticipate more private surroundings.

"I am indeed eager to listen to such commercial chatter, but maybe second."

"Well, guess what."

"What?"

"*Meu cona* is gonna do the talking first!"

In bed afterward, Nellie, naked, suddenly jumped up and ran to her unopened luggage. I admired every angle and quiver of her active, agile form. She came back with a small squat can, from which she pulled the pop top. She dug her forefinger into the dark fragrant goop inside and made me lick the stuff off.

"Holy Christ, is that delicious! What is it?"

"*Doce de café.* Coffee pudding, made with coffee from Fogo."

Fogo is one of the islands that make up Cape Verde, and we were already importing bags of their unique beans, one of our best-selling items.

Nellie explained. "I knew this stuff would go over big, but you could only get it fresh till now, in a restaurant there or maybe here. No one thought of canning it. Not quite as good as fresh, but it's still great."

I had to agree. A little qualm overtook me. "So what did it take to make this happen?"

Nellie looked adorably serious, or seriously adorable. "I had to write a check for fifty thousand, Glen. That's our investment in the factory. I hope that was okay. You know it's all to help my people, right? They are so poor on the islands. Here as well, but not quite so much. Anyhow, we are going to get rich, too. Not right away, but eventually!"

"Yes, sure, of course."

But even as I said it—and meant it—I couldn't help doing the math. Fifty thousand was one tenth of our capital. I was certain we'd get it all back, plus profits. For an untutored gal only twenty-some years old, Nellie had a visionary entrepreneur's head as good as Elon Musk's. She had never taken a wrong step yet. But the tight margins and limits on our funds still made me nervous. I wanted not to have to worry about such piddling amounts. I wanted the freedom represented by the five million dollars that had actually been in my hands before everything fell apart.

As I finished licking the pudding off Nellie's fingers and my own, I couldn't help wondering how Stan was doing with those plans of his for a big score of some kind.

Feeling a little guilty about entertaining such thoughts during—or at least, immediately before—our lovemaking, I told Nellie later that evening about meeting up with our old friend.

"That is so great!" she said. "How is he doing? Can we see him and Sandy soon? I want them to try the *doce de café*, too!"

I explained Stan's current situation to Nellie, and she immediately expressed concern.

"Oh, no, Glen, this is too sad! We have to help them!"

"Don't worry," I said. "I'm doing all I can. But I have to wait for Stan to call me."

"Okay. Just don't wait too long. Maybe you could drive over there."

But I didn't have to drive over to see Stan, because he drove over to see me.

In an eighteen-wheeler as big as a humpback whale.

7

The enthusiastic blaring of Zeus' own air horn brought me to the window of our condo a day or two after Nellie's return. I'd swear I could feel the building shake, although that was surely just my imagination. Looking out past the nice blue-and-white embroidered curtains Nellie had found—after dragging me along on a daylong purgatory of shopping at stores such as West Elm and Pottery Barn—I saw the big rig parked at a slant across a dozen reserved spaces in the condo's lot. Luckily, at this midday hour, all the possessive and litigious owners of those spots were at work.

Standing outside the tractor's cab, clad in matching sand-colored work pants and jacket, his feet encased in safety boots that would have looked big on Dr. Frankenstein's creation, stood Stan, yanking on the horn's lanyard and wearing a smile as broad as the Mississippi.

I opened the window and hollered out, "Hey, lay off! This isn't the stockyards! I'll be right down!"

Just to demonstrate that he could not be forced to do anything against his own desires, Stan triggered one final resonant blast, then gave me the finger.

Nellie had joined me in the front room. "*Ai, mamãe,* what's all this *barudju?*"

"Stan's down there," I said. "With a truck."

Nellie squealed in glee. "What are you waiting for? *Mas dipresa!*"

We hurried out to Stan, who stood proudly in his Carhartt uniform—though I noticed that neither the sides of the truck nor the breast of his jacket bore any company's name or logo. He looked beefier, more like his old self, as if he had been eating better lately. A nice new cell phone protruded from the shirt pocket. Nellie, seeing her former coconspirator for the first time in months, wrapped herself around him like a liana around a giant mahogany tree. He didn't seem to mind. I could only imagine how much a man of his generously randy nature was missing Sandralene.

"Have you actually gotten a real job?" I said after Nellie had undraped herself and begun climbing enthusiastically and admiringly through the cab on a self-guided tour.

Stan dropped his voice. "Well, in a manner of speaking. Actually, that's what I wanted to talk with you about. I can use your help. You'd make a cool two thousand for about forty-eight hours' work. Interested?"

I thought again about how fast our little importing enterprise was leaking money, as well as the general costs of living without a real income. "Yeah, that sounds like decent pay," I said. "But remember, I used to bill two hundred an hour as a lawyer."

"Yeah. And remind me, how much are disbarred lawyers billing these days?"

"You have hit upon a true income-limiting issue," I said. "So, what's involved?"

"I can't tell you here. I don't think you want Nellie knowing anything about this job. So we gotta take a little ride."

Nellie emerged from the cab. "Very, very *bunitu*, Stan. Is it yours? You buy it? Or maybe lease it?"

"Naw, I got no dough to do that. Glen told you how I went broke, right? The rig belongs to my, ah, employer. I'm just a hired driver. But it's a start."

"Well, I am so proud of you, Stan. I knew you would get back on your feet fast. You are a man of much *koráji*."

"Much courage, huh? Thanks."

Nellie had come innocently into our lives on the assumption that she was going to teach us her native Caboverdean language, easing us into our nonextraditable retirement in those paradisiacal islands. I had never learned that much of the creole, although I had certainly picked up additional key vocabulary, most of it filthy, from living together, and was mildly surprised at Stan's comprehension.

"It is only the truth, Stan."

"Thanks, Nell. When I get rich enough to support two women, I will definitely keep you in mind as Sandy's pinch hitter."

Nellie thumped Stan on the chest with her small fist. "Ai, you *buru*! You know it's only Glen for me."

"The offer still stands."

After showing Nellie and me the spotless empty interior of the trailer, Stan said, "Girl, you mind if I take your man for a little ride?"

"Can't I come, too?"

"Well, everyone's got to be belted safely in, and there's only room for one more up front besides me. You don't want me to get a violation on my spanking-new commercial driver's license, do you?"

"No way!"

"Okay, then, I'll take you next."

Stan vaulted easily behind the wheel while I clambered more awkwardly into my seat. Leaning out his window, Stan said, "We might be a little while. I want to get out on the highway and show Glen how smooth a ride this mother gives at cruising speed."

"I'll be here."

Stan went through his preflight ritual with reassuring confidence, then shifted into gear and pulled smoothly away from the condo lot.

"How the hell did you learn to drive something this size?" I said. "You never knew how before we met, did you?"

"Nope. Four-week course since the last time we saw each other. Instructor said I was a natural."

"And who paid for that?"

"Gunther and company."

"And they own the truck, too?"

"Natch."

"So I take it this job involves Gunther's trade in counterfeit goods?"

"A-yup."

We came to a zebra crossing where a bearded hipster was lollygagging as he studied his cell phone. Stan cut loose with a burst of air horn that made the guy jump and twist and spasm so violently, he actually lost one of his Tevas. Retrieving his shoe, the abused fellow scampered off.

"So," I said, "what's the deal?"

"I think I'll let Gunther tell you."

Of course, we did not get on the highway at all but merely drove surface streets to the warehouse in La Punta. Given the full-to-capacity parking on adjacent streets, the parking spots in front of the warehouse were unnaturally empty, as if the locals knew better than to use them. Stan parked curbside, taking up a good third of the block, and we entered the dimly lit warehouse.

An office space of sorts had been constructed at the back of the building by erecting three plywood walls against the rear wall of the warehouse. The resulting cubicle was just slightly higher than Stan's head. Inside the enclosure, under a bare bulb dangling at the end of a long red utility extension cord, Gunther sat behind a folding table topped with various papers and a sample handbag or two. A battered metal cabinet with double doors occupied one corner. A several-year-old calendar from *Lowrider* magazine, featuring a mostly naked and very callipygian model, graced the back of the makeshift plywood door.

The unprepossessing and clerkish Gunther nodded a curt greeting to us.

"Stan fill you in?"

Stan intervened. "I thought I'd let you do that, Gunther."

"Okay, here's the story. We make regular runs to bring goods from transshipment points up to the city for sale. Our usual driver can't do any more trips, so we're trying out Stan, whom we have groomed for the job. I think he'll perform good. He's getting ten thousand per run, so that is some major incentive. We are also trying something new this time. We want to send someone to ride shotgun with Stan. That guy will get two thousand."

"I can't help Stan with the driving."

Gunther sighed—a mix of pity and despair, as if I were his

wife, Alice, doing something particularly boneheaded. "I didn't say anything about driving, did I? I said 'ride shotgun.'"

I was about to remark that just keeping Stan company and maybe helping him stay awake at 3:00 a.m. did not seem to merit my fee, when Stan opened the metal cabinet and got out a long cloth-swaddled object. He unwrapped the thing and handed it to me.

I looked unbelievingly at the alien object in my hands. "This is a literal shotgun."

Gunther rolled his eyes. "Do I hafta draw you a diagram?"

I looked to Stan. "The guy you're replacing?"

"He didn't have one of these, or a guy to use it, when he needed them."

8

The shotgun that Stan had dumped in my lap was a classic Mossberg 500. I had handled this model many times, during my outings with some lawyer buddies who had a thing for skeet shooting. The fad, mostly an excuse for impressing women and engaging in postcompetitive drinking, lasted among us for roughly six months—about as long as the manufactured crazes for blacksmithing, artisanal brewing, and taxidermy. But during my brief tenure as a sportsman, I had gotten semiproficient with the Mossberg. My scores were never very high, but at least the sound of the gun going off did not cause me to drop the weapon, as it had the first time I fired it.

But I did not tell Stan or Gunther any of this. Instead, I just said, "Okay, I'm on board."

"Great," said Gunther, with his customary lack of enthusiasm. "Stan will let you know when the first run is."

Stan took the gun back, rewrapped it, and stuck it in the cabinet.

"Best to leave this here for now," he said. "It's not exactly street legal. We'll try to get you a chance to practice a little with it later."

We left our dumpy traffic dispatcher to contemplate the charms of Ms. September's bounteous tush. Loyal as he was to the declining Alice, Gunther could still dream.

Back in the truck's cab and pulling away from the curb, Stan said, "I really appreciate you signing up for this job, Glen. I need somebody along who knows me and who I know I can count on in a pinch. I still remember you didn't lose your nerve against Nancarrow and his goons."

"I hardly saved the day then."

"Maybe not. But you didn't panic at a gun aimed your way, and that's what counts."

"I appreciate your confidence," I said. "But I've got to tell you right now, there's no way I am going to fire a round at another living human being."

"Aw, it won't come to that. It's just for show and some intimidation."

"Well, then, what happened to your predecessor?"

Stan rolled his eyes. "He was just plain stupid. He was riding solo and he stopped at a nowheresville roadhouse along the way, got slightly sozzled, and started boasting about what he was carrying. The guys who hijacked him were a little too liberal in their application of a tire iron to his skull. Otherwise, he woulda recovered fine and still been on the job. But we are not going to make any such fuckwitted mistakes. We'll arrow down to get the goods, then zip right back here, stopping only at heavily frequented Triple-A-approved gas-and-gulps, where we will employ the buddy system even to take a piss. This is gonna be the easiest dough you ever made, son."

I had to stare out the window for a few seconds before responding. "So is this the big score you had in mind that you thought we could share? Because although the money is somewhat decent—especially your share—it is not exactly what I would call beaucoup bucks. It's more like having a normal job—a lifestyle for which both you and I have expressed our well-considered disdain. Also, in this endeavor, your chances of apprehension and disaster increase with every run, whereas a one-off scam, I think, offers odds a little more in our favor, assuming we are careful and competent."

Stan made a dismissive raspberry sound. "No way is this gig the major move I want or imagined, Glen. No, that is yet to come. I've got some feelers out that I can't talk about right now. Meanwhile, this trucker drudgery is gonna put some cash in my bank account that I can invest in our eventual scheme. You didn't think I was gonna ask you to front the lion's share again like last time, did you? Also, I will have some dough to use in going and getting Sandralene back, and to support her once she's here, in a style that goddamn Caleb Stinchcombe, fuck his hairy ass, would never even be able to approximate even if he sold his prize mule."

"I really don't think Sandy is staying away because you're not buying her silk stockings and taking her to four-star restaurants, Stan."

"Nah, me neither. But I don't want to bring her back here to that sty I'm living in now. There's so many rats there, they have to hump in shifts. Anyhow, now that our parole is up, we are free to go get my woman!"

Stan tugged the horn's lanyard long enough to rupture every eardrum within a hundred yards of the rolling truck.

"Hey, if you get a cop issuing us a noise citation, that's not gonna be a good omen for this trip."

"Let 'em try! I'll just say I was trying to get the attention of some bugger who was texting and driving."

We were approaching the parking lot of my condo. I could see Nellie still outside, waiting patiently for her turn to ride with Stan. I experienced an instant unease and sense of guilt at having to keep this mission a secret from her. But I tamped it down with the thought that she would appreciate as much as I would the extra freedom this money would bring us.

I climbed out of the parked truck and held the door open for Nellie.

"Gas, grass, or ass—nobody rides for free," Stan declared. Nellie just giggled, and it suddenly struck me how much younger she was than Stan and I, and how much less jaded and coarsened by life. I blessed the luck that had brought us together, and, as she motored off with Stan, vowed not to do anything that might ruin her childlike faith.

* * *

The next time Stan called me was four days later. I was braced for the start of our run, but he only wanted me to come and practice with the shotgun. We couldn't bring the illegal weapon to a public range, of course, so I drove us way the hell out into the boonies, to a parcel of land that, just a few weeks ago, had been legally open for May's spring turkey season. Now, in mid-June, it was technically closed. But enough poachers still ignored the rules that I figured any shots would not arouse much comment or suspicion. Locals were leery of summoning the authorities, anyhow. Certainly, we would attract less attention here than elsewhere.

We drove down a dirt road that dead-ended at the edge of a large overgrown glade, and parked. The day was warm and sunny. Birds serenaded us.

Stan took out the gun and some shells. "Here, let me show you how—"

I took the Mossberg from him, checked to make sure it was unloaded. Putting in the nine shells of its capacity, I brought it to my shoulder, flicked off the safety atop the gun with my thumb, then pumped off nine shots that shattered to shreds an innocent, doomed sapling some hundred feet away.

Stan's jaw made contact with his clavicle. This was the only time I had seen him thus gobsmacked.

When he regained the power of speech, he said, "Why the hell did we even come out here?"

"Just to see that expression on your face."

"You sly bastard."

I had prepped Nellie for my upcoming absence by saying that Stan and I intended to go camping—a real guys' bonding expedition. I was going to make it sound as if we might even start a drum circle. But as it turned out, I never even had to use that excuse. Two calls came in nearly simultaneously. One was for Nellie, about a crisis at the pudding factory, which was on the island of Santiago. She must fly out immediately.

The other call was for me, from Stan.

"We are ready to roll."

9

We had been driving for nearly ten hours and were past the outskirts of Detroit. I had heard enough inane talk radio to catch up on all the latest conspiracy theories, my butt was numb, and my tongue had a patented fast-food coating that approached Varathane for impenetrability. I had endured an endless stream of shaggy-dog stories from Stan—mostly true anecdotes of his wildly miscellaneous criminal doings, some going back to child-hood. Many of these tall tales had been hilarious, some heart-breaking, and all of them narrated with his signature untutored flair for storytelling. In turn, I had supplied anecdotes from my own less colorful past.

This exchange was the deepest communication we had shared in all the time we had known each other. Stan stood revealed to me now, even more so than before, as a complex bundle of honor and chicanery, wisdom and folly, cunning and openness. At the halfway point of this road trip, I felt a deeper rapport than ever with my coconspirator. I hoped Stan felt the same with me. We had only each other to rely on.

Stan's new smartphone was emplaced in its plastic mount on the dash, guiding us over the busy surface roads toward our rendezvous. For inconspicuous easy access, the shotgun was hidden under the mattress of the comfy bunk just behind our shoulders. The slick, high-tech interior of our Peterbilt Model 587 resembled some 1950s *Popular Science* dream of a passenger cabin on the Cunard route to Mars.

I wished I could stretch out on that inviting mattress and grab a few winks. But I knew that Stan's boundless energy—he showed no real signs of fatigue after all the tedious yet demanding driving—would serve as a silent reproach to my wussiness. And besides, the time to nap would have been earlier, not now when we were almost at our destination.

The hour was approaching 6:00 p.m. Other cities would be jammed with commuter traffic at this hour, but not Detroit—or at least, not this particular part of the city. So hollowed-out had the city become that vast stretches of it resembled the time-blasted ruins of some dead civilization.

We had entered the city on Route 75, then branched off onto a different highway, finally taking an exit for West Davison Street. Our ultimate destination was 3033 Bourke Avenue.

I thought about Nellie, thousands of miles away across the Atlantic, and wished I were home with her. Stan had gone quiet, and I imagined him to be daydreaming something similar about Sandralene.

We picked up Bourke at last, and I began to suss out the neighborhood. Hardly any retail, just a scattered handful of small, modest houses with a few sheltering trees, each estate isolated on a checkerboard of weedy lots that had once held similar homes until they went vacant, got foreclosed and boarded up, or succumbed to weather and looters before finally being razed. In the warm early-June evening, brown kids played gleefully up and down the lawns and lots, seemingly unaware of the squalor and hopelessness all around them. They took little notice of our big truck—a fact explainable by the presence of several low industrial buildings consorting cheek by jowl with the houses.

Bourke Avenue terminated in a grassy cul-de-sac with a chain-link fence demarcating the big empty parking lot on its far side. Arriviste junk trees, promiscuous flowers, and shrubs gone wild added a feral touch to the urban locale.

The building that bore the stenciled label 3033 BOURKE was painted a sky blue that had weathered in patches to the shade of Paul Newman's eyes. A sprawling single-story structure filling a whole square block, it featured rusty barred windows obscured from within by a hodgepodge of venetian blinds, sheets of cardboard, and repurposed laminated lawn signs for real estate agents, politicians, car washes, and church bazaars.

Stan retrieved his phone from its mount, then climbed down from the cab. So did I. We both stretched.

"I feel mildly but unpleasantly numb and sore," I said, "like someone's been thumping me with a Nerf bat for ten hours straight."

"Are you dissing the comfort of the Peterbilt Five-Eighty-Seven seats?" Stan replied. "Because if so, I'm going to have to report you to my union."

As we walked to the entrance, I said, "Why Detroit? Why not just get the stuff delivered directly to us?"

"Most of these knockoffs come from China and into

Vancouver. Ottawa rolls over for these guys. The authorities just don't seem to care. Over seven hundred billion dollars in traffic might explain some of their attitude. Then the stuff gets hauled by truck across the Rockies and, finally, over the border to Detroit, which is nice and central for further distribution. Also, this city needs any kind of commerce so bad, they ignore blatant illegal shit almost as hard as the Canucks."

"The Good Neighbor policy in action," I said.

"Something like that."

The building had a flaking black-painted office door at the head of two concrete steps. Stan climbed up ahead of me and knocked. While we waited, he scrolled up a photo on his phone.

"This is the guy who's supposed to meet us. Name's Nestor Jassruddin."

Jassruddin's candid head shot revealed a hawkish young face of indeterminate ancestry, with skin somewhat darker than Stan's or mine.

As I contemplated the image, the door's locks and chains rattled; it opened, and the man himself stood there. His slim form was clothed in a baggy plain white T-shirt, denim cargo shorts, and expensive and colorful limited-edition Nike LeBrons without socks. He appeared to recognize us.

"You guys are early."

"Yeah," Stan said. "We made good time."

"The loading crew isn't here yet. You shoulda texted me."

"I tried, but you never texted back."

Jassruddin dug out his phone, studied it, then inexplicably dashed it to pieces on the concrete floor.

"Fucking battery on this cheap-ass thing! Won't stay charged for shit!"

"Well, not now, it sure won't," Stan observed.

"It's just a burner, so screw it. Okay, here's the deal. Get the truck around to bay number one, then come inside to wait."

Jassruddin retreated behind the closed door, and we returned to the truck.

"Backing up is one thing I don't do with my usual finesse and savoir faire," Stan confessed. "You're gonna have to spot me."

"*Finally*, I feel like I'm earning my money!"

Between the two of us, with much halting and repositioning, we got the truck out of the cul-de-sac and rear-ended against the ragged bumper at the designated bay. The big door rolled up, and Jassruddin hailed us inside.

"Wanna play some poker while we wait?"

"Sure," Stan said, and not wanting to appear standoffish, I nodded.

The way toward a lighted office led past towering stacks of cartons.

"This our stuff?" Stan asked.

"Yeah."

"Mind if I have a look?"

"Knock yourself out."

Stan slit open a carton with the penknife on his key chain. I got ready to see some exotic luxury item, but instead he pulled out a can of baby formula with the familiar Similac label.

"What the hell?" I said.

Stan rotated the can admiringly. "Nearly forty bucks retail for the forty-ounce. Twelve to a carton, five hundred or more cartons per trailer. You do the math."

"Holy Christ, that's a quarter million dollars for one trip! No wonder they can pay you ten grand."

"It's not all profit, though," Stan said. "This stuff must cost the Chinese at least a couple of bucks a can to make."

I had a twinge of guilt. "Is it any good?"

"Well, it's not poison. True, it might not have a hundred percent of what it says on the label. But with modern levels of obesity, you don't want kids getting too fat too soon, do you?"

I shook my head in disbelief, trying my best to morally rationalize my involvement in this scheme as a case of "if not me, then someone else." This fake formula had been flowing for a long time, and no one had died or even gotten sick, although maybe they hadn't quite spurted up to national-average growth levels at their yearly checkups. But maybe a lot of poor households had been able to buy nourishment, albeit of an inferior grade, that they couldn't otherwise afford. I figured I could live with it, seeing as how my involvement was temporary.

We had time for just four hands of poker, during which Jassruddin and I lost about a hundred apiece to Stan, before the moving crew showed up: three easygoing, muscular, jokey young black guys eager for a night's under-the-table pay. They started hoisting the unpalletized cartons with a will, and in just a tad over one sweaty hour, they had nearly filled the forty-five-foot trailer with over six hundred cartons.

Stan signed some paperwork, and we said goodbye to Jassruddin and the three guys resting on bales and drinking cold beers, then got back in the cab.

By now the sun was going down, and the air felt cooler. The neighborhood looked a little sketchier in the twilight. The playing children had all gone inside, probably so they wouldn't get shot.

"You're not going to start the drive back now, are you?" I said.

"Yeah, why not? I just wanna get out of the city a ways, to feel like we're making progress. Then we'll find a rest stop and pull over for a nap."

"Who gets the bunk?"

Stan grinned. "You remember who was top dog in our sleeping arrangements in that crappy old Impala of your uncle's, when you me and Sandralene first arrived at the lodge?"

"I hope the shotgun under the mattress is a real princess-and-the-pea situation for you the whole damn night."

10

Over three hours of hard nighttime driving brought us to the Brady's Leap Service Plaza on I-80, not too far from Youngstown. Neither of us had had much of anything to say during the run, although I did broach one topic with Stan—something that had been bothering me ever since the loading of the truck was finished.

"Is that real Similac in those cans?"

"No. It's real fake Similac."

"It's not cocaine or fentanyl or smack?"

"Are you fucking insane? There's like six fucktons of powder back there. I don't think all of South America makes that much coke in a year. Besides, why should Gunther and company get their hands dirty that way when there's plenty of money in fakes? And if you get caught, the penalties for selling this harmless stuff are a slap on the wrist compared to what you get for moving dope. And besides, you think I'd be part of such a killer enterprise after going to so much trouble to *kick* the stuff? No, my man, this is not any kinda *Midnight Express*-style shit, so you can rest easy."

"All right, then. My conscience can go back to sleep."

Sleep. That sounded good. By this hour, closing in on midnight, both Stan and I had been awake for over twenty-four hours, and I certainly had to crash. I couldn't imagine Stan wasn't whipped, too. But first, toilet and grub, in that order.

Outside the truck, I made all my bones pop and creak with stretching. Stan locked up, and we ambled like two aged war veterans over to the main building. Circular and domed and futuristic, blooming with radiance in the insect-plangent night, it resembled a docked flying saucer. Three flags hung limp from their tall poles in the hot, still air.

Leaving the john, my face wet from a cold-water spritzing (try drying your face with one of those Dyson Airblades), I felt almost human. We surveyed our limited food choices and settled on the PZA franchise. Stan demolished two meatball subs, and I wolfed down a sausage calzone. Stan favored Mountain Dew, and I had a Coke.

Back at the truck, Stan kicked off his shoes and stretched out on the bunk as far as his long legs allowed. I reclined my comfy seat, and was gone before I could even say, "Now I lay me down to sleep ..."

Someone was shaking me after what seemed like just a few minutes of blessed unconsciousness. Stan crouched between the two seats.

"Time to get rolling again, son."

"How long did we sleep?"

"Three hours. That's plenty. Here, have a pill."

I knew that Stan occasionally used uppers, and his supply had helped us out before, during our earlier conspiracy. I took one and washed it down with my warm leftover soda.

"I gotta piss one more time," he said.

"I'll come, too."

In the men's room, the guy at the adjacent urinal, plainly another noble beer-bellied knight of the road, spoke to Stan without prompting.

"Haven't seen you boys around before."

"No, cousin. Just got this run."

"Thought so. Well, figured you should know. The weigh station on I-80 outside Clarion, PA, is operating tonight."

"Thanks muchly."

As we walked back to the truck, I said, "What's that news mean for us?"

"Means we are getting off the highway before Clarion. I don't want no government boys poking around our goods. Chances are, we could get by, but maybe not. So why risk it?"

Back on the freeway, I could feel the drug taking hold and my remnant fatigue burning off. We drove for an hour or so before I noticed Stan paying more attention to his side mirror than the traffic warranted.

"What's up?"

"Could be someone's following us. Maybe laying up at the stop wasn't the best idea—might've allowed news of our cargo and route to circulate."

"What can we do about it?"

"Well, they ain't gonna try nothing on the expressway. And even when we get off, so long as we keep rolling there's no way they can stop us. And after our detour around the trucker fuckers, we'll be back safe on the highway again."

"Maybe it'd be smarter to risk the weigh station."

"Naw, getting off the freeway's the best idea. Anyone following us will stick out like a hipster at a 4-H Club."

Despite Stan's reassuring words, I began to check and recheck the reassuring presence of the shotgun under the mattress, my nerves amphetamine-taut.

"For Christ's sake, will you quit that! If you need your bazooka, I'll tell ya!"

We got off I-80 onto I-79, heading south toward Pittsburgh.

"Anyone following us?"

"Hard to tell."

Stan was fiddling with the directions app on his phone, and soon we left the superhighway behind for a succession of smaller roads.

The next time I could make out a route marker caught in our headlights, it claimed we were on PA-68. The narrow two-lane semirural road took us past scattered darkened homes and long stretches of emptiness, where either fields or scrub forest bordered the pavement. At this hour, there was not another vehicle on the unlighted highway, and I began to relax.

Until we came around a corner and I saw a pair of police cars, about two hundred yards away, their dome lights flashing, parked to block the road.

"I guess this is it, Stan," I said. "Should I toss the gun out the window now?"

Stan's answer was to tromp down on the accelerator, and we surged from forty-five to sixty.

"What the hell are you doing!" I gasped.

"Those are not real cops. A barricade in the middle of nowhere at four a.m.? Fuck me if it's real!"

"Maybe they're looking for escaped prisoners or drunk drivers, or something!"

"I say they're fakes. Roll down your window and get your gun ready."

Not seeing much recourse, I did as I was instructed. The damp loam-fragrant air rushed into the cab.

I could see several men standing alongside the "police" cars, in full expectation that we would do the sensible thing and stop, but in the dark and at this speed, I couldn't tell whether they were even wearing uniforms.

The land on the left-hand side of PA-68 at this stretch was a grassy field. Stan dropped the wheels on his side of the tractor onto the field. The cab dipped and swayed, and I was sure we were going over. The left wheels of the trailer followed onto the grass, and we steadied somewhat. Stan sped up, with half our wheels on pavement and half biting through the turf.

Realizing we weren't going to stop, the "cops" began shooting at us. Bullets zinged into our cowling but, luckily, missed the windshield.

I got the shotgun's barrel braced on my windowsill, but the truck was bucking so wildly I couldn't aim.

"Let 'em have it!"

I pulled the trigger as the truck jounced around like college students screwing on a waterbed, and the shot went wild. I fired twice more.

And then Stan clipped the front bumper of one of the parked cars.

For all the noise of rending metal and shattering safety glass, our massive truck hardly slowed. The struck car seemed to rear upward and around like Trigger in an action photo op.

Then we were past the barrier, and Stan had wrestled the truck and trailer fully back onto the pavement. We zoomed away at top speed.

"Okay, now," he said, "if no fresh reinforcement cops intercept us farther on, you'll know I was right."

"Do you think I hit anyone with my shots?"

"Ha! You did more damage to *us*. Look at that fucking mirror."

The mirror on my side hung in shreds from its wiring. The sight was so absurd and pathetic, I started giggling like a lunatic, and Stan joined in.

"If Gunther wants us to pay for that repair, it's coming out of your share, Glen, my man."

"Just so long as you pay for what is undoubtedly one truly messed-up paint job and grill."

We got back on I-80 eventually, with no further interference from police, real or bogus. Stan refrained from rubbing in the rightness of his decision.

"What do you think would've happened to us back there if we had stopped?" I said.

"Best case, a long walk. Worst case, a long, long dirt nap."

At that moment, a wave of deep fatigue and enervation swamped me, leaving me feeling like a pit bull's chew toy. It took the rest of the ride for me to recover any semblance of energy or normality.

We pulled up to Gunther's warehouse in La Punta around 10:00 a.m. We had been gone about thirty hours, though it seemed like a month.

Gunther greeted us in his cubicle office. "Any trouble?"

"Not that we couldn't handle."

"Good, good. The starving infants of our fair city are in your debt. And just so I won't be, here's your cash."

I took my two grand gratefully, and we left Gunther to arrange the unloading of the truck. We said nothing about the damage.

Out on the street, Stan said, "I am gonna eat a large steak and some home fries for breakfast. Then maybe a piece of blueberry pie. Come with?"

"Sure."

When we had finished our meal and sat sipping our fourth cup of coffee, Stan said, "Do it again soon?"

Sitting there with a wad of cash in my pocket, I thought about the whole trip, the tedium and panic combined, and how I could just have sat at home counting my pennies of interest as they accumulated.

"Hell, yeah!"

PART TWO

11

Over the next three months, Stan and I did six more runs together, none of them involving any further deadly interference from mysterious road pirates. The rituals and rhythms of our Detroit jaunts became almost placid and predictable. The roadside plazas and other landmarks of Interstate 80 began to feel as familiar as my childhood backyard, and my share of the ongoing poker losses that Nestor and I forked over to Stan could have been included in my monthly budget as fixed expenses. I was afraid my handsome shotgun would rust from disuse or that my position as stagecoach guard would, *strictissimi juris*, be deemed supererogatory. (Every now and then, my long-gone tenure as a sleazy lawyer popped words and ways of looking at things into the forefront of my mind. I nearly always succeeded in clubbing them down.) But Gunther kept wanting me to accompany Stan, and I was not averse.

One day, sitting in the Inn at Turkey Hill—a Pennsylvania spot that we favored mainly because they brewed several nice lagers and ales—Stan and I sat savoring the remnants of our meal before hitting the highway again.

"What do you think scared off the hijackers?" I asked Stan.

"Probably Gunther's connections."

"His connections?"

"What're you, a schoolkid or something? I thought you were a savvy guy. You figure that Gunther, who lives in a La Punta chicken coop with his skipping-a-groove wife who he can't even afford a babysitter for, and who dresses like he shops exclusively at Aunt Sally's, is fronting all the money for this operation and masterminding the whole thing? He's just middle management. He's running it for someone else."

"Who would that be?"

"Vin Santo is my best guess."

The waitress came by, looking to tactfully dislodge our butts for new paying customers, but Stan placated her by ordering another Barn Dance Blonde Ale. A couple of pints never seemed to impede his driving, though it tended to make me drowsy.

I recounted my brush with the mobster late last year, not long before Stan and I reconnected.

"Oh, so Santo thought you were hot stuff, huh? Maybe that's why you're being kept on despite not doing anything more than filling my tractor cab with warm farts."

"At least half the flatulence may have something to do with your sudden mania for an exclusive diet of Taco Bell bean burritos."

"Aw, c'mon, you know I was just joking. I totally rely on your confidence-inspiring presence. I never in my life felt so safe from rogue side-view mirrors."

"If you hadn't mistaken an eighteen-wheeler for an off-road ATV, I might've been able to aim better."

"Next time I'm saving both our fucking lives, I'll try to drive like your uncle Ralph, who, as I recall, never goes over a brisk thirty-five miles an hour on his way to the track."

I stayed quiet, having no rejoinder for this accurate representation of Uncle Ralph's driving habits as he ferried his lady love, the formidable Suzy Lam, back and forth to their daily handicapping pleasures, abetted by the bankroll of twenty grand I had given them for their help with our earlier scam.

Stan pushed back his heavy chair and stood. He threw down a fifty as a tip. Then, on the way out, he ordered a growler to go.

* * *

On those six runs, besides more baby formula, we hauled loads of fake clothing, fake toys, fake sneakers, and fake cigarettes. Not that any of those goods were fake enough to be unusable—they merely did not bear the actual imprimatur of the companies they allegedly represented. I began to believe that I had seen all the kinds of counterfeit goods there were.

But I was wrong. On the seventh run, the one mission I did not accompany Stan on, the cargo was of an altogether different type. And that proved to be the product that would launch us on our joint venture.

Keeping Nellie happy about my new role as Stan's migratory assistant involved a little creative storytelling. I had accomplished the first trip—luckily, the only dangerous one—while she was absent and unwitting in Cape Verde. But I could not count on her being out of the country every time I needed to ride with Stan. And so I had come up with a plausible reason for Stan and me to be gallivanting around the country.

"Stan's a car transporter for Hertz now, Nell."

"*Fixe!* I am so happy! He can make some good money now maybe? Get back on his feet?"

"Oh, sure, maybe even fifty thousand a year."

Fifty thousand for about every ten days' work, I might have said.

"You wouldn't mind if I rode with him now and then, would you?" I said. "I don't have much really to occupy me day to day, and it would be kind of a break from my routines. They get a little stale. This man-of-leisure lifestyle is not what it's cracked up to be. You wouldn't know, because you've got your business to keep you occupied and happy. Not that my hanging with Stan would really steal much time away from whenever you and I want to be together."

Nellie, with her usual loving exuberance, hugged me and said, "No, of course not! So long as Hertz does not mind you riding with him while he does his job."

"Hertz is not going to care at all."

So the next three months went swimmingly. Stan and I did our thing together, with me socking away each mission's fee in the bank to help fund Nellie's work and our incidental expenses. And whenever I wasn't on the road—which was most of every month—Nellie and I continued to lead our happy domestic life. That included occasions when Stan joined us and regaled Nellie with totally fictitious stories about driving for Hertz, some of which bordered on the implausibly outrageous. Yet she never twigged.

But inevitably, a conflict arose. Now that my period of parole had expired, taking with it any travel prohibitions, Nellie had been urging me to accompany her to Cape Verde. She was starting to get disappointed at my general lack of enthusiasm for such a trip—ostensibly, this importing venture was as much mine as hers, although really it was her baby—and I knew I could not put her off any longer. Nor did I really want to let her down. So I arranged our international jaunt for October. She had been flying no-frills into Lisbon, then to Praia, the capital of Cape Verde, on the island of Santiago. But this time, I told her, we were going to do it up right.

Her beautiful face lit up like the sunrise over her beloved homeland. "A week in Paris first! *Oh, minha nossa!* This is too much, Glen! Can we really afford it, even with all the money I've been using for the business?"

"Yes, we can, thanks to some good investments on my part."

"Then I am going to start packing my sexiest outfits right now!"

I went to tell Stan about the trip.

"No problem, partner! Odds are, Gunther won't need me while you're gone. And if he does, I'll just pocket your two thousand without one shred of guilt."

"So long as you think you'll be safe without me."

"I can always drive with one hand and shoot with the other," he said. "There is no good reason why the mirror on my side should go unpunished."

I hadn't been to Paris since my libertine-lawyer days. But of course, the eternal city hadn't changed. Except that being in love and having Nellie along made Paris even more fun. Her bubbling, contagious, unforced enjoyment of every pleasure made me feel as if I were some minor wish-granting jinni—although I had never read in *One Thousand and One Nights* where the jinni got repaid for his efforts with champagne-fueled, chandelier-rattling sex.

Then we flew to the islands, and the shoe was on the other

foot. Nellie took over as guide, hostess, and civic booster. We went to markets, restaurants, clubs, and historic sites in the Cidade Velha until I felt pleasantly exhausted by the end of each day. An endless train of relatives showered us with endless drinks and endless delicious meals. We stayed at the Hotel Pestana Trópico, whose saltwater pool was invigorating for weary tourist bones. The October temperatures were still in the low eighties, allowing us to swim and cavort along the beaches—arguably the least beautiful sands in the island chain, but still a welcome change from home.

And in between all the fun stuff, we tended to the demands of the pudding factory.

The slightly shabby but well-tended facility on the southern outskirts of the city was run by a fellow named Onésimo Dambara. He proved to be a moderately handsome middle-aged guy, whose dark complexion carried evidence of some really severe adolescent acne or other affliction. He dressed impeccably in linen trousers and floral shirts and had the habit of smoothing his lush lothario's mustache and grinning whenever he addressed Nellie. I began to get a little jealous, especially when they exchanged rapid-fire Criolu that I, of course, could not comprehend. But I tamped down the emotion, realizing that I would never sleep if I contemplated Nellie fooling around all those times when I wasn't with her.

Dambara complained of having trouble with his supply chain of ingredients for the *doce de café,* and so we ended up visiting various plantations and dairies until we straightened things out. And then, before we were half ready to leave, it was the day of our flight back home.

Nellie cried as she boarded the plane, and I got a little wistful, too. I had visions of an unlived alternate life—of how this would have been my pleasant permanent home if our earlier scam had succeeded in making us self-exiled millionaires.

Our fair city at the end of October seemed cold and gray compared to Cape Verde. But it did feel good to be back.

I called Stan, and we arranged to meet for a beer.

"Glen, you are looking at a guy with seventy thousand bucks, more or less, in the bank, and a plan to make even more."

"Yeah? Tell me about it."

"I will do so eventually. But you have to help me with something first."

"What's that?"

"We are going to go get my woman back."

12

"Did you see the steamy look that babe gave us?" Stan said. "I swear, she woulda jumped right into the back seat and peeled her pants off if we'da asked her to."

"Stan, that woman was doing all she could do to keep from falling down laughing. We are driving a mobile recruitment poster for Jimmy Carter's Peace Corps, not some babe magnet."

"Women love quirky."

"This car is not quirky, Stan. It is as far beyond quirky as … as Pluto is beyond us. It is a monument to the unlamented era when pop culture's bad taste assumed the stature of sacred writ."

"You can toss your word salad about Mickey's dog with all the extra dressing you want, son. There is no way I'm going to see this vehicle as anything less than a rolling love wagon."

"Delusional," I said. "And besides, my lust-goggled friend, that thoroughly respectable woman had to be forty-five if she was of legal drinking age."

"I know you like 'em young and dewy, Glen, but someday you will come to appreciate the charms of older females. And those heels she was rocking said, 'I'm easy!' plain as day."

I threw my arms skyward in exasperation, whacking them on the hard roof of our joke of a car.

We had just pulled out onto Hedgesville Road after a satisfying meal at Bernice's Philly Steak and Subs, a neat, efficient hole-in-the-wall diner sharing part of a tawny-brick building. The woman who was the focus of our debate had been climbing into her car in the parking lot and had stopped midway to gawp in horrified wonder at our wheels.

We had taken Stan's new car on our mission to rescue Sandralene. We certainly could not have driven the eighteen-wheeler on this road, even if Gunther had been willing to loan it to us. And Nellie needed my Lexus to get around town on her own errands—especially since she had a trip planned upstate to Centerdale, where her parents lived. Not only did she relish a visit with them—she had still lived happily at home with her tight-knit clan before I spirited her away into a life of sin and entrepreneurship—but also, the sizable Cape Verdean population in that burg made up the initial market for her imports, and she had to conclude arrangements with various merchants. Not that she was planning to stay local for long. She had big dreams about the appeal of her line to nonethnic consumers and hoped she could someday take her brand national. I found myself always cautioning her not to move too fast or get too big before she had a solid foundation.

So Nellie, who knew and approved of this mission to rescue Sandralene, was now somewhere behind the wheel of my sweet luxury ride while Stan and I tooled down this neat, moderately busy two-lane street of modest homes and the occasional strip mall, in what could be charitably classified as a campy antique.

With some fifteen thousand dollars of his bankroll, Stan had bought a Jeep. But not just any Jeep. It was a CJ5 limited model made in 1973—and, I had to admit, in mint condition. The archetypal nonaerodynamic body, like a cracker box on wheels, was mostly a lurid white. I had never imagined that white could be lurid, but this somehow was. The roof and the upper back portion of the car that wasn't big smoky windows gleamed an electric royal blue that would have been judged too overpowering for the uniforms of the Toronto Blue Jays. So far, so tacky. But the kicker was the detailing. Groovy undulant red and blue stripes traced the contours of the Jeep, with occasional cartoony white stars jittering against their patriotic backdrop.

And, of course, not only was the beast a rolling punch line, but its 1973 amenities consisted mainly of ashtrays for every occupant. Of its lack of safety features, I prefer not to speak.

And this was the chariot with which Stan intended to woo Sandralene back into his arms.

I had to admit, Stan was never one to let practical considerations sway him from embracing his authentic vision of a life well lived.

I looked at him and had a sudden insight.

"Are you talking like a horndog because you're nervous about seeing Sandralene again and what she'll say?"

Stan only frowned and kept us rolling down the road.

The drive from home had taken not quite five hours at moderate speed. After our many Detroit jaunts, the journey south seemed like just rolling out of bed to trot down to the corner store. I realized now that Stan deliberately went slow to give himself time to ponder tactics and strategy. I had refrained from offering any advice on how to win Sandralene back. Indeed, I wasn't even convinced that any such campaign was necessary. I found it hard to believe that a few months apart while she tended to her sick mother would have served to alienate the two soul mates—even if complicated by the interested presence of one Caleb Stinchcombe.

I had tried to get Stan to share details of his new get-rich scheme, but all he said was, "When this whole Romeo crap is over, that'll be plenty of time."

Our first stop in West Virginia had been our lodgings: the Thomas Shepherd Inn in Shepherdstown, a large two-story brick Federal-style structure dating to 1868 and painted a café-au-lait shade. Those were the closest accommodations we could find to Hedgesville proper, about twenty minutes distant.

Our hosts, a husband-and-wife team who resembled Santa and Mrs. Claus from the *Rudolph* TV special, had greeted us with effusive warmth, plumping pillows and rearranging chairs before leaving us in our room.

"They think we're gay, right?" Stan asked.

"Hey, if it gets us extra French toast at breakfast, I'm willing to play along."

Leaving our bags unpacked in the room, we had set out for Hedgesville and lunch.

And now, after just a mile or three of additional driving, passing a fire station and a school and a Shell station as well as some neatly tended mobile homes, we were arriving in the center of Hedgesville, such as it was.

"There's the house," I said. Its small, narrow porch was separated from the road only by the width of a sidewalk and a grassy strip. "Number two-oh-one."

Stan turned into a moderate-size paved lot next to the picket-fence-bordered yard of 201. He cut the motor and we stepped out.

On this late-October day, the temperature hovered in the midsixties, and the sun seemed still to be fondly dreaming of the summer just past. I knew that the snaky Potomac, the border with Maryland, was just a short distance away, and I fancied that I could smell its riverine essence.

We realized we were in the parking lot for the Zion Church, a tidy red-brick building with a pointy steeple. Across Hedgesville Road, roughly opposite number 201, stood a larger white wooden church. Any such concentration of churches always seemed to me to imply a proportionate amount of sin that needed preventing or atoning for.

I sized up the house where Sandralene must reside. Three stories high, planted off-center on a quarter-acre lot with plenty of vegetation both cultivated and wild, it sported beige vinyl siding except on its porch, whose bare wood could do with a paint job.

The presence of two guardian churches around the Parmalee ancestral manse seemed to imbue Stan with a good feeling, as if nothing too terrible could happen within their godly sphere of influence. He adjusted his trousers and shirt for a less rumpled look.

I noted a historical sign at the margin of the parking lot. I walked over to read it. It told of the founding of Hedgesville: "Site of a stockade fort built during the early Indian Wars ..."

Stan came up beside me and read the sign, too. I sensed his continued reluctance to face Sandralene, who, of course, knew nothing of our intentions.

Finally, Stan turned to regard the house. "Okay, no more stalling."

"I'm not the one stalling," I said.

"Glen, when you're right, you're right. Let's go."

13

The narrow porch, which was empty of furniture and useless for sitting, really, was a mostly symbolic architectural shield against the nearby flow of traffic. Standing there, I got a deeper impression of the house. Genteel/shabby, as if it had once been better maintained but now suffered from lack of resources and a hollowing-out of its inhabitants, who probably still loved the place but with a sort of melancholy despair.

The doorbell button had a swatch of duct tape across it. A hand-lettered sign, thumbtacked above the bell and faded by the weather, said to PLEASE KNOCK LOUD. The door had a curtained window.

Stan banged with his big fist on the wooden part of the door, and we waited for a response.

"You ever been here before?" I asked.

"Naw. Sandy and I met in the city, and I never knew squat about where she hailed from. She just didn't like to talk about her past."

The curtain twitched aside just enough for an unfamiliar eye and slice of wrinkled cheek to manifest itself before the gauzy fabric slipped back into place.

Another ninety seconds passed, and then the door swung inward.

Sandralene stood there with an old-fashioned straw broom upright in her hand. I had an instant flash of *American Gothic*—if the painting had been drawn by Bill Ward of *Torchy* comics fame.

When I first met Sandralene, her physical magnificence had left me speechless, as if viewing Kilimanjaro for the first time. Proportioned along Amazonian lines, Sandralene inhabited her lush physique with the composure and unassuming self-possession of a jaguar. Her mass of dark wavy hair further accentuated her resemblance to some big, sleek prowling feline. And yet, a Zen-like placidity of expression—resting Buddha face, I called it—left the male beholder feeling as if he were trying to interpret the emotional state of a galaxy whose center contained an insatiable and all-devouring black hole. After knowing her for nearly two years, I was still just as much in awe of her as ever.

Today, Sandy wore a pair of cowboy-cut Wranglers with ripped knees and an untucked men's white oxford shirt. Her hair was gathered up in a red bandanna, and her shapely feet went bare. Even this modest attire, which did not cling to her curves, still seemed pushed to its limits to contain her plenitude.

Stan opened his mouth to speak, but Sandralene beat him to it.

"Stan Hasso, you can just get right to work! There's too much here for just me to do!"

She thrust the broom at Stan, and he reflexively took it.

"Well, what are you standing there for, like two hydrants waiting for a dog to piss on 'em? Come inside."

The front door opened into a hall of sorts. A few steps in

front of us, a staircase with well-used rubber treads headed up. A doorway on the left and one on the right opened onto the rooms at the front of the house while a third doorway, alongside the foot of the stairs, led to the back of the house. A worn braided rug and a teetering vintage side table served as the hall's furnishings. The room on the left offered a view of a sprung sofa, while to the right I could see ladder-back chairs around a large pedestal dining table whose veneered surface had last gleamed about fifty years ago.

"Follow me," said Sandralene with vast authority, and we did.

To my amazement, the normally voluble and in-command Stan had yet to say a word.

We marched through the house, where the other furnishings conveyed the same worn and beaten-down air, and out the back door and into the yard. On a long clothesline hung four or five time-abused rugs.

"Get all the dust out of those, Stan. It isn't good for Mama's condition."

Stan gave one of the rugs a tentative one-handed swat with the broom, but evidently without meeting Sandralene's standards.

"Come on! Show me some of those muscles you're always bragging about!"

Stan gripped the broom with both hands and walloped the rug. A cloud of dust and dirt big as a tumbleweed sprouted.

"Good! That's it! Keep at it!"

Grinning, Stan seemed actually happy to be venting his emotions in a useful physical way, and he laid into the innocent carpets as if they were the guys from Lake Superior Bijoux who had lost him all his investments.

I looked to Sandralene. "Uh, should I beat some rugs, too?"

"No! You come with me and help me get lunch ready."

"But, Sandy, Stan and I just ate."

"So? Mama and I haven't had lunch yet, and Stan'll be hungry again when he's done, and if you're not, you can just watch us all eat."

I meekly followed Sandy back into the house. This new decisiveness and air of command had left me cowed even more than her mere proximity usually did.

We did not proceed immediately to the kitchen, however, but went into a back room that must once have served as a kind of manly den. A table held fly-tying gear, all plainly untouched in years. Ranked on the room's shelves were what appeared, judging by the few titles I could immediately glimpse, to be a complete run of *Reader's Digest Condensed Books* from about 1980 until they had petered out in 1997 with some offerings by Grisham and Crichton. A modern digital TV exuded the anachronistic air of an invader from the future.

A fully extended Barcalounger, whose gray fabric exhibited a variety of daubed but ineradicable stains, held Sandralene's mother in a drab housedress.

I had expected some ancestral similarity to Sandralene's stature, but her mother was of only modest size, her frame perhaps shrunken by age and illness. I estimated her to be about sixty-five. Vestiges of her former good looks indicated that if she had not endowed Sandralene with height and bust and hips, she must still have been a fetching gal in her youth. But now wispy white hair and a pallor diminished her former attractiveness. She wore nose clips leading to a portable oxygen unit. Big tanks stood beside the chair.

"Sandy, honey, could you hook me up to the tanks, please? This little gizmo just ain't got no oomph."

"Of course, Mama."

Sandy made the switch and then introduced me.

"Mama, this is my good friend Glen McClinton. You know how I've talked about him so much. Glen, this is Lura."

"Very happy to meet you, Lura."

Her smile still held some traces of youthful zest. "Likewise, Glen. Are you down here for any special reason?"

"Just to see Sandy."

"Good, good. She's been plenty lonesome these past few months. If it weren't for Caleb's visits, it'd be just her and me sitting here like two warts on a frog."

"Mama, I'm going to make lunch now. Do you feel up to joining us, or would you like to eat here?"

"Here, if you don't mind, dear."

"No, that's fine."

We left Lura fiddling with the television remote.

On the way to the kitchen, Sandralene said, "It's not cancer, just COPD. But that's plenty."

"I guessed as much."

In the kitchen, while Sandy was at the fridge, I took stock of the old-fashioned sink and ancient stove and worn linoleum. Everything was spick-and-span.

Sandy carried prepacks of cold cuts and plastic tubs of coleslaw and potato salad over to the counter. She set them down, and then she burst out sobbing.

"Oh, Glen, what am I going to do!"

She threw herself at me, and I felt as if I had caught someone jumping from the fourth floor of a burning building. The undeniable carnality of her pillowy embrace instantly recalled to me the one time we had sex. Her tears activated my innate sense of protectiveness and aroused me at the same time.

And then, of course, Stan walked in.

14

I released Sandralene and jumped back as quickly as if she had suddenly said, "Flame on!" and revealed herself to be the Human Torch.

"Stan, let me explai—"

Stan regarded his woman and me with a lack of emotion scarier than any jealous anger. "First things first. Who does a guy have to murder around here to get a goddamn cold drink? That carpet-beating gig is frigging hot work!"

Sandrelene sniffed and dragged the back of one hand under her nose, then used the back of the other to swab the tears from her cheeks. "Just hold on one lousy minute, you big greedy ape."

She poured almost a quart of Country Time Lemonade into a repurposed GoMart cup. Stan glugged it down and gave a sigh of appreciation.

"All right, now. What do I have to know, who is going to tell me, and how pissed will I be?"

I had regained my composure easily enough, in light of my innocence. Also, my incipient woody had disappeared, lending my words credence, or at least not directly contradicting them.

"To take your questions in reverse order: Not pissed at all. It's me, your true-blue buddy Glen, telling you. And what you need to hear is that Sandy just wanted a friendly familiar shoulder to cry on, since she faces overwhelming stresses, demands, anxiety, worries, and the necessity to make sandwiches not only for her visibly sick mother and herself but also for two uncouth, unmannerly louts who dropped in without warning."

"Okay. This is the kind of no-bullshit explanation I enjoy hearing. Thank you, Mr. Glen."

"You're welcome."

"And just for the record, I got friendly familiar shoulders, too."

"Oh, Stan!"

Sandralene flung herself into the embrace of her long-absent paramour, and the freshets of tears resumed as if she had been saving them just for him. Stan ran his big hands soothingly up and down her back. But soon they began to stray south of her waist, to the rondures of her shapely bum, and Sandralene's sobs began to acquire a certain lascivious moaning quality. She lifted her wet face from his shoulder and they began to kiss.

"Uh, guys, are you sure this is the place …?"

Neither of them paid me the slightest heed. I might as well have been Jiminy Cricket trying to dissuade Pinocchio from running away to Pleasure Island. The kissing continued to progress into something more.

I left the kitchen and returned to the den, where Lura Parmalee was absorbed in watching *The View*. Mercifully, the decibel level approximated that of the squadron of Harryhausen harpies who attacked Jason and the Argonauts.

"Lura. Lura!"

"Yes, Glen?"

"I think lunch is going to be delayed!"

"That's fine. My appetite's not so good these days, anyhow."

Despite the racket emanating from the TV, I could still hear unnerving sounds of copulation-engendered destruction emanating from the back of the house—dishes breaking, wood splintering, chairs overturned, and the like. So I went out to the car to wait. With the mild breezes of West Virginia wafting through the windows, I almost fell asleep.

Forty-five minutes later, Sandralene appeared in the backyard of her house, at the fence that separated the property from the church's parking lot. The radiance of her resting-Buddha face said all there was to say.

"Lunch is ready!" she called, then trotted merrily off.

I discovered a dilapidated gate in the fence and reentered the house by that route.

The kitchen had been restored to some approximation of its original state, and its small square metal-topped table was set for three: paper napkins, paper plates, plastic cups; chemical-based drinks poured, overstuffed sandwiches sliced diagonally, and uncapped salad containers sporting serving spoons. I assumed that Lura had already had her lunch delivered to her.

Stan was already seated. His broad grin matched Sandralene's, and his face showed a recent scrubbing.

"Damn, I am hungry enough to eat week-old road kill!"

"You consumed an entire three-meat-special sixteen-inch pizza barely over an hour ago," I pointed out.

"A mere appetizer, son. And don't forget how hard I been working."

I sat down and scooped myself some potato salad. The first bite of my sandwich revealed bologna with mayo on white bread. I don't believe I had had such a concoction since I was ten years old.

Stan and Sandralene did not seem inclined toward conversation. I didn't mind. They alternated eating with making goo-goo eyes at each other. I still didn't mind. But when they started feeding each other bits of broken-off sandwich, I had had enough.

"Sandy, your shirt is inside out. And, Stan, that hickey on your neck looks like a lamprey got you."

Stan sneered. "Jealous much?"

"Just tell me you did it on the counter and not on this table."

"Wouldn't you like to know?"

Sandralene had the dignity to blush—not in an especially repentant fashion, but rather as if nostalgic for what had occurred not so many minutes earlier.

"Boys, please!"

Before Stan and I could continue our repartee, there came a loud knocking at the front door.

Sandrelene shot to her feet.

"Oh. I forgot Caleb was coming today!"

15

The four of us—Sandy, Stan, newcomer Caleb Stinchcombe, and I—stood clustered around Lura Parmalee's recliner like diplomats paying their respects to a recumbent head of state. The TV had been muted, thank God. Sandy had rushed us all into the room directly upon greeting Caleb at the door, as if Lura's presence was the only thing she could rely on to enforce good behavior between Stan and Caleb. Penelope never handled the return of Odysseus among her suitors more deftly. So far, Stan and Caleb had not had a free second in which they could bump chests, bare their canines, or engage in any other simian territorial gestures.

I took the opportunity to size up Sandralene's childhood pal.

Caleb Stinchcombe could not properly be termed a redneck, although he walked the narrow edge of falling into that category. Above his Red Wing boots, he was dressed completely in faded blue Dickies work clothes. His shirt had long since been rendered raggedly armless. Perhaps this modification had been for warm-weather comfort or ease of physical action, but it had the additional effect of highlighting very large biceps and massive forearms. Indeed, he was built generally along the same impressively burly lines as Stan, and they could glare at each other with eyes on the same level. But his blond buzz cut and aquamarine eyes contrasted with Stan's darker looks, and his face also featured a kind of apple-cheeked artlessness that, along with a certain air of humility and signs of a moderate intelligence, counterbalanced his shit-kicker indices.

Sandralene turned her attentions, I was glad to see, to Stan first.

"Mama, I want you to meet Stanley Hasso, my boyfriend, about whom I have said so many wonderful words across these many years."

Lura perked up at confirmation of Stan's special status as potential son-in-law. "Mr. Hasso, you've been very good to my little girl, from what she tells me."

I suppressed a snort at the "little girl" characterization as applied to Sandralene, who could have hoisted Sheena of the Jungle over her shoulder and swung one-armed from a vine. Nor did I mention Stan's recent bankruptcy and his attempts to regain solvency through the interstate transportation of counterfeit goods.

"It is surely no effort, Lura. She is a woman who brings out the best in a man, and she deserves everything good. And I plan to keep on treating her special for just as long as she lets me."

"I'm very glad to hear that ... Stan."

Lura's moderate initial affection for Stan seemed genuine and unforced. But when she turned to Caleb—who had been examining Stan intently during his presentation—she practically glowed. She reached out with both hands, and Caleb took them gently.

"And, Caleb, dear, it's so wonderful to see you!"

Caleb's voice was well modulated but with a certain restrained brusqueness, as if he were used to having to yell at featherbedding underlings who weren't living up to his standards. "Always a treat, ma'am. I hope you're doing well?"

"As well as these old creaky lungs allow. What brings you here today?"

"You must've forgot, ma'am. Today's the day I was gonna look at your roof and see how much work it's gonna take to fix it."

Lura's face grew solemn. "You know we can't pay you, Caleb."

"That's funny, Miz Parmalee, I don't recall ever speaking about money here."

Sandralene laid a hand on Caleb's bare arm, and Stan's eyes narrowed as if he were a warthog contemplating a rival.

"Caleb, someday, *some*day you'll get repaid. I promise."

"Aw, Sandra, just forget it, all right? I owe your family more than I can ever make up."

"How's that?" Stan asked with a mix of interest and belligerence.

Caleb fixed him with a straightforward and unabashedly solemn look. "Sandra's daddy saved my life."

Stan looked disbelieving.

"It's the simple truth," Sandralene confirmed.

"Sandra and I were ten years old. Her daddy—Danny—was a fisherman. Just wild for the sport. One Saturday in August, he took us up to the Potomac, near Little Georgetown. Sandra and I went swimming while he fished. Boy, could he cast a right smooth line."

Sandralene took over the story as if part of a well-rehearsed stage duo. "Caleb dove under the water, kinda showing off wild-like. And then he didn't come up. I started screaming."

Caleb scratched his blond fuzz with embarrassment. "Hit my fool head on a rock and then got tangled in a snag somehow. Next thing I know, I'm on the bank of the river and Mr. Parmalee's doing CPR on me."

"Daddy knew CPR from being a volunteer fireman."

"Didn't have no cell phones back then. Even if we had, it woulda taken the nearest ambulance company way too long getting there to do me any good. No, like Sandra says, it's just the simple truth that Danny Parmalee saved my life. You never can work off that kinda debt."

Lura was sniffling. I looked away out of politeness, and my gaze fell on the fly-tying setup across the room. Suddenly, that far-off day seemed vividly present. I could almost smell the river and feel the August heat.

Even Stan seemed quietly impressed. "Sandy, your daddy sounds like a real hero."

Caleb, Lura, and Sandralene exchanged looks of chagrin but kept strangely silent. Finally, Sandralene spoke.

"There was a lot to admire about my father. But he had a dark side, too."

Lura chimed in. "My Danny, he liked to drink too much. He turned mean when he had a skinful."

I asked, "Is that why you separated from him, Lura?"

Sandralene replied for her mother. "Mama never divorced Daddy. He died in prison. A brain aneurysm."

"Mr. Parmalee got in a bar fight," said Caleb. "One punch was all it took. The fella hit his head on the curb and died two days later. Involuntary manslaughter. He only got a sixteen-month sentence, what with having a family to support and never being in any real trouble before. But then the brain thing took him while he was still behind bars. Only upside to the whole mess was that he died in seconds. Sandra was just fifteen."

Lura began to weep, and Sandralene bent to comfort her.

"Mama, Mama, don't cry! That was all a long time ago. Daddy's been at rest forever. All anybody remembers now is the good he did. That's what brings Caleb here today."

We three men stood helplessly by. Eventually, Lura ceased weeping, and Sandralene got her TV show going again. We left Lura watching as Rachael Ray laughed and broke eggs into a mixing bowl.

Back in the front hall, Caleb said, "Let's take a look at the inside first. You can show me where it's leaking."

"I know something about construction," Stan said. "I'll help."

I refrained from saying that so far as I was aware, Stan's expertise with buildings had less to do with repair than with how best to burn them down.

We climbed the creaky stairs and found ourselves in a second-floor hall. The narrower set of stairs at the left end obviously led to the third floor. Sandralene led the way, and I came last.

The others were ascending when a partially open door caught my interest. I poked my head inside.

This was Sandralene's childhood bedroom, and the unmade bed with its frilly white coverlet showed she was still sleeping here. The walls were painted pink. A poster of the Backstreet Boys circa 1997 loomed over a collection of stuffed animals. A small shelf of books chronicling the adventures of the Babysitters Club also hosted an array of souvenirs from nearby attractions: a cream pitcher labeled SENECA CAVERNS, an embroidered patch from the Monongahela National Forest.

I picked up a framed photo of an adolescent Sandralene standing next to her father. Both were smiling broadly with an arm around each other.

Danny Parmalee was revealed as the source of Sandralene's monumental physique. He looked like a bluff, devil-may-care good-time Charlie—fun to be around until he got ticked off.

And, in fact, he reminded me a little of Stan.

I put the photo back and caught up with the others on the third floor.

Caleb was busy knowledgeably inspecting stains on the slanted plaster ceiling. Stan echoed the expert's interpretation of the house's condition. Sandralene nodded her head quietly at the running diagnosis. Eventually, the inspection ended, and we all went down and outside.

In the adjacent parking lot sat Caleb's hard-worn black pickup truck, with white lettering on the doors.

STINCHCOMBE ROOFING

AND REPLACEMENT WINDOWS

"WE DO 'EM ALL, BIG OR SMALL!"

"It's like I thought," said Caleb solemnly. "Whole roof needs replacing. Best I start tomorrow. I'm between jobs now. If I can get up to the Home Depot in Hagerstown before nine, I can be back here by ten."

"Sounds fine by me," Stan said. "I plan to be right up on that roof with you."

16

Caleb Stinchcombe drove off in a cloud of exhaust and the noise of an ailing engine that could use a valve-and-ring job at the very least. I had a hunch then that his business was not doing so well and that his immediate easy commitment to work on the Parmalee homestead was not going to discommode other waiting customers.

Stan turned to Sandralene. "Okay, babe, where am I sleeping?"

"What do you mean?"

"Well, me and Glen got us a room over in Shepherdstown at this froufrou doily-and-doughnut place. But now that you and me've made up, I figured—"

"Well, you figured wrong, mister. What happened a little while ago in the kitchen was very nice, I won't deny it, and maybe it's even a step back to our old times together. But I can't have you here overnight, lolloping around the house like a horny walrus. Mama's too sick for that nonsense. She needs her peace and quiet, and my first duty is to give her all my attention."

"You sure you just don't want me out of the way so's you and Stenchy can get together behind my back tonight?"

"Stanley Hasso! Caleb and I are not an item. He is just my oldest friend and a very, very important piece of my past. And if I ever did want to get sweaty with someone else, I'd do it right under your goddamn nose in the middle of Main Street at high noon!"

I felt suddenly moved to clean off some road dirt from the Jeep's taillights.

Stan raised his hands in surrender. "All right, all right. No need to pump up the decibel level; I hear ya. In that case, Glen and I are gonna hit the road. But we'll be back first thing in the morning so's I can help with the roofing."

Sandralene proffered her cheek for a chaste farewell kiss. Then she went back inside the house with perhaps a little more hypnotic swaying of hips than strictly required for locomotion.

Stan tossed me the Jeep's keys. "You drive. I got some thinking to do."

"I'm not sure I can pilot this vehicle without my Evel Knievel jumpsuit on," I replied.

"Hardy-har-har."

Apparently sincere about his intention to muse and meditate, Stan remained quiet all the way back to the inn. Even in the room, where he threw himself down on the bed with his dirty shoes on, he kept his silence. I used the opportunity to phone Nellie.

"Hi, honey."

"Glen, *meu konbósa*! I miss you so much! Where are you? What's happening? Are Stan and Sandy back together?"

"Stan and I are back in our B-and-B now for the evening. We met Sandralene's mother and that friend of Sandy's, Caleb.

Stan and Sandy have made some small moves toward getting back together again. They are fine with each other, I'd say. But the big issue is still her mother's health. Sandy doesn't want to leave her alone anymore, I think. And that kinda throws a crimp in all of us returning to the city together."

"Oh, Glen, you are so smart and Stan loves Sandy so much, I'm sure you will work something out!"

I looked over at Stan. His brow was furrowed as I had never before witnessed, even when he was plotting the maneuvers involved in conning Barnaby Nancarrow, and he was paying no attention to my phone conversation.

"I think you might have our roles reversed."

Nellie laughed. "What, Stan's the thinker and you love Sandy? Glen, you are so funny!"

"What's up with you?"

"*Algun kuza grandi!* I got Gaipo's Market to agree to carry our line!"

"That's great," I said. "They have like, what, four locations?"

"Six now!"

"I hope you have a mansion already picked out."

"You joke! But I could make us rich someday!"

Nellie's talk of earning honest money naturally inclined me to recall Stan's assertion, before we left town, that he had some kind of sketchy get-rich-quick scheme at least partially doped out. I resolved to convince him to spill the beans sooner rather than later.

Nellie and I exchanged some more inconsequential talk before hanging up. When I had finished, Stan suddenly spoke.

"Let's get something to eat. My belly button is humping my spine."

We tracked down a little bistro, not too touristy, not too hipsterish, called the Blue Moon Café, on the corner of Princess Avenue and High Street. It was airy and friendly and, as it turned out, the source of some tasty food. Stan ate two pulled-pork barbecue sandwiches and a mountain of fries while I had the veggie quesadilla. My meal order prompted the most dialogue from him since we had left Sandralene.

"You in training for the Fearless Girl Olympics or some such?"

"My gut is still churning from baloney and synthetic lemonade," I replied. "I had to put something healthy in my stomach to counteract the effects of your woman's 'cooking.'"

"Well, this barbecue sauce is righteous. Burns like Sandy's kisses. It would restore your probiotic balance."

I laughed. "Do you even know what 'probiotic' means?"

"Yeah, sure. It means 'I'm a wuss who woulda died young if I lived in the caveman days.'"

"Listen, if you want to insult my dietary choices, you should at least go into a bit more detail on this new racket you've hit upon."

"No, not now," he said while saturating his second barbecue sandwich with hot sauce. "Let's get this mess settled first. And besides, I don't have all the angles down yet. I need to talk it out with you. But only when we've got Sandralene back home."

Twilight was coming on when we ended our dinner, and for some exercise we strolled toward the riverfront, eventually ending up at a little park that featured a quintessentially American obelisk dubbed the Rumsey Monument. It stood on a granite pavilion at the head of a few stairs, on a bluff high above the Potomac.

Stan found a few pebbles and began chucking them into the waters below. The distant *plonks* in the gathering darkness sounded lonely and futile.

Eventually, Stan ran out of ammunition for his assault on the river. "Okay," he said, "I figured out how we're gonna convince Sandy to come back with us."

"Great. Let's put your plan in motion so we can get home."

"But there's one other thing I have to do first. I have to show up this Caleb guy for the useless jerk he is."

"Oh, Stan, really now? Can't you just let him be? Especially if we take Sandy out of his reach. And besides, he seems like a nice guy."

"All the more reason Sandy should think he's a jerk."

"I know better than to argue with you. Do what you must. But don't count on me to sabotage Caleb."

"You won't have to help. Me and him will do it all ourselves."

We were back in Hedgesville by nine the next morning. The breakfast at our inn had indeed consisted of baked stuffed French toast, of which Stan, with the beaming indulgence of the proprietor, scarfed down more than his share.

We had time for only a brief chat with Sandralene—Lura was still abed—before Caleb Stinchcombe arrived with a load of shingles and nails and roofing felt and tarps. Shovels and other tools occupied the passenger seat of his truck.

"Sandra," said Caleb, "I think your daddy used to have a good ladder or two in the basement. Figured it would save me toting mine."

"Maybe. Let's look."

We discovered a couple of solid old-fashioned wooden extension ladders in the musty, cobwebbed cellar and brought them outside.

Surveying the house, Caleb said, "We've got a little extra work cut out for us since we can't dump shingles onto the street-side property. Too narrow—they'd end up all over the road, puncturing tires and feet. Probably shouldn't dump them in the church's parking lot, either. So that leaves the side yard and the back. Let's get the tarps spread out."

Using the ladders, Stan and Caleb secured the big green tarps so they formed a kind of fabric slide on two sides of the house, from the roof level to the ground, protecting the windows and siding from falling debris. Sandralene and I watched admiringly. When they were finished, Caleb said to Sandy, "I was going to hire a roll-off dumpster, but then I thought it'd be, um, kinda expensive. So if you don't mind the mess, I'll just truck the old shingles away. It'll take longer, but I've got a deal with the folks at the transfer station."

"Whatever you think best, Caleb."

Stan frowned at Sandralene's admiring tone.

"Okay, then, let's get busy ripping stuff up."

Caleb and Stan ascended their ladders with shovels and pry tools and began shucking off the old shingles, periodically sending shovelfuls over the edge of the roof to skitter down the tarp slides. Although the October sun was mild, the work still looked hot and onerous.

"Can I help?" I yelled.

"No room up here for ex-lawyers!" Stan yelled. "Just go give Sandy a hand."

So I went inside, where Sandy put me right to work on the many chores she had been unable to tackle alone. All day long, the noisy rain of asphalt roofing provided a soundtrack for the domestic chores.

Looking tired and sweaty, the two men came down for a quick lunch, then headed right back up. By suppertime, the whole roof was stripped, all the recalcitrant nails removed, and the surface swept, and the bed of Caleb's pickup was filled with the first load of debris.

Sandy had already thanked Caleb effusively and was now inside, tending to Lura's needs.

"Tomorrow, we'll truck the rest of the junk away," Caleb said. "Then we can get busy putting down the roofing paper. Oh, I want to use roofing jacks, too. Much safer."

He eyed Stan meaningfully.

"I told ya, I'm like a mountain goat up there," Stan said. "No need to worry about me."

Caleb nodded without much conviction, then got in his truck and drove off.

When he was gone, Stan said, "I'll give him this much. He knows what he's doing, and he's no slacker."

"I'm sure you can work around his good qualities."

"Huh."

We went back to our inn to wash up and ate again at the Blue Moon Café. This time, I put away two barbecue sandwiches while Stan had four.

The next day, the yard was clean of debris by eleven, and the tarp slides dismantled. Then began the laborious work of toting heavy rolls of roofing felt up the ladders. Stan made the task into a competition.

"Hey, Stenchy, let's see who can get the most rolls topside the fastest."

Caleb did not respond to the insulting nickname but simply accelerated his pace to match Stan's.

I was kept busy inside trying to figure out what ailed the Parmalees' old washing machine. Eventually, after several YouTube videos, I thought I had the problem figured out. I went outside, where Stan and Caleb were grimly continuing their race as they stapled down the tar paper.

"Hey, Stan!" I yelled up. "I have to use the car to go to Hagerstown for a washing machine part!"

Stan didn't bother to say anything, pausing only long enough to toss me the car keys.

When I returned, the whole roof wore its completed protective undergarment, and Caleb was getting the system of roofing jacks in place. These were sturdy red steel brackets, nailed to the roof in a line and bridged by a plank laid across them to afford the workers safe and solid footing as they applied the shingles. The whole affair could then be repositioned as they worked their way higher up the roof.

"That's enough for today," Caleb finally decreed, and they came down.

Back at the inn, a sore and groaning Stan had to have a long, hot soak before he could even go out and eat.

"That son of a bitch is as hard to stir up as a hornet's nest at the bottom of the sea," he growled. "But I'll make him show Sandy he's nothing but a weak sister in the end."

"You'd better hope you aren't just one big blister before that happens."

They began shingling the next day, and Stan never let up on Caleb for a minute. I had been given the task of mowing the backyard—with a push mower, no less—and trying to tame the wilder thickets of shrubs, weeds, and perennials. So I witnessed the whole thing, starting with two men silhouetted three stories high against the pellucid West Virginia sky. When Stan's chatter picked up, I ceased the clatter of my mower's blades, fearing the worst.

"Hey, Stenchy, who ever taught you how to hold a hammer? Where'd you get these cheap-ass shingles, anyway—the Dollar Store? You call that a tight seal? This house is gonna leak worse than before!"

Caleb soldiered stolidly on, but even from this distance, I could tell that Stan's stream of insults and derision was starting to wear on him.

The men had started at opposite ends of the supporting plank, working in toward the middle of the roof. Now they were practically shoulder to shoulder.

"Gimme room, Stenchy; gimme room! You ain't showing off now to your little gal pal in the river where you nearly screwed the pooch!"

Caleb calmly slid his hammer into the loop at his thigh and stood up on the plank. Stan immediately stood up, too. But from the stiff way he moved, I could see that he was exhausted and his bum knee was troubling him.

I was debating whether to rush up the ladder, call Sandy, or yell "Murder! Help!"

"You don't ever mention that day again, you hear?"

"Who's gonna make me?"

Caleb cocked his arm and swung.

Stan, not at his quickest after three days of hard physical labor, shuffled his feet to avoid the blow, as he would have done adroitly on the ground. At the same time, he swung up his arm in a defensive move that shifted his center of gravity. And so he lost his footing on the plank.

17

The next few seconds unspooled in a sort of slow-motion horror ballet that went something like this: Stan's right foot, closest to the edge of the plank, slipped off just as Caleb's punch arced over his head. Windmilling his arms, Stan then began to topple forward and down until his chest and forearms and maybe chin, too, smacked down onto the freshly nailed-down rows of shingles. The awkward impact jarred his left foot off the plank, and with his legs now hanging over the plank's edge, nothing but the friction of his torso against the asphalt shingles held him in place. And then his considerable weight counteracted that meager friction, and he began to slide down the slope.

At the same time, Caleb reacted by dropping solidly to his knees on the plank as Stan continued his slide toward the abyss. Somehow, Caleb had gotten his claw hammer out of its loop and into his right hand and hooked it into one of the solid "steps"—a length of two-by-four nailed into the roof above Caleb and Stan's row of jacks. Caleb then twisted around from facing the roof to grab at Stan in midslide.

Now, maybe Stan would have managed to catch the plank and save himself. Maybe, failing that, he would have grabbed the gutter and held on—if the flimsy aluminum gutter held somehow—until I could maneuver a ladder over to him, and all before he could fall thirty feet to a serious if not lethal impact. But maybe instead, he would have failed at both saving moves, or even dislodged the plank and brought Caleb down on top of him. No one would ever know, however, because Caleb saved Stan's sorry ass.

A powerful left hand grabbed Stan's right wrist, arresting his downward slide. I could see Caleb's bare right arm, holding the hammer, tauten like a ship's hawser. But everything held. Then, in a Herculean demonstration perhaps not replicable outside this extreme moment, Caleb pulled himself upright by the hammer in his right hand, while hauling Stan up by the hand clamped around Stan's wrist, until Stan's scrabbling feet could again find purchase on the plank.

With the danger over, I suddenly realized I was not alone— Sandralene held my arm in a death grip. I must have let out a shout of alarm when the drama began, bringing her rushing out the back door and into the yard, where she had apparently witnessed the whole affair.

Caleb had both hands on Stan's shoulders, and Stan was nodding his head. Thus reassured, Caleb guided him along the plank to the ladder.

"What happened?" Sandy said.

"Stan was fucking around."

Her anxiety did not disappear, but I could tell it was now tinged with anger.

Soon both men were on the lawn, shaky but sound. Sandralene ran to embrace Stan first. But then Caleb received an equal measure of corporeally expressed gratitude as his reward.

Finally releasing Caleb, Sandy pivoted and, without warning, punched Stan in the gut.

"You big, mean, thoughtless idiot!"

Her well-timed blow caused Stan to whuff out all his breath. After gasping for a few seconds, he recovered without any show of resentment. In fact, he looked positively un-Stan-like in that moment.

"I guess I oughta thank you for that, darlin'," he said. "And my thanks to you, too, bro. I take my lumps as I deserve 'em. But if it ain't too much extra to ask, where are the goddamn cold beers me and handsome Johnny Reb here so richly deserve?"

"Allow me," I said. "It's not every day I get to witness a command performance of the Flying Wallendas in action."

I was glad to leave the three of them alone for a few minutes to straighten out any lingering issues, so I checked on Lura first. She appeared to have slept through the whole thing in her recliner while the TV blared its daytime inanity.

Outside again, I handed out the beers and we all sipped in grateful silence under the warm October sun.

Then Stan said, "Okay, that killer roof ain't gonna shingle itself. Let's get back to it."

Happily, Caleb had the good form not to ask whether Stan was okay or up to the task, but just said, "I don't think we can quite finish it today."

"Fair enough. One day at a time, son, one day at a time."

"Right," I agreed. "And I've got to whip the gardens at Versailles into shape. That's a big job, too."

"Oh, boo-hoo for you," said Stan.

Sandra regarded Caleb and Stan with silent admonishment that did more than any words could to let them both know they were on her strict parole. She went inside, the newly sociable roofers ascended, and I returned to my push mower.

On the way back to our B&B, Stan didn't speak for the first few miles. Then he said, "Now I owe you both big-time."

"Owe both who what?"

"I owed you already for saving my life." Stan referred to our first meeting, when I had blasted a hit of Narcan up his snout after he OD'd. "And now I owe Stinchcombe for stopping me from taking a thirty-foot nosedive. That's debt enough to make a fella weary of going on. Maybe I should just change my name and take a powder."

"Or—and I admit, this is a long shot—you could try being a better person."

"Ain't gonna happen, Glen boy. But don't worry, neither is the other thing. You and Johnny Reb are stuck with me for a good long while yet."

Before dinner, lying on his bed in our room, Stan said, "I gotta make a couple of private phone calls."

"You know how to find your way downstairs to the street."

"I figured you could leave me the room so I could rest up a little more. I've had a very demanding day."

"Oh, Christ, what a big baby! All right, I'll meet you at the Blue Moon."

When he showed at the restaurant, Stan seemed quite pleased with himself.

With a wariness born of experience, I said, "Care to tell me what's going on?"

"Nothing but the smoothing of our domestic troubles, and the paving of our road to riches. You'll find out soon enough."

"It's not 'our' domestic troubles. Nellie and I don't have any disagreements."

"I am generous to a fault, Glen, and what's mine is yours."

* * *

The shingling job was finished by midafternoon the next day, and I had made as much progress as I could with the unruly flora, short of taking a flamethrower to the entire lot and starting from scratch. Now the four of us—Caleb, Stan, Sandralene, and I— sat around the kitchen table, sweaty and rewarding our sense of accomplishment with a cold pilsner.

Stan spoke up. "Reb, you thought about my offer long enough?"

"I have. And I'm going to take you up on it." He looked to Sandy and me. "Like I told Stan, my roofing business is on its last legs. Work has dried up almost entirely. I was about ready to throw in the towel anyhow, when Stan asked me to go north and help him with his new enterprise."

"New enterprise?" I said.

"Just hold your horses, son. You'll hear all about it on the drive back home. Now, Sandy, honey, what did Lura say when you told her about our plans?"

"She's all for it, Stan. She's very grateful and she even started to cry. She said you're like the son she never had."

"What plans?" I said.

"Lura's coming back to the city with us."

"You're putting her and Sandy up in that tiny hovel you call an apartment?"

"No, Reb's gonna live there. And quit making the place sound worse than it is."

"Where's Lura going to live, then?"

"With your uncle Ralph and Suzy Lam. Old people love having other old people around."

"With Ralph and Suzy! What do *they* think about this?"

"Why don't you call them?"

I took out my phone and dialed my uncle's house. Suzy Lam, Ralph's racetrack coconspirator, main squeeze, and Chinese-auntie-style force of nature, picked up.

"Nephew! You in town yet? We can't wait to meet Sandy's mom. She looks like Wonder Woman, too, maybe, huh? And that rent money she brings—too generous. It will help us so much! This shitbox car of mine goes through oil like a goddamn battleship!"

After I managed to extricate myself from Suzy Lam's enthusiasm, something dawned on me.

"If Caleb's living in your apartment, and Lura's at Uncle Ralph's, where are you and Sandy going to stay?"

"Right with you and Nellie, son! We gotta keep our heads together twenty-four-seven to pull this operation off!"

18

We were approaching the city limits, and I was still trying to fathom all the convolutions of this new scheme of Stan's. Only partially sketched out, inspired by a chance occurrence, and certainly requiring a much larger investment than he and I could cobble together, the whole megillah seemed dicey and a little daft.

On this gray, chilly October Monday—goodbye, temperate West Virginia clime!—with drizzle flecking the windshield, and the antique car's lack of a working heater a distinct inconvenience, the two of us were the only occupants of Stan's Bicentennial Super Jeep. Much as Stan had wished to play the conquering hero ferrying Sandralene and her mother north, Sandy's calm and cogent reasoning had finally prevailed on him to admit that his car did not constitute a suitable conveyance, especially for Lura.

"That oversize Hot Wheels toy is a rolling death trap," Sandralene had told him. And it's got no shocks to speak of. I am *not* going to have Mama shaken to pieces before she dies in a fiery collision."

And so, despite Stan's barely suppressed grumbles, it was Caleb who got to shepherd the ladies home. His silver 2005 Buick Park Avenue—payment in kind for fitting out some tract mansion with storm windows—appeared to be a sort of shabby-luxe West Virginia status symbol. He was quite proud of it, and it did seem like a limousine next to Stan's ride. So our cramped back seats held only Lura's modest luggage. The trunk of Caleb's car was stuffed with his clothes and vital possessions, including a complete set of roof-shingling tools, "just in case this here plan of yours goes tits-up."

Both Caleb's home and the Parmalee manse, with its new watertight roof, were sealed up snug for the duration of this change in residency, and under the watchful eye of one of Caleb's many cousins.

"Call up Sandy and see how they're doing."

"You just talked to her twenty minutes ago."

"I want her to know I care about her and her mama."

"Jesus, you'd think you two had just agreed to go steady while sipping frappés at the local soda fountain. Did you give her your letter sweater yet?"

"Today is the first day of the rest of your motherfucking life, Glen. That's how I try to live."

"Maybe we should start up a line of inspirational posters instead of this harebrained enterprise you have barely begun to elaborate."

The impetus for Stan's dreams of quick unearned wealth, I learned, had been his last delivery of goods from Detroit—the trip I bailed on in favor of lolling about in the Cape Verde Islands with Nellie. (He had quit his driving job at that point, or at least arranged an indefinite leave of absence. In either case, he and Gunther had parted on good terms.) The journey had been unexceptional—no hijackers or cops or snoopy weigh-station personnel involved. But the cargo had been atypical. And its ultimate disposition had been totally snafued.

Stan had transported not fake baby formula or fake Victoria's Secret lingerie or fake Le Creuset cookpots, all of which he and I had delivered before. No, this time he hauled a trailer full of fake Intel Core X-Series microprocessors, each packaged tastefully in its black-and-gold box whose printing quality was only slightly muddier than the real thing.

Five thousand of them, each with a retail value of fourteen hundred dollars. That is, the real ones from Intel fetched that much, and these would presumably sell in roughly the same ballpark, even considering the discount for their illegitimate provenance.

Seven million dollars' worth of bogus computer chips.

If I had entertained any illusions that penny-ante Gunther, who picked up beer money at flea markets with his fake handbags, was the mastermind of this racket, this news laid them to rest.

Certainly, Vin Santo, the presumed whale behind this speculative endeavor, stood to make some nice money if he could sell all these little gizmos. And there had apparently been a guaranteed buyer—before they got busted.

Stan had shown me the headlines on his phone.

COUNTERFEIT GAME CONSOLE DISTRIBUTOR ARRESTED

MILLIONS OF DOLLARS IN ESTIMATED ILLEGAL SALES

BEFORE BEING SHUT DOWN

DISTRICT ATTORNEY EARNS GRATITUDE OF RETAILERS

Now the five thousand fake units were sitting in Gunther's warehouse without a buyer.

And Stan thought he could parlay them into at least a million dollars apiece for us.

"What did you have in mind?" I asked him. "Just step into the shoes of the guy who was arrested, in possession of more fake PlayStations and Xboxes?"

"No way. The local cops and the feds are all over that market, just waiting for the next sucker to try it so's they can chop his head off, too. No, we have to turn those chips into some other kinda digital whatsit. Everything digital is hot these days. Your ePads and your iDildos and all like that. We find someone who can use those chips, then we go to Santo and arrange to broker the deal for a cut. I figure he's pretty desperate by now to unload that stuff, which is just taking up space on his shelves, and recoup his investment."

"Sure. But would he really cut us in for such a big percentage of the deal? Two million out of seven tops?"

"I figure it depends. If he can't find a taker himself and we make it easy for him, then we'd be worth it. But I ain't gonna settle for less than a million apiece. I'm sick of nickel-and-diming it."

"But what if he finds a buyer himself?"

"Then we're out in the cold. That's why we have to move fast."

"And how do you suggest we go about locating a client for these chips?"

"We are going to get a solid lead from your buddies who rooked me."

"Chris Tabak and Jess Inkley, from Burning Chrome? As I recall, they did not precisely 'rook' you. It was more like you dumping wheelbarrows of cash at their feet."

"Those are the bums, whatever they did or didn't do. I figure they've got tons of leads, even if some are investment opportunities that weren't quite up to snuff for them."

"You know," I said, "you might actually be onto something there."

"And why are you surprised at my genius? No, wait—no need to jeopardize our friendship. Now, get Sandralene on the phone. I want to make sure they know how to get to your uncle Ralph's house."

I called Sandy and established that they were not far behind us, having made an additional bathroom stop to accommodate Lura, and that Sandy did indeed recall where Uncle Ralph lived: on Greenwich Street in a modest working-class neighborhood dubbed, with unmerited pomposity, the Swales.

After I hung up, Stan said, "Still not gonna call Nellie to let her know what's up?"

"She knows we're returning today, and she's back from her own road trip. But there is no way I'm going to tell her over the phone that you and Sandralene are coming to stay with us. That is the kind of news that has to be delivered face-to-face."

"Aw, you know Nellie loves me and Sandy. That little girl has had a sweet spot for me ever since I rescued her from a lifetime of wage slavery at Micky Dee's."

"And involved her as an accessory in a grand-larceny scheme from which she emerged unpunished only by the grace of who knows what overgenerous deities. It's still a miracle that she ever forgave me for all the lies you forced me to tell her."

"Ha, that's a good one! You whomped up more lies than I ever did. Bigger and badder ones, too—mainly because that's what lawyers do."

"No, that's what *crooked* lawyers do. And God knows, ever since I became one long before you stepped on the scene, I have lied my way into and out of more trouble than I ever before imagined. But I don't seem able to stop."

"Because you don't want to be a normie, no more'n I do."

"This much is true," I said. "But let us return to the topic of your moving in with Nellie and me. Being good friends with someone does not necessarily mean you care to share living quarters with them."

"Quitcher old-lady fussing about it, will ya? It's only temporary. Didn't we all live together at the motor lodge?"

"Yes—in separate cabins."

"What if I promise not to use your toothbrush?"

"Was that ever even a likelihood?"

We were almost at Uncle Ralph's, so I tabled the discussion.

At the front door of the modest, frowsy ranch house, I had an overwhelming sensation of déjà vu, taking me back to when I had lived here postincarceration, after my stint at the halfway house, before Stan and company ever entered my life. It seemed eons ago, and I wondered what new changes this phase of my life would bring, and how I would feel looking back on this day from some distant point.

Suzy Lam greeted us as if we were from the Lottery Commission, bringing her one of those giant publicity checks. Her cheerful, roly-poly Asian bountifulness always made me feel good. I was glad Uncle Ralph had her in his life.

"Where's my new sister, boys!" she whooped. "I got her room all fixed up nice. Now, Glen, I know it used to be yours, but there is no moving back in now!"

I thanked her and went inside to see Uncle Ralph. As usual,

his wrinkled, whiskery vitality as he bounced up out of his comfy chair conveyed a mix of Uncle Sam and a billy goat.

"Glen," he said, "you're looking fit as a fiddler crab. When are you and Nellie going to take us to dinner again? I could chow down at Red Lobster any old time."

"Soon, Uncle Ralph. Once things stop being so busy all the time."

Through the front window, I saw Caleb's car pull up.

Sandralene ushered Lura in with daughterly solicitude. Introductions were made, with Caleb receiving a generous share of Suzy's bonhomie, and the arrangements of the house were disclosed, down to how to stop the toilet from running on forever after a flush.

"It's a swell place," Lura said. "Thanks for having me. I'm glad not to be alone in that big old house, and to free up Sandralene. I just hope the winter isn't too cold up here."

"Colder than a well-digger's ass most years," Uncle Ralph said helpfully.

"Goodness!"

"Mama, don't listen to him. If you feel settled, I'm going to go now."

Sandralene and her mother kissed goodbye, and we left the house.

"Reb, I'm gonna show you to your new place before we go brace Glen's woman about us moving in. I figure not having a stranger around will make things simpler with Nellie. But we'll all get together for supper tonight. Sound okay?"

"Sure. I don't want to be a monkey wrench in anything."

I was a little uneasy at how fast Stan was railroading Caleb, so I asked the big, easygoing Southerner, "Are you sure you'll be okay alone for a while, here in a strange city? You've got our phone numbers ..."

Caleb gave me his trademark broad, guileless grin. "Oh. Sure, Glen, thanks for asking. But you know, I'm a big boy now, and this is not my first time in a standoffish northern city. Why, back in high school we had a class trip to New York. Stayed overnight, too!"

Stan rolled his eyes. "So your passport's got a shitload of exotic stamps in it. Let's get a move on."

We drove in two cars to Stan's ghetto apartment. I had never actually been inside since Stan and I reconnected at the flea market and was surprised to find the third-floor walk-up less squalid than the exterior of the building and the generally dismal tone of the block had led me to imagine. Caleb trotted up his stuff from the car, then flopped down on the couch.

"I won't mind a break," he said. "Kinda tuckered out. This is more changes than I've had to go through in the last ten years."

Stan returned from the bedroom with a suitcase of his own clothes. Sandralene's things from West Virginia had already been transferred to the Jeep.

Sandralene bent down to bestow a kiss on Caleb's cheek. "Thanks so much for all you've done, Caleb. We'll try to make all your troubles worthwhile."

"The landlord lives on the first floor," Stan said. "I'm gonna tell him which car is yours; then it shouldn't be messed with."

With Sandralene along in the Jeep, I got demoted to the cramped back seat along with the bags. Luckily, it was a short ride to my condo.

Nellie must have been watching for us, because she met us down in the lobby with kisses and hugs and a huge smile.

I felt grateful to be back in comfortable, familiar surround-ings. It seemed that lately all I had done was travel. I got ready to deliver my carefully formulated speech to Nellie about our new very temporary lodgers, when Stan blurted out, "Nellie, babe, Sandy and I have to crash with you guys for a while. That okay?"

Nellie gave an excited squeal. "*Fixe!* We will make everything like a big *fésta* all the time!"

While Nellie was hugging Stan all over again, he managed to give me a look that said, *The fun's just starting, kid!*

19

In my lawyer days, I had gotten so I could spot an MBA with some certainty from across a crowded shark tank. My skills were so refined that I could almost name the alma mater of any venture capitalist my work brought me into contact with. But tonight over our business dinner, I learned that although I had known them cursorily for some time, my radar had failed to discriminate properly in the case of Chris Tabak and Jess Inkley. Or maybe I was just out of practice. To my eye, the trim and preppy Tabak looked totally East Coast, and I had always pegged him as a graduate of the Columbia Business School. Staid and dull Inkley, on the other hand, had about him a corn-fed air not so far removed from Caleb's down-home manner, and I had subconsciously assigned him to the University of Chicago's Booth School of Business. In fact, their alma maters were exactly reversed, proving that you can't judge a crook by his sheepskin.

But whatever their deceptively dissonant matriculations, the two men and their agency, Burning Chrome Ventures, had a reputation as smart, savvy, relatively aboveboard private-equity guys. Sure, they had come a cropper with Lake Superior Bijoux and thus deprived Stan of his nest egg, but there had been nothing sketchy about the deal. At the same time, like all such guys, they liked to skate on the edge of convention, respectability, and government-approved best practices, in search of the biggest payback before any crew of like-minded rivals could swarm in. So Stan and I had high hopes that they could point us to a buyer for the fake Intel chips—some high-tech start-up looking to cut corners, who maybe wouldn't peer too closely at the provenance of the goods.

We had decided to leave Nellie and Sandralene home while meeting with the Burning Chrome duo. It wasn't that we intended to keep it a permanent secret from the women, or even that we necessarily assumed they would frown on our venture. We just figured that the fewer complications at this stage, the better.

Before we sallied out to supper that night, I had asked Stan a question that was bugging me.

"Do these counterfeit chips actually work?"

"Well, the video game guys who were snapping them up didn't have any complaints. But I don't think they actually offered, like, any warranties that lasted much longer than a round of *Monster Hunter Two*."

"So we could be held accountable if these chips had a high failure rate?"

"Aw, come on, Glen boy, put that scheming lawyer brain of yours to use. Exactly how is some schnook who knew from the get-go he was buying and reselling fakes gonna come after us? What would they say if they even got us in court? 'Your Honor, these for-shit rip-offs I bought at a crazy discount didn't hold up to the standards of the real things I shoulda purchased if I was an honest businessman'? No, once we dump these fakes, we are golden. No refunds."

"Well, then, I guess, if you say so …"

"I say goddamn so."

I had picked a restaurant where I once dined pleasurably with Tabak and Inkley years ago: the Auroch and Dodo, whose specialty was exotic meats. Surprisingly, the place enjoyed a good reputation among the hipsters and the coolhunters and the socially enlightened since all their meat was sourced from fair-trade ranches in Africa and South America and impoverished parts of the USA that practiced sustainable farming.

The server had given us menus, set us up with drinks, and told us the specials.

"The Everglades Pizza is a favorite. Alligator, python, and frogs' legs."

Stan said, "Are you fucking shitting me?"

The server, an impeccably turned-out young fellow with a man bun and a way of talking that indicated his favorite director was Wes Anderson, remained unperturbed. "I can bring you a sample."

"No way. What're you guys having?"

"The capybara was delicious last time I was here," said Tabak.

"Okay, put me down for that."

We had appetizers that involved ground camel meat on focaccia and chatted about nonbusiness topics for a while. Tabak and Inkley politely made no reference to my past transgressions and jail time. Our entrées arrived, and Stan took a tentative bite. Finding it to his liking, he chowed down enthusiastically on the slabs of pale meat in gravy. I had made the comparatively safe selection of *beshbarmak*—horse, with noodles and onions.

We finally got around to the real matter of the evening.

"Chris, Jess, we need your advice," I said. "And please, we expect you to bill us for this consultation." I explained how we hoped to sell the Intel units that had recently come into our possession, while omitting any discussion of their genuineness.

The two men put their heads together figuratively, employing the semitelepathic communications of longtime business partners. *"Do you think—?" "No, that's not quite right." "Maybe ...?" "What about—?" "Nope, can't see it."*

Finally, they had to admit to drawing a blank.

"C'mon," Stan urged impatiently, "there must be some Bill Gates type just getting started in his toolshed who needs what we got. They won't go cheap, but if you guys are financing him, he could maybe swing the deal."

Tabak looked at Inkley. "What do you think of Luckman?"

"It's the only real possibility, even though it's a slim one."

Stan got excited. "Luckman! I dig the name already. What's his story?"

"Well, he's got an invention. And that's about it. No business plan really, no investor interest. We thought he was too risky for us. But the invention just might be marketable. And from what I understand, each unit would use one or more processors. If he was ever going to launch his line, he'd need those chips of yours."

I said, "But he's got no current backing? Is he independently rich?"

Inkley chuckled. "Not so's I could see."

"Then how could he afford to buy our chips? No, this seems like a dead end."

"Hold on. Hold on just a damn minute," Stan interjected. "We could get in on the ground floor of something here. Maybe we wouldn't just sell him the chips and book it. Maybe we'd be more like partners with this Luckman."

I could see that Stan was falling prey to the same fever that had seduced him into bed with Lake Superior Bijoux. "Stan," I said, "this is way beyond our original scope."

"Glen, my man, you have to know how to recognize an opportunity when it presents itself, and how to grab it. Besides, all we're gonna do is approach this Luckman cat and see what he's all about. No commitments unless it looks good, right? What could we lose?"

"All right, I suppose it's safe. We've got no other avenues."

"Give us the contact info on this Luckman bird."

Tabak texted me the man's name, phone, email, and address: Dr. Ronald Luckman, resident in a nearby suburb outside the city.

We got through coffee and dessert, I paid for everyone, giving Man Bun a decent tip, and we made our goodbyes; then Stan and I were out in my car.

"I got a real good feeling about this," Stan practically crowed.

"You sure you're not just feeling that plateful of giant rat you just ate?"

"What're you talking about?"

Still parked, I googled up a picture of a capybara, with its designation of world's largest rodent, and showed it to Stan. He studied it intently for a moment, then handed me back my phone. He looked slightly green.

"Well, I said lots of times I was hungry enough to eat a rat's ass, so I guess it serves me right."

20

A frustrating week had passed since the dinner with our investment advisors, and Stan and I had not yet contacted Dr. Ronald Luckman. When we called his house and spoke to his wife, he was out of town at some professional conference. Then we decided that before hitting up the doc, we should try to feel out Vin Santo, owner of the languishing Intel chips. No sense in putting a lot of work into this scheme if the chips had been sold or if Santo was not interested in working with us. But he, too, proved to be on the road—in Vegas, at what was surely a very different sort of professional conference from Luckman's.

Meanwhile, life moved on.

Caleb Stinchcombe had found his temporary niche in chauffeuring Lura and her dutiful daughter around on innumerable trips to various new doctors to get Lura's health issues under control. He seemed as happy living in Stan's digs on his own savings as a clam that had escaped the chowder pot. Lura, meanwhile, was basking in all the attention and happily adapted to life with Uncle Ralph and Suzy Lam. And Stan evinced no jealousy that I could detect.

When Sandralene wasn't tied up with her filial errands, she had taken to assisting Nellie with the mechanics of getting Tartaruga Verde Importing up and running at full steam. Sandralene claimed that she couldn't just sit around our apartment all day but had to feel useful. So Nellie had put her to work on the computer, designing labels for various products. Despite having no experience or training, Sandralene proved to be a quick learner, surprisingly talented in coming up with attractive imagery and layouts once she knew her way around the software. Adorably, she employed both hands when using the mouse.

"*Kon serteza*, Sandy is no Caboverdean," Nellie told me. "But she has the eye and mind of the average customer. And she really wants to help!"

"That's good, sweetheart. Maybe you could even take her on your next trip to the islands."

Nellie's look turned serious—an expression that I always thought made her look like a perplexed teenage beauty queen contemplating which pimply boyfriend got to take her to the prom. Not for the first or last time, I marveled at my good fortune.

"But Sandy and Stan do not have a lot of money, Glen. And what they do have, Stan is saving for some investment, I think. *Talvés*, it could be we have to buy Sandy's ticket. Would that be okay?"

"Sure. Totally deductible."

"*Nháku!*" Nellie hugged and kissed me. "This would be next best to going with you. Only thing missing would be me riding your big *pichoti* on some quiet secret beach."

This randy talk and some immoderate snogging led to impromptu afternoon sex in a providentially empty apartment—a romp that I needed immensely. Having Sandralene sharing these living quarters had, as I had feared, led to a more or less perpetual low-level state of arousal. The first time the big, curvy woman had sat her exquisite rump down at the breakfast table, clad only in creamy silk pj's that Nicki Minaj would have rejected as too incendiary, I had to force into my mind's eye images of baseball, chess, and tile showrooms. Thank God Stan was still lazing abed. So sending Sandralene away with Nellie to Cape Verde would be like experiencing a period of blissful, relaxing monasticism.

After Nellie and I had cooled off, still lying in bed, she asked me, "So, Glen, you know what Stan has in mind? Are you in on it, too? Please tell me it's not something dangerous like when you messed with that *cabeca ma biroti* Nancarrow."

"Yes, I do know. And yes, I am on board. And no, there's no danger at all. It's just a chance to make some real money. You know we could use some income, the way we're spending on the import business."

I hadn't meant to guilt-trip my lover, but the unintended effect was useful in gaining her wholehearted agreement. "Oh, Glen, you must know how grateful I am for all your support! You are making *nah sonhu* come true! Anything you and Stan decide to do is fine by me. I don't even need to know nothing specific. You just tell me when everything is *kompletu*—or before then if you need my help."

So, with Lura, Caleb, Sandralene, and Nellie all cruising along happily engaged in their various pursuits, Stan and I felt confident of tranquility on the home front when we showed up for our meeting that night at the door of Vin Santo's nameless blind pig.

"You got your game face on?" Stan said.

"I've never been gamier."

"Good one."

Santo's manager was the same obnoxious young twerp with the postmodern buzz cut who had failed to run me off on my first visit. This time around, he showed some grudging deference as he ushered us past the wheels, cards, slots, and boozy clientele into the unadorned, pedestrian quarters from which Santo reigned. Even a supercilious lout could smarten up, I supposed.

Seated at his commonplace desk, the mercenary monarch still resembled some tubby borscht-belt stand-up comic with awkward secret vices and the fashion sense of an Albanian sugar-beet farmer. His perpetual Big Gulp stood within easy reach. The same two stooges, or clones thereof, who had shadowed my earlier meeting with Santo stood guard just inside the door.

"Welcome, gentlemen," Vin said with the closest thing to a smile that we were ever likely to get from him. "I know one of you personally, even if we don't go too far back. Glen McClinton, how ya doing?"

"Pretty good, Vin. And you?"

"Can't kick. I haven't had to kill anyone in at least the past half hour. That makes it easy on my delicate nerves."

For my peace of mind, I decided to assume he was joking, and so I just smiled in response.

Santo turned to Stan. "Now, *you* I know by reputation. The best torch in town. Once worked exclusively for Barnaby Nancarrow, until he did you dirty."

"That useta be my CV in a nutshell, Vin. But it's out of date.

You can add that until recently, I was driving one of your rigs, under your boy Gunther Stroebel. Never lost a cargo. And I aim to add a few more lines to my résumé. Glen and I are now legit brokers, like. And we come to you with a proposal."

Stan outlined in broad terms how we thought we had a buyer for the fake Intel chips that were still presumably languishing in the warehouse, and would be happy to take a commission on them. Naturally, he did not name Dr. Ronald Luckman as our prospect, but he did say the guy was an inventor.

Santo seemed intrigued by this. "An inventor? With some kinda new high-tech gadget? That shit is how you really clean up big these days."

When Stan tried to speak in the manner he imagined a venture-capitalist representative of Burning Chrome would speak, it came out like a duck trying to impersonate a dog.

"We believe this to be so. But we have not fully sussed out his potential nor the marketplace applicability of his product."

Santo seemed impressed. "This could be very lucrative if we did more than just dump the chips on him and screw. A nice conduit for laundering certain moneys. You think this brainiac is open to taking on some silent partners?"

Stan lied with bald-faced confidence. "We do. In fact, we were already thinking along those lines ourselves, having some residual profits from our last enterprise, which we wished to put to work. But if you want a piece of the action, Vin, we'd be more than happy to cut you in."

Santo sipped his plastic bucket of candy-flavored swill and pondered our offer for a moment. "Okay," he said, "here's how it's gonna go. You brace this guy and come back to me with a solid assessment of his gizmo. Glen, I'm relying on you and your investment paisans for this judgment. Then I will decide if I am prepared to do this deal, and how much capital I'll put into it. Does that suit?"

"It suits us fine," Stan replied.

"Then let us seal this stage of our affairs with a drink."

I thought for one crazy moment that we were all going to have to take turns with the Big Gulp, slurping from the oversized straw as if it were a peace pipe. But Santo ordered up some nice champagne, and by the time the three of us had emptied two bottles, we all were chattering away like old army buddies.

And so it would be, I supposed, as long as we didn't do anything that made Santo need to kill us.

PART THREE

21

Yet again Nellie and Sandralene were out accomplishing vitally important business errands in my beautiful car, which, it seemed, I hardly ever got to drive. I suspected that part of their day would be devoted to purely self-indulgent shopping, but I didn't mind. Keeping our women happy and busy and out of our hair was an essential part of the scheme Stan and I had worked out. And riding in Stan's clown car was a small price to pay.

We had followed my phone's GPS out of the city, to the bedroom community of Hayfields. As the name implied, the district had, once upon a time, featured farms and cows and similar arcadian motifs whose pastoral charm our hardworking ancestors had failed to preserve down to our time. And so the land had long ago been platted out in middle-class houses, seeded with a few strip malls of restaurants and yoga studios, and devoted to weary workers who had moved on up from the immigrant origins of their parents.

As we turned onto Greenwood Street and I began looking

for number 1300—Luckman's address, as provided to us by the boys at Burning Chrome—Stan said, "I'm gonna let you make our pitch to this Poindexter. You know, suss out what his invention is, how many of the chips we can reasonably unload on him, what we can charge. The investment angle, if any. All that good stuff. After all, you gotta start carrying your weight in this enterprise sooner or later. And I figure you'll relate to some overeducated nerdburger a lot better than I will."

"Thanks, Stan. Operating on those principles, I should allow you to talk only to brain-damaged three-card-monte dealers who moonlight as trade union enforcers."

"Ha! I know you don't mean that, Glen. I know you got real respect for my brains. Why else would you keep on tagging along with me and backing my brilliant schemes? After all, who hit on this whole play of brokering the computer parts?"

"Oh, you've got street smarts, sure; that much I give you. But that wouldn't be enough to convince me to follow you. No, your real seductive gift is some kind of mystical good luck that always saves your ass and makes you come out of the pile of horseshit smelling like the proverbial rose."

Stan seemed to consider this seriously. "Like having you in the car behind me with a hit of Narcan just when I OD'd."

"Why'd you have to go and remind me of the biggest mistake of my life?"

"Biggest smart move of your life, you mean, you ungrateful bastard! For one thing, without our connection and everything that happened, you'd be jerking off every day instead of tapping your cute little brown shorty."

"Maybe instead, I'd be an honest lawyer again, about to get nominated for a state supreme court judgeship."

Stan laughed so hard, I thought he was going to drive into a mailbox. When he could talk again, he said, "You are so permanently bent, you could not even walk into a courtroom without giving yourself a black eye from the doorknob."

"Here's Luckman's house, on the right," I said to bring the frustrating conversation to a close. Stan pulled into the short hedge-bordered driveway of a colonial with an attached garage, both in need of a paint job, sitting on an unkempt quarter-acre lot.

We had finally made an appointment with Luckman, so he was expecting us. And indeed, the door swung open almost immediately after we rang the bell, and Dr. Ronald Luckman stood revealed.

The scientist was of average height, not precisely burly or fat, but rather, cylindrical, keg-shaped, without many natural contours. The punch line to an old joke involving scientists popped into my head: *First, postulate a perfectly spherical cow ...* This odd quality extended even to the formation of his skull and his pan-shaped face, which could reasonably be called, in a way, good-looking despite its oddity. I realized that what he most resembled was a living Lego sculpture.

Luckman's short sandy hair was threaded with gray, and I realized he had to be at least in his late fifties—older than Stan and me by quite a few years. He wore wide-wale corduroy pants and a much-laundered checked flannel shirt against the November chill; argyle socks, and scuffed boat shoes.

"Mr. McClinton? Mr. Hasso? Won't you come in, please."

His baritone voice, though educated and composed, conveyed some level of incertitude, lack of self-confidence, or weariness, as if life had delivered to Luckman more than his share of beatdowns.

The house's interior displayed an absolutely average array of furniture and decor, except perhaps for an excess of overstuffed bookcases. But I had little time to scope out the environment before Luckman said, "Let's go right out to my workshop. You'll be able to see the project for which I need your chips."

Off the neat kitchen, a door opened directly into the garage. As he stepped through ahead of us, Luckman flipped on the overhead fluorescents.

The chilly place was filled with shelving stuffed haphazardly with various electronics, components, tools, and complete devices. A portable heater unit radiated scant warmth. The smell of old motor oil and fried transformers filled the air. A large stained workbench centered on the concrete floor held a soldering station, pliers, spools of wire and solder, and an open laptop next to a gadget that I assumed was Luckman's project.

The gadget was a gray metal chest with a shoulder strap and a hinged lid, rather resembling a carry case designed to hold a hundred music CDs. But the interior was instead filled with a welter of complicated circuitry, connected to various readouts and controls and a tiny LCD display like a phone's screen. I assumed that the innards were exposed to be worked on and would be hidden in the finished state. From the case emerged a slim electrical cable terminating in a pistol-grip device that reminded me of a point-and-shoot video game controller.

I noticed Stan taking everything in with acute discernment and judgment.

Luckman's attitude as he approached the gadget became that of a beaming father ready to introduce his child prodigy. His dour face lit up with real enthusiasm and affection.

"Here it is, gentlemen. The result of over a decade of research and labor, all on my own nickel. No institutional backing—a hindrance that slowed my progress considerably. But that leaves all the patents and rights in my name. I call it the Luckman Blast Agent Sensor—LBAS, for short."

The name didn't help clarify anything. "Exactly what does the machine do?" I asked him.

"It's an explosives detector. Let me demonstrate." Luckman took down a glass jar filled with a quantity of pinkish granules. "ANFO—ammonium nitrate–fuel oil. The stuff McVeigh used in Oklahoma City. Now, watch this."

Luckman powered up his detector, and various colored LEDs began to glow, while numbers flickered and waveforms appeared on the little display screen. The whole affair reminded me of a clunky tricorder from early *Star Trek*. He picked up the pistol grip and held it over the vial, squeezing the trigger. Nothing happened, and he frowned. He adjusted some controls and tried again. Nothing. More adjustments, and finally a beeping like the backup indicator on a forklift sounded. Luckman appeared relieved.

"You see? Once the sensors are calibrated precisely, perfect detection every time, even through a glass barrier. And it doesn't work only with ANFO. The LBAS detects any kind of explosive you can name."

Stan gave me a look that asked, *Who's nuts, him or us?* I really couldn't decide.

"Each unit uses one Intel chip such as the kind you are offering for sale. I will need a large number of such chips, at a suitable discount, if I am to start mass production of my device."

"Do you have a buyer already?" I asked.

Luckman frowned. "No, not exactly. But the market for sensors such as mine is large and robust. The military, both domestic and international, places great store in such devices. Police and fire departments around the globe, also. Transportation security. The demand for a really accurate and reliable explosives detector is practically unlimited! The ones that exist now are primitive. But if I can only get mine to market before any of the next-generation rivals, I'll be able to establish a dominant position in the marketplace. That's why I'm eager to secure your chips."

"How would you pay us?" said Stan. "These babies go for fifteen hundred apiece."

Luckman's face fell. "Well, you see, I was hoping for credit, perhaps in return for a partial stake in the enterprise. My capital at the moment is limited—I've invested so much in R and D over the years already. And I'm afraid a professor's pay—I teach physics at the State University, you know—goes only so far."

The longer Luckman talked, the less I believed in him. He just seemed like an eccentric loser. Maybe his machine could do what he claimed. But more likely not.

"That's asking an awful lot from any partner, Dr. Luckman," I said. "We have to limit our risk, you see."

"Oh, but there's very little risk! Sales are practically guaranteed. Just look!"

On his laptop, Luckman brought up a recent news article from the *Wall Street Journal* that detailed the demand for such devices.

BIG AEROSPACE FIRMS GEAR UP FOR INCREASED

BOMB-DETECTION SALES

I was starting to reconsider the potential here when Stan cut right to the chase.

"How much would one of these babies go for?"

"Oh, given its superior performance against any competitor, I estimate somewhere between twenty and thirty thousand dollars apiece, based on prices charged for other, more limited devices."

We—or Vin Santo, to be precise—were sitting on five thousand chips worth fifteen hundred each on their lonesome: seven and a half million dollars' worth. Almost 100 percent profit, since Santo had paid peanuts for the initial load of junk hardware. That was a figure that could stoke a man's greed.

But now, inside one of Luckman's gadgets, each chip would suddenly be worth up to twenty times as much.

The math was easy enough even for a law-school grad. A hundred fifty million dollars gross. And again, while there were bound to be expenses, the vast bulk of that take would be pure gravy.

And Stan and I were nothing if not gravy hounds.

22

I knew that Stan had instantly run the same astonishing numbers in his own head as well. I gave him a look, which he correctly interpreted as a desire for a confidential talk. He addressed the professor.

"Dude, sir, me and my partner need to exchange a few private words."

Luckman seemed thrilled that we had not dismissed him and his proposal out of hand. "Of course," he said. "I understand completely. You two stay right here and have your discussion. I'm going back inside. I'll ask my wife to make some coffee for us."

Luckman left the garage and respectfully closed the door to the house behind him.

"So, whaddya think?" Stan said in a lowered voice. "Does this fossil got something valuable or not?"

"I'm no expert, Stan. I know that explosives detectors really do exist and that there's a deep market for them. That's about the extent of my wisdom on the topic. His gadget *seemed* to register the sample material after he fiddled with it for a while. But maybe he just pressed a button that set off the beeping manually. We don't know."

"Well, the more I think on it, the less it matters whether the gadget works like he says or not. All we gotta do is convince a buyer or three that it works. Maybe not the Pentagon, but somebody lower down the food chain and a little more gullible. Look at this thing, all them wires and dials! It's impressive enough to bamboozle that Apple guy Jobs, even, if he was still around."

"Maybe yes, maybe no." I pondered Stan's argument for a moment. "So you're saying we can build a fake detector with a fake chip inside and still sell it and get rich."

"Absolutely. You're a respectable and competent con man, aren't you? This looks like a perfect scam. No harder'n selling fake pocketbooks at the flea market."

"But what about the financials?"

"Obviously, we gotta bring Santo on board. You and I don't got the nut to get things rolling. Let's say we cut Vin in for eight million off the top for his chips. Another couple for whatever the production costs are, which he's gonna front. Call it ten. After we sell all the units, that leaves a hundred and forty million to split four ways."

"*Four* ways?"

"You, me, Santo, and Dr. Doolittle here. What's that work out to, roughly? Thirty-five million apiece. And you thought we were gonna score big off Nancarrow! We'd be set for life even if we paid legit taxes! With that kind of dough, we could spit in the eye of anybody we please."

"As Groucho said, 'If that's your idea of fun.'"

"Whadda ya say? Are you on board this gravy train or not?"

I considered the matter for a short interval. "It'll be a lot of work. We've got to babysit Luckman, keep Santo happy, make sure the girls stay blissfully in the dark, oversee production of the gadget, line up buyers, run the dog-and-pony show ..."

"You want your thirty-five million for doing nothing? Where's your goddamn work ethic?"

"Let's do it."

"My man! Okay, we just have to make sure Luckman don't go looking for no other backers; then we convince Santo we are onto a major deal and we know what we're doing. Let's get our asses in gear."

We opened the door into the kitchen. No one was there, but an old coffeemaker was dripping dark brew into its pot and filling the air with a pleasant aroma. We went on into the front room, where Luckman had first received us.

The bulky inventor was kneeling on a throw pillow in front of a modest side table in a wall niche. With no lamps lit, it took me a minute in the gathering November late-afternoon gloom to recognize the setup as a small, modest Christian shrine. A decorous statue of the Holy Virgin, an unlit votive candle in its painted glass jar, a set of rosary beads lying flat on the table at the foot of the statue, a framed photo of an elderly couple whom I instantly assumed were his venerated parents, probably long deceased. Luckman's head was bowed, his hands clasped, and his lips moving almost imperceptibly.

Hearing us come in, he unhurriedly finished his prayers, made the sign of the cross, and stood up. His guileless face exhibited no embarrassment whatever. Hardly my reaction or, I suspect, Stan's. Funny how Luckman's innocent piety disconcerted us more than if we had stumbled on him in flagrante with his wife.

Approaching us with an eager yet anxious smile, Luckman guided us back to the seating area. "Gentlemen, I hope you've reached a favorable decision on investing in me and my machine."

"Yes," I said. "Yes, we have. Your demonstration was most impressive. All this is contingent on approval by our superiors, of course, but I feel fairly confident in giving you our pledge of support. All that remains is to work up the exact agreement."

Luckman beamed and began shaking both our hands exuberantly in seemingly endless rotation. "Mr. Hasso, Mr. McClinton, this is the culmination of a dream. I can't possibly convey what this means to me. Oh, I know our success is not guaranteed, but I sense nothing but a clear road ahead of us. Let me get my wife in here with the refreshments, so I can tell her the good news. Rosa! Rosa, we're ready for the coffee now!"

In from the kitchen stepped a striking, elegant, yet somehow humble-looking woman in her fifties. Slim and small-bosomed, Rosa Luckman wore a simple brown sheath dress in an almost indiscernible plaid design and coordinated flats. Her wavy black hair, falling just below her shoulders, exhibited some proud streaks of gray. The few age lines on her face enhanced rather than detracted from her well-wrought full lips and large green eyes. She carried a tray with coffeepot, cups, and a plate of supermarket doughnuts.

Rosa Luckman turned her generous attention first to her husband, giving him a big smile. Her gaze flicked to me, then to Stan.

She stumbled, nearly losing the tray. Her face had gone solemn and pale. With an immense effort of will, she regathered her composure, but her pleasant voice quavered when she spoke.

"Forgive me, the rug ..." She hastily set the tray down on the coffee table. "Ron, please, all of a sudden I'm not feeling well. I have to excuse myself. I'll hear all your news later. I'm so sorry, gentlemen. Goodbye."

She turned and hastened out.

I looked at Stan. His face mirrored Rosa's. I had never seen him so pale and aghast.

Luckman, however, seemed to detect nothing odd. He made gentle excuses for his wife, poured us coffee, talked about a dozen random topics. It seemed to take forever before we could break away.

I waited until we were in the car. Stan seemed to have trouble finding reverse. Out on Greenwood Street and motoring away, I said, "Okay, you want to tell me what that was all about?"

"I know Luckman's wife from way back. Twenty years ago, she was Rosa Saxby."

"And?"

"And she was my fucking wife!"

23

The pleasant, manicured suburb of Hayfields seemed to acquire a *Twilight Zone* aura. Strangers in the street looked like alien mimics still learning their craft. A sheen of sweat on Stan's brow confirmed the depth of his unsettled state. I felt as if certain assumed foundation stones in the relationship between Stan and me had crumbled to dust. What the heck could explain this bit of ancient history, previously sealed away? And what line of questioning could I take that wouldn't further upset Stan and possibly earn me a bop in the snoot?

Luckily for me, Stan started talking first.

"You knew I grew up in the Gulch, right?"

"Sure, a real old-school slum. You had to walk uphill both ways to and from school through snowdrifts you could barely see over—that is, when you weren't shoplifting, rolling drunks, and shooting dice."

"Hardee-har-har. Easy for a rich guy's kid to make fun of us poor slobs."

"My dad never made more than thirty-five thousand dollars a year. Hardly rich-rich."

"Yeah, okay, but at least, you *had* a dad. And a mother, too, I know. That's being rich in the only way that counts. My old man croaked when I was seven. Too much booze all the time, and then one night he decided to take a little nap on the train tracks."

"Holy fucking Christ. I never knew. I'm sorry, Stan."

"Thanks. I try not to make a big deal out of it. All water over the bridge. And plenty of other chumps've had worse things happen to them. Lucky for me, my mother held it together and kept the family going."

I chose not to inquire at this moment about siblings, including the quasi-mythical trampy sister. I figured Stan would mention any such relations if they figured into his tale.

"But Ma died when I was sixteen. Cancer. I had no relatives—at least, not any that wanted to take in a stray kid. And I was a minor. The state was gonna put me in a group home. I couldn't stand the idea. I was all balled up inside, confused, half crazy. Plus, I was pretty wild to begin with. You weren't so far off the mark with your joke about shoplifting and shit. Except it was more of a grand-theft-auto thing. The idea of having to live with a bunch of strange kids and follow some dumb-ass rules and do what a bunch of busybody adults told me to do—it drove me nuts. I was all set to hit the road. Christ knows what woulda happened to me as a runaway. Sure, I was big for my age, and tough. But that's no proof against anyone bigger and tougher and meaner. I'd seen too many other kids go down that path to an early grave. But that was when Rosa stepped in."

"Rosa Saxby, who was—"

Stan took a sharp turn onto a wide avenue without really slowing down enough, as if he were trying to outrun the memories.

"Miss Saxby was our science teacher."

"And she took an interest in you because you were such a promising student?"

"Shove it! She had an interest in me because we were already screwing our brains out."

"Stan."

"Yeah?"

"You are my new retroactive role model for my own teenage years. You were living the *American Pie* dream. I doff my figurative hat to you."

"You can joke, but the whole deal was not like the fantasy. There was a lot of sneaking around and nerves and guilt. Rosa coulda lost her job, got prosecuted for sex stuff. She was almost twenty years older than me. But we couldn't quit it. There was just some badass unstoppable chemistry between us. It was like we went crazy when we were alone together. It wasn't all sex, though. She meant a lot to me, and I guess I meant a lot to her. Because of what she did when my mother died. I came crying to her about the group home and running away. And she said she had a solution. We'd get married. That'd make everything all legal and safe."

"You married a thirtysomething gal at age sixteen?"

"Sixteen and a half. You make it sound like it never happened to anyone else before. Didn't you ever hear of Jerry Lee Lewis?"

"I know you're big on the blues and rockabilly and such, but Jerry Lee Lewis' life does not present the greatest model for ethical or emotional smooth sailing."

"Well, maybe neither of us was thinking straight. But that's what we did. And, of course, Rosa had to quit her job anyhow when we went public. You can picture the scandal. Lotta frigid old maids got their panties in a bunch. Anyhow, we set up housekeeping together, and thanks to some odd jobs and pinching pennies, we managed to stay afloat. But it only lasted about a year and a half. There was too much tension; we were too far apart in who we were and what we wanted and how we looked at the world. Sure, I remember lots of good times from that year and a half. But on the whole, it was a really rough patch for us both. So as soon as I turned eighteen, I hightailed it outta the apartment and outta her life. Rosa got in touch with me a short while later to file for divorce. But we never saw each other after that. Twenty years. I never tried to look her up, and she never came after me, neither, far as I knew. Just too much pain involved."

"And now here she is. Mrs. Luckman."

"Yeah, I wonder how that happened."

"Happily for you, my friend, we live in an age of miracles. Allow me to consult my crystal ball."

It took me all of three minutes online to learn that Rosa Saxby Luckman had been the secretary for the State University Physics Department for fifteen years, until her marriage to Professor Ronald Luckman a few years ago resulted in her voluntary retirement from that position.

The news seemed to relieve Stan of some small measure of unease and anxiety. "She had an okay life, then, I guess. I useta picture her in bad circumstances when I thought of her at all, and it always tore me up."

"Is her presence going to interfere with our plans?"

"I don't know. I don't think so. But I'm gonna have to get her alone and talk about things."

"Maybe you can catch her when Luckman's in church."

"Oh, you are just the funniest goddamn comedian since Pauly goddamn Shore."

24

Stan and I were showing up at Vin Santo's illicit dice-and-drinks dive so often that we should have been given loyalty cards. Get nine punches and your tenth lap dance is free. (I seemed to recall, from my first drunken visit, a back room where such frivolities occurred, although Stan and I had not visited it since.) Instead of a suspicious reception at the entrance, we were waved in with a gap-toothed smile from a scar-faced doorman whose formal training must have taken place at the box office of cockfights where the mortality rate among the patrons rivaled that of the roosters in the pit. Even the two goons stationed as bodyguards inside the sanctum sanctorum honored us with stone-faced nods of recognition, as if to say, *We now deem it somewhat unlikely that we will have to blow your heads off, but we continue to stand ready to do so anyhow—although with maybe the faintest scintilla of regret, should the occasion arise.*

Driving here with Stan the night after the day of our interview with Dr. Luckman, I had silently assessed my partner's mood after the shock of yesterday's chance meeting with Rosa Saxby Luckman. We hadn't discussed the event any further during the past twenty-four hours. I wondered what, if anything, he had said to Sandralene. But whatever unburdening he had done, he seemed to have made some inner accommodation to the revelation. He appeared alert and on top of things, although a trifle less cocky than usual. I guessed I could count on him to whatever extent I always did.

This evening, the ill-proportioned Santo wore a nicer-than-usual suit, complete with a dashing boutonniere. It raised his appearance from his customary Catskills tummler to Olive Garden sommelier.

Sensing my attentions to his fancy dress when we were ushered in, he explained, "You're lucky to find me here, gentlemen. Just back from a funeral."

I did not choose to inquire into Vin's relationship with the deceased, or the deceased's mode of death. "I hope it wasn't too painful an occasion, Vin."

"Not at all. I was able to console the widow in a very meaningful way."

Stan leered. "I been there, too, Vin."

"I doubt it. Not unless, as matters eventuated, you likewise were able to pass on nearly five hundred grand that was owed your untimely demised partner."

Stan managed to sound contrite. "Pardon my foolish presumptions, Vin."

"No biggie. Now, I assume you boys are here to inform me of what came to pass with this hotshot inventor guy you went to interview."

"That's exactly right, Vin," I said before Stan could utter anything else off-key. "And we're happy to report that this affair is shaping up to be a bonanza for all of us. Not only are you going to offload those chips, but you are going to turn them into solid gold, thanks to our research and initiative."

I then laid out all the details of Luckman and his invention, and our plans to monetize it, deploying all my salesmanship and jury-swaying eloquence. Santo nodded with seeming appreciation at intervals, sipping on his soda all the while. When I felt I had engaged his interest and greed sufficiently, portraying the venture as a business challenge and a diversion from his usual rackets, I ventured to propose the four-way split that would come after he had recouped his sunk costs off the top.

When I had finished speaking, I sat quietly and nervously alongside Stan, awaiting a response. Stan had one leg crossed over the other and was rubbing the knee that had been shot, either because it pained him or as some kind of good luck talisman, or perhaps just as a nervous tic. Whatever the cause, it struck me as a kind of tell, and I telepathically sent Stan a message to desist. But my ESP must have been offline.

Santo set down his drink, clasped his hands across the Brooks Brothers tattersall vest that encompassed his considerable belly, and looked ruminatively up at the stained ceiling of his shabby office. After a wrenching ninety seconds, he lowered his gaze to our level.

"Boys, I like the way you think and the forthright manner of your presentation. But I will immediately propose a minor change to the terms, without which there will be no deal. I stipulate this due to the largeness of my investment and risk as against the zero-to-chickenfeed nature of your stake. I am reclaiming my up-front money first, of course. And then I am assuming fifty percent of whatever else we take in. Let's say, for instance, there is a hundred and twenty million left after my expenses. I get sixty, and then you two and the prof split the remaining sixty as you see fit."

Twenty million apiece? Or more, if we could con Luckman somehow? It was a step down from thirty-five million, but still nothing to sneeze at.

I looked at Stan, and although he was frowning slightly, he nodded yes.

"Vin, we are all on the same page."

"Excellent! Then I believe we can get this show on the road pretty quick. And to demonstrate that I am not taking my extra share for nothing, I am going to move right away to recruit, through my extensive network of pals, a valuable component into this enterprise, the necessity of whose skill set you have so far overlooked."

"And who might that be?"

"I don't know their name yet, just their job. You need someone experienced in the international arms trade—a salesman. Some joker who hangs out with the right people. You can't just run an ad on Craigslist for these pricey suckers. You gotta use someone with contacts and experience—a broker, like. And I'm pretty sure I can find the right guy for you."

I had to admit, Santo was absolutely right. Stan and I would not have had the barest idea how to solicit buyers for the Luckman Preemptive Blast Agent Sensor. We needed a person well versed in the marketplace, someone with real contacts.

"Vin, this is just another example of why you sit at the top of the free-enterprise pyramid in this region. You're always thinking one step ahead of everyone else. Now, this broker—he'll work for a flat fee, not a share?"

"You will have to negotiate that detail yourselves. But it seems unnecessary to cut in a mere freelancer for any large sum."

"I like it," Stan said. "Just a hired gun."

"Not literally," Vin replied. "But I can provide those, too, of course, should any such urgent need arise."

25

Her ecstatic yelps ceasing, Nellie rolled off me and onto her back. Her ardent activity, now at an end, rendered her a compact, moist, toffee-colored landscape of hills and vales and oases, like one of her native islands, rising from a sea of rumpled blue-green sheets. Her thick billows of black hair might have been a raft of seaweed or a dangerous oil slick laving the shore of the headlands. Or perhaps that was where my metaphor-making facility broke down.

"*Deus!*" she gasped. "You knocked all the stuffing right out of me. I can't even remember no more why I was worried."

I replied, "I can't even remember what century it is."

"Ai, Glen, you are always *tantu loku*! Maybe that is why I love you so much."

"I must be *loku* to share my bed with a wild-eyed nymphomaniac."

"I am just a healthy girl with normal needs. *Meu cona* gets to burning sometimes."

"That must explain why I can't even move."

She suddenly jumped up. "Oh, but we have to move now. Look at the time! You and Stan have your appointment, and I have to be at the bank by three."

Nellie had reached a point, in her ramping-up of Tartaruga Verde Importing, where our personal bankroll would no longer suffice and was, in fact, dangerously close to zeroing out. I could not tell her yet that we would soon be so rich that I could personally fund a score of small businesses. And in any case, those riches lay in the future, inaccessible for any current needs. And so Nellie was seeking to arrange a line of credit. Fear that she would not get approval had been preying on her mind, and I had suggested a pleasant bedroom interlude as at least a temporary balm.

Having Stan and Sandralene out of the apartment at this moment was added incentive to make the most of our freedom and privacy. Not that our housemates exhibited any reciprocal courtesy. Lately, I spent a lot of time in our laundry room, the farthest I could get from the noises of athletic sex emanating with uncanny frequency from behind the closed door of the guest room Stan had commandeered upon our return from Hedgesville. The uninhibited clamor of their lovemaking featured half-strangled bellows from Stan and oscillating whoops from Sandralene, evoking the clash of the Titans.

Nellie headed into the attached bathroom for her shower. I didn't jump up yet, nor did I find a need to pull the covers over me. The heat in the condo was running against the mid-November cold, but it was on much too high for my taste. Neither Nellie nor Sandralene was responsible for the abusive temperature setting, however. Rather, it was Stan who proved a self-indulgent baby in the face of any ambient chill.

"I spent too many damn days freezing my ass off indoors when I was a kid," he said. "And the last winter in that dive where we currently got Caleb stashed was miserable. I never want to go back to being cold again inside a house. Now that I can afford it, I like things tropical."

"Now that *you* can afford it?" I replied. "I haven't seen you kick anything into the utilities kitty just yet."

"Keep your pants on, Glen boy. I'll write you a check at the end of the month."

I figured I should get up and get dressed. Stan and Sandralene would soon return from their visit to Sandy's mom at the Uncle Ralph and Suzy Lam ménage. My dissolute uncle and his squeeze had even started taking Lura to the racetrack with them. Then Stan and I had to go visit Gunther Stroebel. As Vin Santo's property manager of sorts, Gunther had been delegated the task of finding us an appropriate building to convert into a factory for the manufacture of the LBAS. Gunther had phoned to say that he had something good lined up and we should come take a look. Once we approved, we'd swing around to Luckman's place with the agreement that Santo's army of attorneys had crafted, get him to sign—he hadn't minded waiting a couple of days—and the assembly and stockpiling of the units could begin.

Our eventual customer or customers were an unknown quantity and would remain so until Santo sent to us the experienced broker who would presumably hook us up.

Meanwhile, we had Nellie and Sandralene happily bamboozled under the carefully cultivated impression that Stan and I were still employed by Hertz in its mythical car-transport business, but in a more elevated capacity that did not involve so much interstate travel.

All the parts of our scam seemed to be falling nicely into place, and I had the same feeling of warmhearted pride and satisfaction I had gotten whenever past larcenous gaffs were humming like a top.

So far as I could see, the only unsettled matter was Stan's relationship with Rosa Saxby Luckman. The two had not staged a formal private reunion since that chance meeting in Luckman's living room, and I hoped any such reconciliation would go smoothly. The last thing we needed was an aggrieved Rosa trying to turn Luckman against us.

Nellie's reappearance in the bedroom, swathed in a big white towel, motivated me out of bed to play a bit of grab-ass. Eventually, we both managed to get dressed.

Out in the main room of the condo, Nellie gathered up her coat and hat and my car keys. "Wish me luck, *bebe*," she said. "If this goes through, I'll be off to the islands again. You'll miss me a little maybe, huh?"

I tried to convey my imminent longing for her by cupping her lovely bum through her coat and giving her a long, juicy kiss. Then she was off.

Sandralene and Stan returned just fifteen minutes later to find me dressed and ready. When Sandy doffed her cold-weather gear, I sent a silent prayer of thanks heavenward that Nellie had already rendered me relatively immune to spontaneous arousal. Looking like a Deadhead girl circa 1971, our West Virginia Hippolyta wore farmer jeans and candy-apple-red clogs. Under the bib of the overalls, she sported a tie-died thermal shirt, its waffle-weave fabric attenuated by the might of her matchless bosom.

Stan kept his coat on. "Hustle, Glen. We don't want to keep the man waiting."

I got into my jacket. "Sandralene, are you still up for going with Nellie to Caboverde? I can't, and I'd feel better if she had someone with her."

Sandralene's sunny Woodstock smile completed the hippie-hottie allure. "Sure, Glen," she said. "It'll be fun. I've never been out of the States, you know. But I got my passport when we were all planning to go there after the Motor Lodge deal. Do you think it's still good?"

"Yep. Your passport lasts ten years."

Stan managed to take Sandralene's first comment as a mild criticism. "I know I haven't showed you a real good time yet," he said. "But don't you worry, doll. Pretty soon we'll be visiting places a lot more exotic than this old town."

Out in Stan's car, I said, "How was Lura?"

"Man, it's like night and day. She was wasting away down there in Dixieland. Now that all her meds are straightened out and she's got some company, it's like she won the lottery."

"That's good news." I let a few blocks go by in silence before I said, "You had any more insights into approaching Rosa?"

"I just figure when we go out to Luckman's place, I'll get her off to one side and tell her my honest feelings. What more can I do?"

"Happy to hear you trying out the path of righteousness for once."

"Hey, man, I don't mess around with my friends. That leaves everyone else in the world."

I realized that we were not heading directly to the warehouse-district address Gunther had given us, but rather to Stan's old apartment, which was not far removed. Stan responded to what must have been a questioning look.

"We're picking up Johnny Reb," he said. "When I invited him to come back here with us, I had a feeling we were gonna be able to use him somehow, and now I know how. He's gonna oversee the factory. You and I don't wanna do it, right? But someone's gotta be there all the time to make sure everything's running right. And I can tell Luckman's not up to it. His head's in the clouds."

"You think Caleb will agree?"

"He already has."

"Well, I guess it's a good idea. But you could've at least consulted me about it first."

"Maybe I woulda, if you didn't always have your nose buried in pussy."

"That is the worst case I have ever heard of someone trying to deflect his own immense load of guilt onto the nearest innocent bystander."

"Yeah, so you say. But what you don't know is, Sandy and me got back to the apartment while you and Nellie were still going at it. I was so damn mortified, and for my innocent girlfriend to hear such sex talk! We hadda leave and go straight to the neighborhood church until we guessed you two were finally done."

"In any such future incidents, I can recommend the laundry room as a safe space."

Caleb was already standing on the sidewalk when we pulled up. He got in the car, shivering.

"Dang, these northern winters are hella cold!"

"This ain't even winter yet, you doofus. Just wait till the snow is up to your pecker."

Caleb laughed. "I'll just get out my drywall stilts and be safe till there's another two feet of the stuff!"

We arrived quickly at a vacant vintage warehouse similar to the one Santo used to store his counterfeit merch, which was only about eight blocks away. Roly-poly Gunther awaited us. We all went inside the vast unheated space, where we could still see our breath. There was no electricity running, but Gunther had come equipped with several yellow plastic Eveready handheld lanterns, and we were able to scope out the interior to our satisfaction. Caleb immediately became enthusiastic, speculating on how he would set up the place for maximum efficiency. He possessed a certain small-businessman's competence that Stan and I lacked, and I could see how he would be a valuable addition to our enterprise.

We wrapped up and went outside. Stan said to Gunther, "Tell Vin it's fine. We'll take it."

"Uh, Stan, maybe I could ask you a favor?"

"Sure, what?"

"You think you could find a job for Alice on the assembly line so's I wouldn't have to worry about her all the time? You know she can follow orders pretty well, despite her troubles."

"Well, let's ask the foreman here." Stan explained briefly about Gunther's cognitively slipping wife.

"Why, heck, I don't see but what she'd be darn useful. Maybe put her in the packing department if she can't handle anything more complicated. She can always fold boxes or something."

Gunther's face wore a look of immense relief. "Thanks, guys. Thanks so much."

Gunther went his way, and we brought Caleb back to his place. Before he got out of the car, Stan handed him a roll of cash.

"First week's salary. Now you can stock up on grits and gravy."

"I'm more of a sushi guy, actually."

It was getting on toward evening when Stan and I headed off for Vin Santo's to pick up the contract.

"Luckman's tomorrow?" I said.

"Yeah," Stan replied. But he did not look as if he relished the prospect.

26

Nothing had changed at Luckman's drab suburban residence in the few days we were gone, except that the rampant weeds of summer had succumbed to frost, rendering them both less obvious and more dismal looking than before, under leaden skies.

Luckman opened the door for us and conducted us inside with his authentic old-fashioned etiquette. Rosa was not immediately visible.

"You gentlemen have the contract, I presume?"

"Of course," I said. "Our silent partner—he's the fellow with the funds, you know, so we always try to keep him happy—was very eager to cut the best deal for all parties. You'll see his signature below on both copies of the agreement, and we'd be very grateful if you would not mention his involvement here, as he prefers to keep a low profile in order to discourage publicity and forestall his business rivals. But you can rest assured that he has a reputation for square dealing."

I supposed that Vin Santo's predilection for putting his adversaries into a long pine box could be construed as "square dealing" if you squinted. But in any case, Vin's actual name could be found nowhere on this document. A shell company with untraceable roots had been set up. Nor was Stan or I down on paper officially.

"You'll see, Professor Luckman, he kept it very simple. It's only about five pages, actually."

"Let's take it into my study so I can go over it with you."

We went into a room we hadn't visited before, featuring an old-fashioned wooden desk, more shelves full of weighty physics tomes, and a pair of leather club chairs with brass studs down the arms. The room smelled like old pipe tobacco, and I spotted an antique humidor and a rack of pipes. Stan and I sat down in the club chairs while Luckman went behind his desk. I noticed a framed photo of Rosa there.

Luckman motored slowly through the legal verbiage, with the intense scholarly particularity of someone evaluating a tricky essay from a hopeful protégé. Stan kept trying not to crane his neck to study Rosa's angled-away picture, but his restive body language steadily betrayed him. Luckman, happily, was too focused on legalese to catch on.

Finally, Luckman had examined the document to his satisfaction, though he continued to hold it above the blotter.

"I see that either party can terminate the arrangement upon thirty days' notice," he said.

"Of course."

"And that you are just licensing the rights to manufacture my device. You make no claim on the patents or intellectual property. All that remains completely mine."

"But of course." What I failed to say was that thanks to this clause, if any remorseful buyers should come after us for selling useless devices, he would be the one left holding the bag.

"And I am responsible, naturally, for providing the schematics for assembly of the device, but also for sourcing the various components."

"We naturally assumed—"

Luckman waved a hand. "No, no, you weren't off base. I know all those suppliers intimately. No point in you reinventing the wheel. Now, as to the division of any profits …"

Santo had written up the terms he had outlined aloud to Stan and me. And in a fit of generosity, Stan and I had agreed not to try to gyp Luckman of his fair share: one third of the monies left after Santo got his fat slice of the pie. I think Stan's ready compliance had something to do with Rosa's stake in the game. But now I suspected that Luckman might consider even this largesse unfair. So I got all my arguments mentally lined up to convince him otherwise.

Luckman laid the contract down on the green felt and regarded us with solemn and perhaps slightly watery eyes.

"Gentlemen, if we manage to sell even just the initial five thousand units—an eventuality that I firmly predict—we all will be coming into an immense sum of money. It beggars the imagination; it truly does. I never really contemplated actual numbers like this before. But your contract makes it all seem quite real, and I confess I don't know how to react. This is a life-changing sum. Are you both quite sure that we face no hidden costs? Could my share perhaps be amended downward to some degree, to maintain a reserve against unforeseen expenditures?"

I felt a small but easily repressible pang at Luckman's naive trust in us, and his willingness to make sacrifices for a couple of undeserving grifters like us. But what the hell. Along with all the criminal liability, he was going to get a decent amount of dough. And if he really felt like being a proper Christian martyr, we could always invent some phony expenses that would siphon some of the money out of his pocket and into ours.

Stan said, "Prof, you can rest easy. This is not our first rodeo. Me and Glen and our big-enchilada third wheel have done this before, and we would not have specified such a division of the kale if it were not all on the up-and-up."

Luckman allowed himself to relax and grin. "Very well, then. I'm signing this now with a happy heart!"

Once both copies were signed, Luckman retained his, and we took ours. He moved to a closed sideboard then and opened it to reveal a few scant bottles of fussy liqueurs—stuff that old ladies drank when they were feeling thirty-nine again.

"We need to toast our arrangement, fellows! Oh, wait," he said. "Let me get my wife. She simply *has* to be here!"

Stan laid a hand on Luckman's shoulder. "You do the pouring, amigo; I'll fetch the missus. Just point me to where she might be lurking."

"Oh, just go looking; the house isn't that big. You'll find her easily enough, I'm certain."

Stan left the study. Luckman consulted me nervously about which weak tipple was sufficiently grand and robust to solemnize such a major deal. I couldn't really pay attention, worried as I was that I might hear a face getting slapped, a shoe connecting with an ass, and Stan being summarily ejected. Time seemed to stretch on forever. But no such crisis intervened, and eventually Luckman settled on a bottle of tawny port. He poured four glasses, and just as he finished, we heard steps approaching.

Rosa Saxby Luckman entered first. She wore a white ruffled blouse and a black skirt, flesh-toned nylons, and flats. Her solemn face was flushed, and one small tail of her blouse had escaped the skirt's waistband. Behind her pranced Stan, looking like a rooster just put in charge of a coop as big as the *Queen Mary*.

Luckman immediately raced to embrace and kiss his wife. I regarded Stan for a second with horrified disbelief, then silently drew my sleeve across my face.

Stan did the same, erasing the lipstick smudge there.

Luckman disengaged from Rosa but kept an arm around her waist. He grabbed a glass and waved us to take ours. Then he said, "Here's to all success for our happy little fraternity!"

27

Stan and I waved at our women as they threaded their way through the TSA line and past the metal detectors. I was glad to see them looking so happy and beautiful and competent together. They redeemed us, they surely did. Somehow, through no discernible merit on our parts and despite all our wickedness in need of comeuppance, we had lucked into these two extraordinary women to walk beside us through the valley of the shadow of criminality into which we had willingly entered. The imbalance of the situation in our unworthy favor almost made me doubt the existence of cosmic justice.

When we could no longer see them, we turned around and went through the busy terminal and out to my car in the hourly lot. I would have exclusive use of it for at least the three weeks that Sandralene and Nellie would spend in Cape Verde, and I relished being behind the wheel again. Riding around in Stan's patriotically got-up anachronism had me feeling as if I were out drumming up votes for Ronald Reagan's reelection.

After we had merged back onto the expressway, I turned to Stan and broached a subject that had been much on my mind.

"What the bloody fucking outrageous hell were you thinking, banging Luckman's wife? And in his own house, *with him there*!"

"Oh, Christ, not that again! It's been, what, five days now and you still won't let it go!"

"I am going to continue to ask you every day until I get some kind of answer that makes sense. Didn't it occur to you that if Luckman found out and got pissed, it could wreck our whole deal?"

"Of course that practical little thought ran through my head, just before and just after. I'm not an idiot, you know. I can plan for the future just like you. Delayed gratification, right? Key to a lifetime of success! But there was nothing neither of us could do. As soon as we were alone together in the same room, twenty years vanished in a flash. It was like I was sixteen again and Rosa was thirty-five. We were swept up in that same crazy-hot blindness to anything else but fucking each other comatose. Before I knew it, I had her skirt up around her waist and her panties down, and—"

"That's enough detail, please!"

"You don't think the prof suspected anything?"

"Now who's repeating himself? I told you a dozen times, he was blind as a pocket calculator to what had just happened right under his nose. All he could see at the moment was that his lifelong dream was going to come true and make him rich."

"Good for him. He seems like an okay joe. Probably worked like an Amish mule all his life, mollycoddling his precious little candy-ass students and sucking up to deans and suchlike. I'da killed myself or, more likely, someone else a long time before I got to where he is. Though he really oughta pay more attention to what his wife is up to. He's a lucky stiff to have someone like Rosa. If she were my wife—"

"And that's another thing! What about Sandralene? Do you think she'd be happy if she knew what you were up to?"

Stan grinned like Babe Ruth in the 1932 World Series, right after hitting his called shot into the center field bleachers.

"I told her just before we left for the plane. She doesn't care. What we got is stronger than that. After all, I don't tug on her reins, do I?"

Stan looked meaningfully at me, no doubt as a silent reminder of the one time Sandy and I had done the deed, with his tacit but limited sanction, so I wisely backed off that angle of attack.

"She actually said," Stan continued, "that she liked imagining me when I was a kid, before she knew me, and that maybe knocking boots with Rosa would be like some kinda fountain-of-youth thing."

"Holy God, you're not going to keep screwing Rosa, are you? Wasn't once dangerous enough?"

"I can't promise anything. Whatever happens, happens. All I can say is, I won't go angling for it. Watch the damn road, Glen boy! That was a 'sixty-nine Porsche Targa you almost dinged! Listen, I want this scheme to succeed as much as you! I'm tired of being poor."

"You've still got the dough you earned from driving the truck?"

"Yeah, but it's going fast, what with rent on Caleb's place and paying him a salary until Vin gets the funding flowing to us, and incidentals like meals and shit and keeping Sandy in Victoria's Secret. I swear, that woman must own six dozen bras."

"You'd never know it to look at her." Sometimes, I can't help myself.

"Ha!"

"Well, we should see some relief in the cash-flow department soon, once the assembly line gets going and we have something solid to show Santo. Let's go see how Caleb's doing."

"Any chore that doesn't involve another lecture from Mr. Keep It in Your Pants Choirboy is fine with me."

"You should thank your lucky stars that I've got your back."

"I thought it was my front you were concerned about."

The paint-exfoliating exterior of the dingy warehouse that was to be the LBAS factory presented a modified appearance from just a few days ago. A new small sign announcing the place as LUCKMAN ENTERPRISES was affixed to the front door.

Inside, the place was lit and heated, at least in the newly framed narrow corridor that led from the entrance to a sizable office. And another change: the corridor was lined with a dozen job hunters, here to apply for work assembling Luckman's gadget. Also, from deeper within the building, came the sounds of hammering and saws and drills.

Stan and I got to the head of the line of applicants just as one of them, a young woman, emerged smiling from the office. Before the next person could enter, Stan and I cut the line with a curt but courteous explanation from Stan.

"Small delay, folks," he said. "Business talk between the owners. Just hang loose; it'll be short."

Inside an office freshly appointed with desk and computer, long side table with application forms, file cabinet, coffeemaker, and minifridge, we found Caleb Stinchcombe and Alice Stroebel, Stan's Alzheimer's-afflicted former flea-market assistant and Gunther's wife. Alice was laboriously filing the paper application of the woman who had just left.

Caleb looked focused and preoccupied but not put-upon.

"Hey, Stan, Glen, good to see you. I was going to report later anyhow. I think we're almost up to speed. We've got nearly fifty good workers lined up, all with some assembly-line experience and all available immediately. Soon as Ron gives his approval to the physical setup and we get our raw materials in, we can start production."

Luckman had shown us the plans for assembling his device, taking hours to go over with us how he had put the one and only working model together. We had brainstormed the process and broken it down into about fifteen steps, to be performed at fifteen workstations, each staffed with a team of three. We also needed shift supervisors, gofers, packers, and even security guards. Altogether, we were looking to hire close to a hundred people. Luckily, the city's crummy employment stats were on our side.

"That's just great, Caleb. Keep up the good work. You, too, Alice."

"I know this system real good, Glen. It's just the alphabet."

We left Caleb and went deeper inside the building to see how Luckman was faring.

The big, open, brightly lit warehouse space swarmed with carpenters and electricians building the assembly stations and lots of shelving. There was really no automation involved, so the construction was simple. We tracked Luckman down at an open bay door that was letting in chill air redolent of auto exhaust. He was accepting delivery on a cargo of parts from a truck driver. The driver was then persuaded, with some reluctance, to offload the stuff himself, with the aid of a hand truck, since we didn't have our staff in place yet. While the guy grumpily wheeled cartons bearing the logo of an electronics supplier over to an empty corner, I talked to Luckman.

"Ronald, how's it going? Any regrets about leaving the university?"

Luckman had abruptly quit his teaching job in advance of the semester break for Thanksgiving. By doing so, he had certainly killed any chance at future academic employment, but he didn't seem to care. He was in the fever grip of this new role as entrepreneur.

"Oh, Glen, it's fabulous! I'm getting a real sense of accomplishment here. And we haven't even begun putting the units together yet!"

"Does your wife have any worries?"

"Oh, no! Rosa's happy as a clam. She's got ultimate confidence in me and the LBAS. I've never seen her so content in years."

Stan had suddenly found something needing his attention at one of the workstations under construction.

"All right then," I said. "Keep at it. We've got to go see our mutual backer now and give him an idea of our progress."

Back in my car, Stan said, "Happy as a clam. You heard the man."

"Yes, well, one application of the happiness treatment will have to last both of you for a good long while."

In Santo's office, we gave our report to the rapaciously alert crime boss. He listened quietly and, when we were finished, said, "This is all excellent news, boys. I am going to tell Gunther to transport the Intel chips over as soon as construction is finished. Meanwhile, Luckman Enterprises now has a bank account at my favorite institution, which has reason not to inquire too closely into any business of mine."

For one fleeting moment, I wondered idly whether that meant Santo had an arrangement with the bank to launder his fake money, but I quickly deemed that kind of federal-level pull beyond even his reach.

The mobster continued. "You'll have credit cards and checks and letterhead and all that other good stuff by tomorrow. That should alleviate any out-of-pocket expenditures."

"Thanks, Vin, we really appreciate that."

Santo waved a fat hand dismissively. "Trivial stuff—just bookkeeping, really. But I got a more important development to share. I rousted up your go-betweens, the smarties who are gonna put you in touch with the buyers, after which all you gotta do is the selling. They're waiting in the next room. Richie!" One of the bodyguards, a crew-cut blond with biceps rivaling Caleb's, jumped to attention. "Richie, show our new friends in."

28

I really didn't know what kind of person or persons I was expecting to see. Years of James Bond and *Mission Impossible* films had left me with the impression that weapons brokers came in basically three types: sleazy and/or fanatical Levantines, icy Russo-Eurotrash; and implacable, cruel-eyed Asians. Also, they were always male, either stubbled or dapper, and certainly steeped in many, many years' worth of vile experiences that would have made John le Carré hide quivering under his bed.

So when steroid Richie escorted in the pair of putative arms-trade experts Santo had dug up, I was a little taken aback.

My eyes went ineluctably first to the female of the pair. I wanted to call her a girl, she looked so young. But I swiftly realized that she put on the gamine persona with the rest of her outfit. Her tall, willowy form and short feathered auburn hair consorted well with a pale face rendered almost childish by its soft lines and small nose. Only on closer inspection did I spot the sophisticated makeup job that concealed her maturity.

She was dressed elegantly and expensively. Her simple white blouse and little black bow tie were not particularly upmarket, nor was the leather skirt whose hem rode at midthigh. Ditto the black knee socks. But her shoes were Gucci mules, the red ones with an embroidered snarling panther face. And her long sweater coat I recognized as the same one I had once scoped out for Nellie: cashmere with a fractal pattern resembling the Painted Desert. I had put off buying it for Nellie because it went for forty-five hundred dollars.

The woman smiled at us as she stepped across the room, and the dissonance of her taut, swaying carriage, posh clothes, and tweener body blasted an erotic charge straight at every male present.

Her associate contrasted sharply but was no less striking in his own unshowy way. He was an East Asian male—Chinese, I was guessing. Equally youthful, he nonetheless looked like someone in his reliable, steady midtwenties, not an adolescent. His short, neatly styled hair was black as licorice, and his bluntish features exhibited a nice symmetry without any pretensions to handsomeness. As with many males of his ethnicity, the skin of his face was smooth and stubble-free. A loose magenta polo shirt showed from beneath his unzipped taupe anorak, the kind with a ridiculous amount of fur trimming the hood. His narrow-legged pants were a dusty shade of lilac, and his brown shoes were that same style of brogan gunboats we used to associate with bog-dwelling Irish terrorists of the 1930s but which had inexplicably become fashionable. He radiated a broad grin meant, I supposed, to assure everyone of his harmless affability.

Between them, the two had pretty much all the seductive-

first-impression bases covered. Charm and substance, outgo-
ingness and reserve, competence and polish. I sensed that they
would make an impressive sales team, and so I quickly began to
recover from the initial shock at their failure to conform to my
stereotypes.

One thing I could not immediately suss was whether they
were just coworkers or there might be a romantic angle between
them.

Santo actually stood up from behind his desk—a magnani-
mous gesture he had never made when Stan and I entered. He
waddled over to the woman first and pecked her on the cheek.
Then he pumped the guy's hand as if he were churning butter, all
before turning toward us.

"Gentlemen, I wanna introduce to you Chantal Danssaert
and Les Qiao. Chantal, Les, say hi to Glen McClinton and Stan
Hasso. They're the fellows in need of your expertise and savvy."

"I'm Glen," I said, and took Chantal's slender, strong hand.
Whether from being recently outside or as an artifact of her
natural metabolism, it was cool as a summer brook.

"It pleases me to make your acquaintance, Glen." Her
charming accent was hard to place.

I found myself still holding on to her hand after our shake.
She made no effort to withdraw, but a delicate flick of her eyes
alerted me to my faux pas, and I hastily released her.

Stan stepped up. He seemed unwontedly awed at Miss Danssaert, as if she were an emissary from some sphere he had never
before encountered, perhaps Fairyland or Oz, and I could almost
hear his estimation of her as "some pretty exotic, high-tone trim."
What he actually said was only a little more decorous.

"If you were a grenade, lady, I would pull the pin and die happy."

Chantal's laugh rang like bells in a carillon. "You would survive any explosion, Stan, I think."

Les Qiao's handshake was firm and his mien respectful yet commanding in the manner of, say, a safari guide, if that makes any sense. He seemed to say, *You're paying the bills, but I'm the one who knows where we're going.*

"Stan, Glen, good to meet you." His voice was a pleasant tenor, and his idiomatic, faintly accented speech and common-place first name suggested American origins, but I thought I'd ask.

"Native to the States, Les?"

"Not at all. Hong Kong. But sometimes I think my parents must've been more British than the queen. Anyhow, twelve years at the International School left me sounding like this."

"Where are your stomping grounds, Chantal?" Stan said. He managed to pronounce her name as if he had read it off a strip-club marquee.

The woman did not immediately answer, but instead took a tin of mints from her coat pocket, delicately selected one, then popped it between her elegant lips, all as if erecting a cordon sani-taire between herself and Stan. "I am originally from Belgium. But I have not lived there for many years."

Vin Santo had stood by patiently enough during these intro-ductions, but now he began to chafe a bit. Apparently, he had other matters to attend to—maybe pulling out someone's finger-nails or cutting a brake line.

"Okay," he said, "now that you four have gotten all palsy-walsy, I'm gonna let you work out your plans without me. Just keep me in the loop, okay?"

The four of us left Santo's office. Out on the frosty sidewalk, I said, "So, where shall we go to talk?"

"We are staying at the Parkside Hyatt for the duration of our mutual endeavors," said Chantal.

"Sweet!" Stan exclaimed. "The lap of luxury."

Chantal rewarded him with a thousand-watt smile. "Indeed. And they have a superb restaurant there. I have already spoken to the chef about preparing a certain dish from my native Flanders. And it is approaching the supper hour, I think."

"Sounds jake to me," said Stan. "Who cares what a good time costs, anyhow?"

"Your devil-may-care flaneur's joie de vivre, Stan, warms a girl's heart."

Stan frowned but apparently chose to interpret her remark as a compliment.

29

Stan took the last thick slab of artisan bread from the woven-porcelain bread basket and used it to wipe the last drips of golden-white gravy from his plate. The bread disappeared in three bites. But for the nice sharkskin suit, one might think he had just hit the soup kitchen after a week of starvation.

"Man, this stuff is like liquid crack. Whaddya call this dish again?"

Chantal Danssaert responded to Stan's gargantuan appetite with cosmopolitan tolerance and a bemused smile worthy of the *Mona Lisa.* "This is *kippen waterzooi.* A kind of chicken stew made with beer and cream. And I must compliment our chef later for his mastery of an unfamiliar recipe that is uncomplicated yet demanding."

"Beer *and* cream, huh? That's like holding pussy in one hand and another guy's dick in the other—ya gotta commit to one or the other."

Les Qiao laughed heartily. "Stan, you're a pip."

In the face of Stan's raunchiness, Chantal stayed cool as the avocado gelato the waiter had just suggested for dessert. "You describe a not-unheard-of scenario, I think, Stan. Such juxtapositions often produce intriguing results, I have found."

Much as I enjoyed hearing a gorgeous woman talking about a ménage à trois, I tried to steer the subject gently back to business. The meal had indeed been delicious, and Chantal and Les proved to be enjoyable company. They each had a vast stock of stories and anecdotes, mostly relating to their vocation as arms brokers, that were delightful to hear. The subtext, of course, was, *Allow me to present my bona fides.* I had listened raptly as they recounted their experiences in May at CANSEC, the big annual arms fair held in Ottawa. To cement one deal involving a certain Middle Eastern client, they had been obliged to find a live camel at two in the morning. Their client had left the reason for his unusual request to their imagination and, now, ours.

Throughout the dinner, while captivated by their exploits, I had tried to scope out whether the two were lovers. I don't know why I was so interested. Maybe just because I was already missing Nellie after just a few hours' separation. Or maybe it was because I always felt that the more I understood about how people were connected, the more handles I had on them for my own manipulative, self-centered purposes. In any case, their behavior had led me to no firm conclusions. Yes, Chantal had laid her delicate fingertips on Les' bare arm, but she had done the same to me to emphasize a point. And Les had leaped up and kissed Chantal enthusiastically when she delivered a particularly funny punch line, exclaiming, "Babe, you're the greatest!" But his lips had only caught the corner of hers, and she had not reciprocated with much vigor. So I was still left puzzling over the exact nature of their relationship.

Tabling the matter for now, I cut to the heart of the matter: money. Having learned that Stan and I were expected to foot all their expenses for the duration of their stay here, I had been working sums all night, especially after making a discreet inquiry to the Parkside Hyatt's registration clerk before dinner, regarding the price of the suite that Les and Chantal had already engaged. She had informed me that we were on the hook for twenty-five hundred dollars per night, though there might be "a small discount for long-term residency."

Suppose this whole scam ran for another month, from assembly of the units to closing a deal. That would be seventy-five thousand dollars just for lodging this pair, to say nothing of feeding them. Not much out of our potential profit of twenty million apiece. But still, I didn't want Vin Santo thinking we were being spendthrift with his up-front dough.

"Guys, I think Stan and I would be relieved to nail down the fee for your efforts in drumming up some customers for our product. Vin never mentioned a number to us. He's our silent partner, so to speak. Did you quote him a price yet?"

Chantal waved her hand dismissively, as if the matter were too obvious or tawdry to consider for long. "We follow the standard rate in our industry: one percent of the transaction."

"Gross or net?"

"Gross, of course."

I found the number astonishing. "With the best outcome, we hope to sell one hundred and twenty million dollars' worth of goods."

"It won't require a calculator, then, to determine our share as one point two million."

Stan whistled. "Not bad dough for some schmoozing and pimping and matchmaking. Hey, maybe there's a Tinder for generals and dictators and secretaries of defense and such, and we could go it on our lonesome."

Chantal's entire bearing instantly assumed a glacial quality impressive to behold, and I got the feeling I was facing not some genteel, well-mannered procuress, but more a Euro version of Madame Chiang Kai-shek or Grace Mugabe. Les stiffened, too, his generally jovial face hardening. But he left the talking to his dagger-eyed partner.

"I can assure you wholeheartedly, Stan—and you as well, Glen—that no such simplistic online resource exists. I can also say without an iota of uncertainty that two rank amateurs such as yourselves would get nowhere without our connections and experience. Your merchandise would gather dust and never sell before it quietly became obsolete. You could hide it up your asses for all the benefit it would bring you. I doubt you have even a single name at the moment as a potential customer, whereas Les and I can readily adduce at least a dozen. I think, however, that in a small-scale deal such as this, we would do better to bring in only two or three buyers and let them bid against each other."

Stan didn't take the slightest offense at this scathing riposte to his gibe, but rather seemed delighted. "You're a kick-ass little gal, ain't ya? But that's exactly what we need. So consider your fee locked in. After all, it's only six hundred grand apiece from me and Glen boy. Why, we drop more'n that on condoms every year. Hell, maybe we'll even kick in a bonus if you can bring us a live camel or two."

Again Chantal's delightful laughter pealed like bells. "We will see what we can do, Stan. One hump or two? But first, let us learn more about the stellar virtues of this product you wish us to tout."

30

The afternoon following our dinner with the arms experts—the bill for the meal had topped out at a mere seven hundred thirty-nine dollars and forty-five cents, exclusive of generous tips for both waiter and wine steward—I wheeled my Lexus into the driveway of Ronald Luckman's home. I had persuaded Luckman to leave off supervising construction at the factory long enough to do a show-and-tell for our new partners. He was so eager for production to begin that he was putting in insane hours.

Hours that his wife must somehow fill on her own.

The four of us got out of the car and into the chilly air. Stan and I went to ring the doorbell while Chantal and Les stood back a way, gawping at the drab suburban surroundings as if viewing the village huts of a newly discovered Amazonian tribe.

Rosa Saxby Luckman appeared, her hair pulled back, looking fine and vaguely regal in a simple blue shift patterned with large white camellias. Her gaze shot right past me to Stan, and I could practically feel the lightning bolt of lust zap between them, crack-ling and sizzling and ionizing the air. Dragging her eyes away from her former prize science student, Rosa said, "Ronald's not here yet. He phoned to say he was running into some traffic. But please, come in."

Mrs. Luckman showed us into the front room, where we took our seats. Les and Chantal continued their silent anthropological assessment of the natives' habitat.

"I'll fetch some refreshments," Rosa said.

"Lemme give ya a hand," Stan offered.

I sighed rather too loudly as the two hustled out of the room. Les was handling a gaudy souvenir made of seashells and twine as if it were the Antikythera device. Chantal appeared to take note of my dismay and to draw from it whatever deductions her imag-ination and worldly wisdom could provide.

The fetching of refreshments involved rather more half-muffled thumps and clatterings than the task typically entails. Les and Chantal refrained from comment. Then the front door opened.

I jumped up and rushed to greet Luckman, hailing him in a booming voice as if we were two hikers on opposite rims of the Grand Canyon.

"Ron! You made it! Shame about that traffic!"

Luckman regarded me as if I were moderately demented. Then his attention turned to the newcomers. He had been informed of their role and was naturally curious and eager to impress them. I made introductions all around, with Luckman effusively welcoming the pair to the USA, the state, his neigh-borhood, his home, and his workshop. While I was officiating, Rosa and Stan emerged from the back of the house. Rosa carried a bamboo tray of biscotti and fine china cups, while Stan toted an insulated carafe and a matching sugar-and-creamer set. This little spread clearly had required some effort on the hostess' part, but one would be hard put to associate it with the banging noises that preceded it.

After we had politely sampled the sweets and drained our demitasses, Rosa excused herself from the business palaver, and the rest of us trooped out to the garage.

Luckman went almost blow by blow through the entire development history of his device. Chantal and Les, to their credit, listened alertly and asked intelligent questions. Then Luckman did his test with the ANFO sample, triggering the alarm. When he had finished, Chantal set her Marc Jacobs purse down on the benchtop near the LBAS and bent over to peer closely into the innards of the machine. She pointed with a manicured finger.

"And this component, Ron?"

Ron lowered his head next to hers, and I could register his instant intoxication. Indeed, Chantal's subtle perfume was alluring even at this remove.

"That?" he answered woozily. "Oh, that's the heart of the unit. I invented that little bit of circuitry myself. I'm afraid I can't disclose its exact nature just yet, even to such a charming business associate as yourself. But when the patents are finalized, I'll be most happy to go over it with you."

Chantal straightened up, drawing Ron with her as if magnetized. She said, "Oh, I understand completely your discretion, but I don't need to know. I comprehend now the complete functions and abilities of your invention."

Retrieving her purse, Chantal led the way back into the house. Rosa did not reappear. All of us had duties to perform, so we didn't linger.

Seeing us out, Luckman said, "I think I won't go back to the factory right away, Glen, if that's okay with you. I'm a little tired, and I fear I've been shortchanging Rosa of my attentions for some days now. I'll see you there tomorrow."

I patted him on the shoulder. "Sure thing, Ron. Don't sweat it. Plenty of time to get it all done."

"I suppose. I just have this sense of urgency somehow. As if our time is limited."

* * *

As soon as we turned off Luckman's block, Chantal spoke from the back aseat. I caught her face in the rearview mirror.

"That machine is useless, you know. You would get the same results waving Harry Potter's magic wand over the sample."

Stan said nothing. I thought to deny the assertion, but then said, "Yeah, we kinda figured as much. But how did you realize it?"

She opened her purse, dug in, and held up a pale waxy block about the size of an ice-cream bar. "Recognize it? No? This is a chunk of C-four. You know, as in plastic explosive? The machine never beeped once."

I had to admire her ingenuity. "So this means our arrangement is off?"

Chantal deployed her enchanting laughter once more. "Of course not! We make no judgment on the wares of our clients. It just means you two have to work very much harder with the people we bring you. And please try most earnestly to succeed in the ruse, not only for your sake, but so as not to soil our reputation!"

Stan said, "I knew from the start that we were all on the same fucking page, doll."

I pulled up in front of the Hyatt, and Chantal and Les got out.

"I think Les and I will take in the touring show of *Hamilton* tonight. I understand the tickets are a bargain compared to the New York prices—only six hundred dollars apiece. Could you write us a check for, say, fifteen hundred then?"

I complied, and Chantal folded the check neatly in half before tucking it next to the C-4.

* * *

Back at the apartment, I flopped down wearily. The first full day of bachelor existence for Stan and me was proving highly demanding.

"You want me to grill some steaks for us?" I asked Stan.

"Nah, I'm going out. Thanks anyhow, though."

I let Stan go without inquiring about his plans, adjudging deniability more important than reassurance.

By ten o'clock, the steak, a baked potato, and half a bottle of red wine had rendered me hors de combat. I didn't even shower but just stripped to my underwear and fell into my too-empty bed.

Around 1:00 a.m., I awoke having to pee a Niagara of transubstantiated pinot noir. I stumbled out to the kitchen for some ice water to wash the fug out of my mouth.

The little living room night-light revealed on the floor a blue dress patterned with camellias, and beyond it a trail of more intimate garments leading to Stan's room.

I sure hoped Ronald Luckman was either a very sound sleeper or gullible enough to believe in overnight bedside visits to a dying grandmother.

PART FOUR

31

By the first week in December, our factory of fakes was buzzing along with the desperate efficiency of a seaport sandbag-packing operation on the eve of a hurricane. Nellie and Sandralene were still in Caboverde, calling at regular intervals to update us on the progress of Tartaruga Verde Importing and to tantalize us with their loving sweet-voiced endearments and promises of sensual reunions. Mama Lura had learned how to handicap horses almost as well as her adopted sister Suzy Lam, while Uncle Ralph, content to live off the winnings of his two female housemates, had ceased his debilitating activities as a stooper, or gatherer of discarded betting slips. And Stan and Rosa, while almost certainly still conducting their dynamite-dangerous clandestine liaison, had slaked their passions down to covert, sensible, and undramatic levels, which served, from all indications, to keep Luckman happily in the dark. I didn't bug Stan anymore about the morality or practicality of his affair, and he certainly didn't bring up the topic with me. After all, I wasn't his minder, and he wasn't my ward.

Meanwhile, the effervescent Chantal Danssaert and the good-humored Les Qiao happily and unanxiously awaited our stockpiling of finished units in quantities sufficient to impress any buyers with our general manufacturing competence and ability to satisfy demand in a timely manner. Only then would they bring in any prospective customers. I deduced that they were suffering no enormous emotional strains, given the steady flow of charges they racked up at various eateries, theaters, clubs, and stores.

Every day, I went to the factory to gauge our progress. I generally found excellent conditions, thanks to the combined efforts of Caleb and Luckman.

Caleb oversaw everything about the factory except quality control and inspection. Responsibility for those departments devolved naturally to the inventor of the LBAS. Luckman circulated tirelessly among all fifteen workstations, doing random surveillance of assembly procedures. Then, when each unit emerged finished at the end, he put it through its paces, proving to his own deluded satisfaction that the miraculous sensor could detect test quantities of any and all explosive substances paraded before it. The off-brand chips served to power and control all the other circuitry in the device and allowed each unit to mount a convincing display of explosives-detecting wizardry. Without our contribution, Luckman's sensors and readouts would have remained inert, although the false results they gave were still basically useless.

Luckman's mind-set in this area intrigued and puzzled me. Did he sincerely believe in his vaunted wonder machine's ability to function as advertised, albeit with some sensitive tuning or tweaking in each individual instance? Did he know that the unit was a farce? Was he trying to scam us at the same time that we were busily scamming him? Or was it some kind of split-brain thing—a willful self-deception by which his surface mind believed the lie while his subconscious brain knew the truth?

No matter how much I talked to him, I couldn't discern the answer—except to all but rule out any conscious duplicity. Luckman was just too sincere and too naive, his Christian belief too real and dominant, to be capable of practicing the same kind of ruse that hardened, unethical atheists the likes of Stan and me were capable of.

Whatever the riddle of his motivations, he was turning out quite an impressive-looking product.

We had found a source for sleek extruded-aluminum cases that did not resemble the clunky prototype. Then we had settled on an enameled color combo of fire-engine-yellow with black stripes, connoting danger and military-grade capabilities. The shoulder strap for carrying was high-tech webbing. The controls and the embedded video display were easily accessible on the exterior of the case. The pistol-style detector no longer looked like a video game zapper, but rather like something a bounty hunter from the future would use to take down a robot nastier than Arnie. If I were a cop or a colonel or head of company security, I would want one of these before I even knew what it was for. I was glad that at least the look of the thing would help sell it and counted on Luckman's techno-nursemaid abilities to breeze convincingly through any demos.

I was equally impressed with Caleb's abilities to perform with utmost equanimity as a one-man human-resources department, combined with purchasing, billing, and maintenance duties.

Alice, as his assistant, had quickly reached her limits, although we kept her on for a few simple tasks, and we had hired a couple of competent helpers for him. Their presence at additional desks in Caleb's office helped fill out what had been an underused space.

I was also pleased that Caleb and Luckman had seemed to hit it off, since they both were so integral to our success and had to coordinate closely all day. They had a lot of traits in common that seemed to draw them together. They both were religious—Luckman to a greater degree—and both navigated the world with the same kind of old-school attitudes despite Luckman's being a big-city academic and Caleb's more blue-collar, rural roots.

I often found the two of them in earnest conversation, and not always concerning business. A common thread seemed to be the degeneracy of contemporary pop culture. And once, in our temporarily empty break room—a few folding chairs and card tables, a Keurig coffeemaker, a couple of vending machines provided by one of Vin Santo's more legit franchises—I came upon them sitting silently in communal prayer and backed out before I could disturb them.

I just felt lucky that they took charge of all the headachy crap that otherwise would have fallen to Stan and me.

Stan was genuinely unstinting in his praise of his former rival. He explained one day when we were schlepping a quantity of packing foam from Gunther's warehouse to our factory.

"I knew when I tangled with Johnny Reb back there in Hedgesville that he was one smart cookie and was gonna help us out big-time someday. That's why I said we hadda bring him home with us."

"Not just because you live by the credo 'Keep your friends close and your enemies closer.'"

"Enemies? Me and ol' Caleb? He's got no designs on Sandralene anymore, I can promise you that."

"Why shouldn't he, after you've kicked her to the curb?"

"I done no such thing! I told ya, Sandy is cool with me and Rosa. And besides, it's different when Sandy's outta town. When she gets back, I ain't gonna be tomcatting so heavy."

"And what's Rosa going to feel about the sudden chill?"

Stan looked a little nervous. "I'm sure she's gonna be a good sport about things. After all, cougars can't be choosers, can they?"

On that note, I left Stan to lie uneasily in the metaphorically burning four-poster he had created.

I thought to sound out Caleb about his own romantic inclinations, just to get his side of things. So one day I made a point of taking him out to lunch at a nearby diner. After we had ordered and chatted a while about how he liked his job and his living conditions and life up north in general—he still couldn't get over strangers not bothering to return a cheerful greeting on the street—I said, "You met any women yet you might fancy a date with, Caleb? I've noticed some pretty gals out on the floor who have a hard time taking their eyes off you when you're out there. Big, strapping, handsome gent like you should have no problem finding some company."

Caleb self-consciously smoothed an errant cowlick, but it sprang right back up. "Well, Glen, it's like this, see? I know this job is probably only temporary, and I'll be heading back to West Virginia with my stake. You fellows are paying me mighty generously, by the way, and I can't thank you enough. But I did leave a good business down there, after all. At least, it'll be good again when the economy picks up, which it always does. And I'd hate to get serious with some local girl who wouldn't necessarily want to stick with me when I relocate."

"Jeez, Caleb," I said, "you can at least have a little fun till then! No need to put a ring on it."

"I appreciate your take on matters, Glen, but I've got to approach things like this as I see fit." He paused. "Besides, there was ever only one gal for me, and not being able to have her is not something a man gets over easily."

That sure sounded to me like carrying a torch for Sandralene, but I wouldn't be conveying that news to Stan. I patted Caleb on the back. "Of course, of course. Well, you just let me know if you need me to act as matchmaker, if you're too shy."

Stan and I had reported in to Vin Santo several times in the past week, and he expressed satisfaction with the way things were going. The very smoothness of it frightened me a little. I wasn't used to such problem-free, stress-free operations. I kept waiting for something bad to happen, but nothing did.

At last, we had five hundred units sitting in inventory, ready to sell. All the bugs had been purged from the assembly process, and we would soon whip through the remaining forty-five hundred chips. For the first time, I thought about the long-term implications of our setup. What if we found a deep market, and Santo could rustle up some more fake chips? Could we shuck and jive our customers with rigged trials long enough to earn Stan and me a hundred million apiece? My brain would whirl dizzily whenever I contemplated such a prospect, and I would have to bring myself gently down to earth by remembering that we hadn't yet sold unit one.

But when Chantal called me and said, "I think we are ready now to bring in our first two clients," it was hard not to dream big.

32

Chantal, Les, and I stood in the airport's unsecured public area, where the disembarking passengers would emerge down a pair of escalators. Coffee smells wafted from the nearby Starbucks booth to compete with the heady outgassing of flame-retardant chemicals from the new carpeting. The essential hybrid bouquet of modern civilization. Busy travelers surged, and expectant families shuffled. A couple of limo drivers held up iPads with the names of their clients displayed.

I had to confess to being just a tad nervous: my typical scammer's stage fright, which would vanish, I hoped, the moment the con began in earnest. But I was also a little uncentered by Stan's absence. I realized how much I had come to rely on his indomitable blend of savvy and crude. But we had agreed that he would hang back from this initial meeting until I had scoped out the nature of our first customer. Stan's rough edges, I felt, might be a little off-putting to certain sophisticated sensibilities. Stan had consented, with only small reluctance and his usual disdain for appearances and conventions.

"Fine by me," he said. "I got plenty to do besides stroking some purchase-ordering paper shuffler who probably never actually even busted a cap before. Rosa and me are going to the track with your uncle Ralph and his harem today."

"Jesus, Stan! Can't you keep a lower profile, for God's sake!"

"Aw, don't pop your vasectomy stitches. The prof don't know your uncle, and for sure he's not gonna show up at the track. This is safe as houses."

"All right, all right, just try to be circumspect."

"I can't be circumspect, cuz my dick ain't never been cut—and I got no plans to change that status."

"Oversharing! Not to mention, a truly dreadful pun. Just go away now."

I resolved at that point that I would try to seek out Rosa later and make a case for tapering off or breaking off this affair. Though I had never yet had a one-on-one with the ex-schoolteacher, I suspected she would be more amenable to logic and caution than her Gulch-bred paramour. Who knew, though?

If Stan's absence undercut my confidence a little, the cool, unruffled professionalism of our arms brokers served to bolster my spirits.

Chantal Danssaert, as always, looked the embodiment of aloof high-fashion competence. She wore a pantsuit of gunmetal-gray lamé threaded with white silk, for an understated striped effect. The lapels of the puffy-shouldered double-breasted jacket intersected low enough to reveal the upper band of her lacy white undershirt. I suspected that her sylphlike build meant she could go without a bra, which was fine by me. In contrast to the severity of the suit, her expensive-looking heels were encrusted with gaudy costume jewelry, as if she were ready for the Cirque du Soleil. She pulled the look off impeccably.

Her business partner, Les Qiao, had ramped up his typical sloppy-chic stylings to a kind of *Matrix*-y all-black Korean rapper / ninja look: Mao jacket, shiny linen pants with enough billowing extra fabric to hold two of him, and jackboots that the book burners out of a Bradbury novel might have worn.

I turned to Chantal now, and she stopped fiddling with her phone.

"So today we're bringing in just the one guy?"

"Yes. I want to lavish all our attention on each buyer individually at first. We will show them great favor for the day or two they are alone with us. But then, when they come together with their peers to inspect the product and see the demo, we will exude impartiality and encourage them to compete with each other. This way, we will get the maximum bid out of each one."

"That's another thing I'm uncertain about," I said. "Why aren't we just going to ask a standard retail price for each unit, rather than conduct an auction? Let everyone buy as many as they want."

Chantal again went through her small ritual of popping an Altoid. It struck me as her securing a Maginot Line against stupidity, and about as useful as that fortification had been. But we all need our superstitions. "You must trust me on this," she said. "Many of these firms and agencies like to have exclusivity on a product. They are rivals and are always looking for an edge. If your detector could just be picked up by anyone, right off the shelf like something from Target, it would not appeal to them as strongly. And besides, Les and I will be happier if our one percent comes from a bigger transaction."

"Okay," I said. "I have to assume you know what you're doing. But I'd hate to have both parties blow us off entirely."

"This will not happen, I promise you."

Les Qiao chimed in. "Gotta believe the Danse, man."

"And we really have to put them up on our nickel, at your hotel?"

"Of course. Do you wish to look like a piker, Glen?"

"I like to look solvent. You guys have already run up some hefty charges."

"You will find that we are worth every penny, Glen." She laid the back of her cool hand possessively against my cheek and smiled. "We are excellent fluffers who ensure the money shot."

Her touch and bawdy talk sent a little wavelet of pleasure through me. Les Qiao seemed not to mind her intimate gesture, and once more I was left wondering about their nonwork relationship.

I glanced at the flight-tracking screen and saw that our guy's plane from DC had arrived at the gate.

I said, "Tell me again about this Smalley guy."

Chantal said, "Peter Smalley is a retired US Air Force major. He now works for Steel Marquee, a private security, risk management, and defense contracting company. They are based in Reston, Virginia, and currently are managing operations in Somalia, Afghanistan, Qatar, Nigeria, and a dozen other places. Their revenue last year totaled nearly one-point-five billion dollars."

Figures on that order of magnitude gave me vertigo. I wished Stan could be here to revel in the giddiness. "So dropping a hundred and twenty million on our goods—"

"Will be, for them, a modest purchase. As would a much nicer two hundred million."

I played with my share of those numbers in my head for a while, envisioning everything Nellie and I could do with that kind of dough.

Chantal interrupted my fantasies. "Here he comes."

I had no trouble spotting Smalley, who had plainly based his look on a swaggering Chuck Yeager–Clint Eastwood clone. Tall and rangy with weathered features, he wore cowboy-cut Wrangler jeans and a black rodeo shirt with white piping and blue embroidered floral motifs on the yoke. His Lucchese alligator-skin boots must have set him back at least five grand. The leather flight jacket, gray ball cap bearing a NASA patch, and Ferragamo aviator sunglasses completed the look.

Carrying only a moderately sized bag that spoke to his frequent-flyer efficiency, Smalley wove confidently through the crowd when he spotted Chantal. He swept her up in a full embrace, lifting her slight body off her feet and twirling her around. He let out an accompanying whoop that drew the attention of anyone within earshot. Men all wanted to be him, and the women wanted to be Chantal.

"Mothering bride of Christ, you sweet little Belgian truffle! How you doing, goddamn it? I haven't seen you since Dubai last year!"

Chantal consented to have both her cheeks kissed, Continental style. I started to wonder whether she was working for me or Smalley.

"Oh, I am maintaining myself quite well, Pete. But I have no need to inquire about you, for news of your exploits in Mali came to me."

"Aw, hell, they don't let me out in the field that often anymore. But when they do, I naturally aim to unfuck whatever situation comes my way, and that sometimes requires lighting up a few idiots who didn't get the memo. Hey, Lester, my son! How's it hangin'?"

"As well as can be expected, Pete. Allow me to introduce Glen McClinton, CEO of Luckman Enterprises."

Smalley had a grip that could have squeezed coal into the Kohinoor Diamond. Happily, he didn't demonstrate on me.

"Great to meet you, Mr. Smalley."

"Pete! It's Pete, compadre, or we don't do business together."

"Well, informality's no hardship."

Smalley turned back to Chantal. "Now, baby, get me up to speed. What's this burg offer by way of entertainment for a lonely business traveler? Last time we were together, as I recall, you and me ended up dancing on a bar."

"Glen knows his town better than I, Pete. I'll defer to his wisdom."

I dug out my phone and punched in Stan's number. I hoped he was back from the track by now.

"Pete, I think you are sincerely going to enjoy meeting Luckman Enterprises' chief operating officer, Mr. Stan Hasso."

33

Stan dropped a cheap white Styrofoam cooler on the coffee table of our apartment. I had been sitting on the couch, scrolling wistfully through texts from Nellie and wishing she were back home. Not only would her presence prove stimulating and enjoyable on its own merits, but perhaps having her around would serve as an excuse to avoid further late-night excursions with Chantal, Les, Pete, and Stan.

Over the past two nights, these four revelers had exhibited the alcohol-intake capacity of an entire frat house, compounded by the exhausting party-hearty ethic of a Range Rover full of victorious female rugby players. Pete Smalley, obviously happy to be out of the office on an extended all-expenses-paid junket, seemed in no hurry to get a demo of the Luckman detector. But I couldn't hack it. By this afternoon, I could feel my liver enlarging and brain cells dying faster than crickets in an early freeze. But Nellie showed no particular yearning to rush home, tied up as she was with the import biz. So I would just have to suffer on for the sake of our eventual big score.

"What's this?" I asked Stan, gesturing to the cooler.

"I figured you could use some protein. Build up your endurance so's you stop turning into a pumpkin at midnight. So I got us some nice sirloins. Oh, and I think there's fish in there, too. That's real brain food, you know."

I now saw that the cooler was embossed with the Omaha Steaks logo. But there was no address label to show that it had been delivered.

"You signed up for this?"

"Hell no! You know me—even a phone plan makes me feel tied down. This is from Gunther's warehouse."

Studying the box more closely, I saw that the logo was a little off register, not quite perfect.

"This is counterfeit meat?"

"Sure. And fish, too. All authentic ripoffs. But just as good as the real thing. I think you and me mighta even driven a load of these boxes on one of our last trips in the semi."

I took off the plastic wrap and removed the cooler lid. The red and gold boxes inside looked authentic enough except for the hazy trademark, and a generous quantity of dry ice had been packed to keep everything frozen, so that the bargain-seeking customer would not die of E. coli and thus be unable to return for more.

"So now we are peddling fake gadgets, while eating fake food and drawing on a bank account possibly filled with fake money."

"Sounds about right to me."

"Doesn't all this fakery ever get to you? Doesn't it seep into your soul, so you start to feel fake, too? Don't you ever want to have something real to hang on to?"

Stan moved away from the frozen contraband and over to the liquor cabinet, where he poured himself a generous shot of scotch. "I got plenty of real things in my life to keep me grounded. Women, for one. Nothing realer. And I don't ever bother with watching what's 'seeping into my soul,' cuz that is one organ no one has ever managed to show me on no doctor's-office anatomy chart. You're just freaking out for no reason at all. Or maybe you're antsy or horny or something, and it's queering your nerves all up. I don't see what the hang-up is, anyhow, about trimming some corners to save a little dough. What's it matter the brand name that's stamped on something? It's all the same stuff. This meat probably comes from the same butcher that supplies the genuine Omaha Steaks. You're not gonna be able to tell the difference."

"But sometimes there is a difference between real and fake," I said. "Sometimes the fakes are dangerous—like fake antibiotics that don't work, or fake airbags that explode when they're not supposed to."

"Take my word for it; these steaks ain't gonna explode. Not the fish, neither, unless you cook them on a leaky propane grill."

I put my phone down on an end table and got up from the couch. I needed a drink now, too. "Stan, you're impossible to reason with. Your skull is as thick as a cape buffalo's."

"You just can't stand to lose an argument, which is why you gotta turn to add-hominy attacks. This is something I have known about you from the first time we started hanging out together. But I don't generally mind, because I know it is the mark of an insecure person."

"Oh, just forget it."

"It is already gone from my consciousness. Oh, yeah, I got

something else for you from the warehouse. It's for Nellie, actually. I picked up one for Rosa and one for Sandy and figured you could use a little help, too, with the old romance thing once Nell gets home."

Stan took a bottle from the pocket of his winter coat and tossed it to me. It was perfume, 24 Faubourg by Hermès—about a hundred and a quarter a bottle.

"Another fake? I can't wait to smell it. It probably features the essence of plastic flowers, with notes of Easter-basket grass."

"Just get those steaks going, will ya? I gotta get over to see Rosa before any clubbing tonight."

Weary of arguing and dreading another night out on the town, feeling somehow insubstantial, as if I were a tenth-generation photocopy of myself, I carried the cooler into the kitchen, defrosted the steaks in the microwave, then started cooking. Mention of Rosa reminded me that I still had not finagled a private talk with her about where she thought her affair with Stan was heading. Maybe tomorrow.

Just as I was sliding plates of meat and fish and some fake Rustic Roasting Vegetables onto the table, my phone rang. Convinced it was Nellie, I scrambled for my cell. But Chantal's ID showed.

"Hello? What's up?"

"You and I and Les will not be going out tonight—at least not for fun. Marquee Steel Pete will have to amuse himself. Our second client is arriving, and we have to meet him. Please pick us up at the hotel."

"Should I bring Stan, too?"

Stan was waving the unheard chore away with his left hand while his right brought a forkful of rare sirloin up to his lips.

"That will not be necessary, I think. Your perspicacity will suffice. We will see you in half an hour."

Chantal ended the call without so much as a polite goodbye, and not for the first time I wondered who was boss of this operation.

I explained to Stan what was happening.

"It's cool you can handle this by yourself, Glen. Much obliged. This frees up my evening to be with Rosa."

"Stan, you know this has to come to an end. What's Sandy going to feel when she gets back and finds you boinking your high school physics teach?"

Stan narrowed his eyes. "Have you been on the phone with Sandy about all this?"

"No, of course not. I'd never interfere like that. Why do you ask?"

"Only cuz she's been acting a little weird with me the last few days, like something's bothering her. She sounds kinda like she did down in Hedgesville. In fact, she said she might come home before Nellie does."

"It's not anything I've said or done, believe me. I haven't even exchanged a single text with her."

"Okay, okay, I believe you. Nobody can figure out why women do things, anyhow. Maybe she just got lonely for her old man. That would be perfectly logical given my irresistible nature."

I made no comment, but wolfed down my meal and dashed out of the condo.

I had expected to find Chantal and Les waiting for me on the sidewalk or in the lobby, but when I didn't spot them there, I texted and got an answer bidding me to come up to their room.

In the luxury suite—faux gaslight sconces, flocked wallpaper, divans—I found Chantal ready to go, all understated fashionable allure as usual, already wearing her elegant camel-colored Burberry wool and cashmere coat. But Les remained on the bed, sitting up against a stack of pillows, fully dressed but unshod, legs crossed at the ankles, and looking equal parts grim and sheepish—half stubborn, half apologetic. His smooth Asian features reminded me in that moment of a petulant child's.

"What's wrong?" I said.

Chantal made a gesture dismissive of all Les' concerns, indicating that her partner was a wimp afraid of shadows. "He does not wish to associate with our new client any more than is strictly necessary, and generally by daylight, in a group. Especially, he objects to riding in the back seat with the man from the airport to the hotel."

"There must be a compelling reason, and I want to know more, of course. But couldn't we solve one problem by having *you* ride in the back seat with the guy?"

Now it was Chantal's turn to be peevish. "I do not care to ride all cramped up in the backseat of a car without a very good reason. And this is not a good reason."

"It is to me," said Les.

"All right," I said, "this isn't getting us anywhere. I assume we have to be at the airport fairly quickly, and we're just wasting time. Why didn't this guy give us more advance notice, anyhow?"

"It is the nature of his business. It is hard for him to get away or to know when he will have free time. It is a testament to my salesmanship and connections that he agreed to come at all."

"Well, who is he? What's he do?"

"His name is Derian Crespo. He hails from El Salvador and is connected with an NGO in that country."

"Nongovernmental, huh? Some kind of demining operation that could use our detectors? Making the countryside safe for farmers? What's his group called?"

"La Sombra Negra."

"'Black Shadow'? Never heard of it. Not very sunny-sounding and upbeat, is it?"

Les' laughter held a bitter edge. "Why should it be? They're vigilantes—a death squad."

34

I wasn't sure I had heard aright.

"A death squad? As in killing people at random?"

Chantal objected. "They do not kill people at random. They kill only the bad people, with maybe a little collateral damage, just like your American drone strikes and superheroes. Surely you have heard of the merciless MS-13 and the grievous problem they represent? The Black Shadow is the only force that can deal with them effectively. The brutal gangsters of MS-13 fear no one except them. That's why the government of El Salvador gives La Sombra Negra its extrajudicial blessing. I believe Derian Crespo actually sports a governmental title apart from his more freelance pursuits."

"But they murder people!"

"You very rationally did not say 'innocent people.' What of your Mr. Santo? Are his hands clean? Yet you are accepting his support and funding."

I sat down on one of the divans. I did not need this ethical and practical dilemma at this moment, when I was already stressed out and juggling half a dozen different chainsaws. The fake sirloin churned in my stomach. I could see why Les might be leery of tagging along with this new client. You endorsed mass graves just by sharing a cab with such a guy, whose motto, I suspected, was closer to "Kill them all and let God sort them out" than to "Imagine all the people living life in peace."

Chantal squatted down to get her eyes level with mine. I noticed for the first time their dove-gray fathomless depth. Her lovely white face seemed carved of marble.

"Listen to me, Glen, this is no time to lose your nerve. If you want someone to buy lots and lots of your toy detector, you have to go where the money goes, and find the kind of people who want this thing. MS-13 is getting into making bombs more and more, even associating with terrorists, and La Sombra Negra wants to be able to reliably detect these dangerous explosives. They have deep pockets and the need for your detector. When we get Crespo bidding against Smalley, who knows how high the price will go? Think of all that lovely money in your pockets."

I tried to follow her advice and envision the easy street I would soon be dwelling on. But all I could think of were the potholes and car crashes on the way to that boulevard of dreams. To mix metaphors, it was like Gatsby having to swim across Macbeth's sea of blood to get to the green light on Daisy's dock.

"What's going to happen when the detector doesn't perform up to snuff back in El Salvador?"

"This was always your concern, no matter who bought it. Surely you knew this. But don't worry. The detector is not *totally* useless, just partially. You can always claim that the operators are doing something wrong, and even earn more money by sending instructors if you want. It will work good enough to fool people for a long time. And by then you will be out of the picture with your profits, leaving Luckman holding the bag."

I hesitated, and Chantal added, "Besides, you're not selling him guns, after all—just life-saving devices."

I stood up, having made a decision. "Okay, let's go meet Dark Zorro."

Les remained planted on the bed, arms folded across his chest. "I'm still not coming. The less time I have to associate with Crespo, the happier I'll be."

Chantal made a noise of resigned disgust. "Be that way, then. You and I will discuss this more when I return."

*　*　*

The car was on the expressway heading to the airport before Chantal spoke again. Her heady perfume filled the cabin, and I guessed it was not counterfeit.

"Les is such a little girl sometimes, I wonder what I see in him."

"You two, ah, are, um, an item, then, I take it."

"Les and I go way back. It is complicated."

"I see."

Her hand resting lightly on my thigh nearly caused me to swerve out of my lane and end my checkered life in a flaming crash. Unlike its coolness when we first shook, that hand now burned through the fabric of my pants.

"It's an open relationship, you understand."

"Oh, I understand plenty."

Chantal removed her hand and said, "But we must attend to our business first."

"Oh, I could not agree more."

A small bubble of space surrounded Derian Crespo as he moved down the corridor among the other disembarking passengers from his flight. Some aura he radiated warned even blithely unobservant strangers not to get too close or hinder his freedom of movement.

Nothing about him was particularly scary. Of average height, not too young but not quite middle-aged, with mocha features of unremarkable handsomeness. A shaved head but with lush, neatly groomed mustache and goatee as if to compensate. His clothing was neither extravagant nor cheap. He wore a nice black down vest over a blue soccer jersey of the El Salvador national team. The shirt and his tight designer jeans showed off an athlete's build. I failed to see a bandolier of bullets or any automatic small arms concealed on his person.

He greeted Chantal first, with a charming smile that nonetheless seemed to convey no more true happiness than the smile of a guy sitting in the husband chair outside a women's dressing room while the Super Bowl is in progress.

"Señorita Danssaert, it is a pleasure to meet again after you did us that good turn at the SCTX in London."

"And I hope to do you another here, Derian. Please greet Mr. Glen McClinton."

Crespo shook my hand with a grip that said, *You are receiving the exact measure of pounds per square inch sufficient to impress you with my superiority without doing actual damage.*

"*Mucho gusto, señor.* I am sure we will be of much benefit to each other."

We claimed Crespo's bag from the carousel and trekked out to the car.

There was not a lot of chitchat on the drive back, since both Crespo and Chantal were preoccupied with their phones.

As we pulled up in front of the hotel, Crespo said, "I must ask a favor of you. I have associates here in the city—they are one reason why I was eager to voyage here—and they have just prevailed upon me to help them with a certain small matter. So I would ask if we might put off the demonstration of your product for a day or two?"

"Oh, sure, no problem," I said.

"I am immensely in your debt, *señor* Glen."

* * *

I watched the pair enter the expensive lodgings and mentally totted up the extra charges the delay would occasion.

Back in the Stan-less condo, I had a long shower that failed to make me feel completely clean, then went to sleep. My dreams that night were filled with images of Sandralene and Nellie running through a tropical rain forest while being pursued by a pack of wild boars, while I feverishly tried to make edible a steak that had been marinated in perfume. Off in the shadows, I somehow knew that Stan was canoodling with Rosa, while Luckman aimed the pistol sensor of his detector at them, disintegrating them with a crackling Buck Rogers plasma ray.

I woke up around 6:00 a.m., unrested but unable to get back to sleep. Stan's bedroom door, open last night, was shut, so, deducing that he was home, I kept the volume of the television low when I turned on the news.

At the top of the hour, the lead story breathlessly informed me of an "underworld slaughter overnight among several Latino gangs!" Apparently, quite a few of the more reprehensible local thugs had met an untimely end. The authorities felt that inter-tribal rivalry explained it all.

35

The last time I could recall feeling this way was when I was ten years old and standing in front of the principal's desk at William Chaloner Elementary, getting reamed for having disassembled part of the chain-link fence around the school's property to fashion a shortcut home for myself. Back then, I writhed under simultaneous and conflicting sensations: acknowledgment of guilt, and irritation at not being able to take pride in a harmless bit of hacking that had made my life easier.

Now, with Vin Santo playing the principal's part, I was experiencing a similar mix of emotions. There he sat behind his big, barren desk, looking as miffed as a horny Apollo when Daphne changed into a tree, while he kept me standing before him. His two "security personnel" shifted uneasily from foot to foot, just waiting to administer whatever punishment he might decree.

Yes, I was in part culpable for what had happened, though my intentions had been straightforward and laudable. Sure, Derian

Crespo was now resident in town, bumping off members of the Mara Salvatrucha gang left and right, only because I hadn't vetted Chantal Danssaert's prospective client more stringently. But Crespo was also a likely purchaser of our gadget, able to make us all stinking rich with money from his oligarchic backers. So shouldn't the balance have swung more evenly between the two extremes of praise and condemnation? Yet Santo preferred to emphasize the negative. It seemed woefully unfair.

This time, at least, I had an accomplice by my side to share the burden of Santo's wrath. Although Stan had not yet even met Crespo on this late morning after the man's arrival, he displayed admirable solidarity, for which I was grateful. He had said only a couple of words in response to Santo, as had I. But just his presence was reassuring.

Having elaborated in considerable detail on the repercussions of letting Crespo loose in our city's underworld to upset the delicate dynamics of mobster collegiality, Santo seemed to have entered his summing-up phase, so I tuned back in to his words.

"Don't misunderstand. It ain't that I am particularly fond o' these fucking beaners, see. Uncivilized, that's what they are. So I got no brief for them. They ain't like me and the guys who work for me. There's nothing old-school about them, no sense of tradition. They are like the fucking Ebola virus, killing the very thing they hope to live on, in the bloodiest way possible. They got no principles, no strategy, no skills. All they know how to do is chop and slice and choke and grab. No long-term plans, no sense of building relationships and cutting a guy a break, knowing he'll owe you one down the line. So it don't crush my heart to see any number of them end up feeding the turtles in the marshes outside town."

I was about to unwisely point out that Santo should therefore be very happy with the janitorial service Stan and I had accomplished by bringing Crespo here. But seeing me open my mouth, he raised a fat paw to silence me, and it proved just as well.

"But, on the other hand, these Mara Salvadouchebags got their uses. They keep all the other spics from horning in on our operations. So long as you supply 'em with enough cash and women, they stay satisfied and will not look to muscle in where they're not wanted. Not that they're even capable of handling the more sophisticated stuff, but they coulda stepped on our toes in several profitable areas, such as making short-term loans. But they didn't. And why? Because of a carefully maintained equilibrium."

Santo paused to peer at Stan, who was digging the nail of his pinkie finger into the space between two incisors. "Hasso, do you even know what equilibrium is?"

"Sure. That's when you and your old lady are doing sixty-nine and she's on top and you are both giving as good as you get."

Santo let out a huge guffaw. "Hasso, you're okay. Sure, I guess that's equilibrium—although I prefer not to imagine doing sixty-nine with these fuckers. Anyway, where was I? Oh, yeah—so there was an equilibrium between me and the spics that is feeling some ripples from these killings, and the outcome is unpredictable. I am trying my best to smooth things over. But if there are any more executions, some truly ass-biting repercussions are bound to come."

I ventured a response. "So it's our job to rein in Crespo. I think we can do that, Vin. After all, we have the demo with Luckman scheduled for tomorrow. Crespo and Smalley will make their bids at the close of that process, and then they'll both be gone. How much trouble can he get into in the next twenty-four hours?"

"Maybe a lot, which is why I am counting on you to keep

him busy. His whack-first-ask-questions-later style might work okay back in his dirt-alley homeland—where, you know, before Columbus straightened them out, the natives useta just cut a guy's beating heart right outta his wide-awake chest without a blink—but it don't fly here."

Santo paused for a refreshing sugary jolt from his Big Gulp, then said, "So, I can count on you two to maintain order and quiet? I'd hate to see all this investment of mine get pissed away, especially because things are humming along nicely so as to earn us all some decent money. But if it all goes fubar, somebody will have to make good on everything, and it won't be Vin Santo."

"Totally clear, Vin," said Stan. "No worries."

I just nodded.

Outside Santo's establishment, which was shuttered at this early hour, I shivered in the cold that the third week in November had ushered in. It dawned on me that Thanksgiving—late this year—was just about a week away. I tried to imagine being free of all cares and responsibilities, sitting down to some big old-fashioned celebratory dinner with all my loved ones. Nellie, Stan, and Sandy. Uncle Ralph and Suzy and Lura. Caleb and the Luckmans. Even Chantal and Les. Maybe Vin Santo would show up at the door like Scrooge, bearing the biggest goose from the market.

Such a vision seemed infinitely unlikely. On Thanksgiving day, Stan and I would probably be sharing the marshes with Crespo's victims or else driving as fast as we could toward the Canadian border. But meanwhile, until everything fell apart, we had to try our best to keep Santo's precious equilibrium intact.

Stan and I got in my Lexus and headed toward the Luckman Enterprises factory.

"I deeply look forward to meeting this Crespo," said Stan. "He seems like a righteous dude. Takes a lotta balls to chase after your enemies in a foreign country, where you don't know the ropes so good."

"I'm sure you and he will have a lot in common to discuss," I replied. "Maybe your arsonist skills will somehow impress him. But meanwhile, we have to make sure everything's set for tomorrow. Then I'll call Chantal and stress to her that she and Les have to help us moderate Crespo's behavior."

"If anyone can do it, that tough little broad can. She's got ice water in her veins—that's why her hand always feels cool to the touch."

"Come on, Stan, she's not inhuman."

"Oh, and what's this I hear? Do I detect a glimmer of kindly sentiment towards the lady? Maybe you had a hand down her pants while Nellie's been gone and I was too busy running everything to notice."

"Don't be ridiculous."

"I just calls 'em like I sees 'em. Oh, by the way, we got another little chore today."

"What might that be?"

"We gotta pick up Sandy at the airport. Just her, no Nellie. And her flight gets in around four."

"You're kidding, right?"

"Why would I do that? Especially about such a special lovers' reunion."

"Why can't you go get her by yourself?"

"I need you around just in case she ain't totally jake with my fooling around. Maybe she brooded over it a little too much. Like I said, she's sounded a little weird lately on the phone. I don't wanna take any chances. You'll be kinda like a referee, to make sure she don't scratch my eyes out, like."

"Okay, I can see that. But you were supposed to give me time to talk to Rosa, to get her to end the affair."

"Oh, I took that into account. I made a date to see her for lunch. But she doesn't know that you're gonna be the one to keep it."

"So you're done with her, just like that?"

"Yeah, pretty much. She was getting a little too clingy. And besides, it's Sandy I love, not her. I don't wanna hurt either one of 'em. But if somebody has to get hurt, better Rosa than Sandy. Sandy's my future; Rosa's my past. It was fun while it lasted, and I think I made her life a little more exciting for a while. That Luckman ain't exactly one for living *la vida loca*. Good provider, loves the hell outta Rosa, and all. But about as exciting as my old aunt Myrtle. Anyway, Rosa shoulda known from the start it was never gonna be no long-term thing, her and me. She's tough; she'll get over it fast."

"I hope so," I said. "She could make trouble otherwise."

"Don't worry, that's not her nature. You just gentle her along. Maybe even tell her she's better off without me, that I'm just a no-good heel anyhow."

I couldn't help myself. "It will feel refreshing to tell the truth rather than lie, for a change."

36

It was amazing what copious infusions of cash and the invoking of Vin Santo's name could do to motivate construction contractors who might otherwise tend toward duplicity and sloth. Luckman Enterprises now boasted a not-too-shabby conference room, attached to Caleb's office. Nice furniture, tasteful carpeting, elegant LED lighting fixtures, a wet bar, and a sixty-inch monitor on one wall. Here was where we would conduct tomorrow's demo after giving Derian Crespo and Pete Smalley a tour of the factory.

Arrayed on the table were several samples of different explosives, some in open glass dishes, others in sealed metal containers. I recognized the familiar pinkish granules of ANFO, the ammonium nitrate–fuel oil explosive, which seemed to be the only substance that Luckman's gadget could reliably pick up. A couple of the snazzy-looking LBAS units brooded impressively between the containers and a stack of glossy prospectuses.

When Stan and I entered, Caleb and Luckman were standing

side by side at the table, intently studying the setup. Luckman had one hand resting intimately on Caleb's shoulder, like a football coach with a player, or a father advising his son. Hearing us come in, they straightened up to greet us.

"Glen, Stan," said Luckman. "Take a look and tell me what you think. Caleb's laid it out beautifully."

All the samples were neatly labeled with their names and descriptions, and one of the detectors was split open to show its complex innards. The other would presumably be used to respond to the samples.

"You sure this gizmo of yours is gonna work okay?" Stan said. "We gotta impress these guys if we hope to sell stuff. And the last thing we need is to fall down and get mud on our faces."

"Of course, of course, I understand," replied Luckman. But you needn't worry about anything. With proper handling, the LBAS is infallible."

Again I wondered about Luckman's state of mind when he uttered such counterfactual pronouncements. Was he willfully deluding himself, or just whistling past the graveyard? Did his pride, sense of self-worth, and perhaps even sanity depend on the efficacy of his gadget? Especially now that he had quit his teaching job and staked his whole future on it?

Whatever the reality of his situation, his cool, assertive attitude was enough to reassure me—and, we hoped, our potential clients as well. I just prayed the machine would perform up to snuff, or at least appear to.

"Would you like to see the video?" Caleb said. "The firm we outsourced it to did a bang-up job, especially given the short window they had."

When I hadn't been otherwise engaged with placating

gangsters, covering for a philandering friend, keeping the funds flowing to my lover's import business, and getting schooled on the arms market from a sexy Belgian, I had whipped up a rough outline of all the LBAS' selling points. I discovered that the process wasn't really so different from coming up with a convincing trial brief. At one point, I even imagined for a moment an alternate career and life for myself, in which I had worked for some ad agency or PR firm and never been tempted into jurisprudential criminality. But any such fancies were fleeting, since I couldn't change the past and must deal with the inglorious mess I had created for myself.

"Sure," I said. "I'm eager to see if they used anything of mine. Let 'er roll."

Caleb already had a laptop cabled into the big monitor, and set the video playing.

The presentation was slick and colorful, fast-paced, and thoroughly professional. The actors employed to embody our workforce and potential customers looked like the cast of some hip new HBO series. The portrayal of the lifesaving scenarios that the LBAS could enable would have brought tears to the eyes of a battle-hardened general. I heard some of my hastily scribbled talking points translated into dialogue. The short passages on-screen of Luckman speaking made him seem less like Professor Irwin Corey and more like Neil deGrasse Tyson. Anyone looking at this clip would have been convinced that Luckman Enterprises was a Fortune 500 company with global reach, and that the LBAS was the biggest contribution to civilization since the microwave oven.

"Beautiful, beautiful. Good job, Caleb. Along with all the pampering and the face-to-face glad-handing tomorrow, this should really seal the deal. One or the other of these guys is going to offer us beaucoup bucks."

Looking a little concerned, Luckman said, "That brings up an important point, Glen. What can you tell me about this second potential buyer? I know he arrived only yesterday, but surely you have his background information already. I was able to do some extensive online research on Pete Smalley and Steel Marquee, and I approve of their corporate stance and track record. They have received good ratings from various ethical watchdogs. They're not perfect, of course—there was that incident with Myanmar—but they seem like good people. And that's of paramount concern. We can't let the LBAS be used by unsavory types. But this Derian Crespo—I couldn't find anything just using his name. What's his firm all about? I understand they're based in El Salvador."

To my great credit, I managed to think fast enough to come up with an answer that would align Luckman's moral compass, playing off something I had said the day before to Chantal. "They want to use your detector for clearing away land mines, Ron. You know how bad the situation is down there in that poor abused country."

Luckman's face relaxed. "Oh, that's wonderful. I couldn't imagine a better use for my brainchild."

On that note, after checking with Caleb that everything was under control and that there was nothing else Stan or I could help with until the next day, I decided to conclude the meeting. The big, buff Southerner gave his thumbs-up to the whole operation. So far as he knew, our product and intentions were utterly legit.

"The thousandth unit just rolled off the line and onto the shelves," he said.

"Super! If we can get one of these guys to pay for the finished thousand and take delivery as a guarantee for the rest of the output, that will breathe new life into our cash flow."

And keep Vin Santo happy.

Out on the chilly sidewalk, Stan said, "You're meeting Rosa at the Seacook Shanty in half an hour. It's a nice little outta-the-way fish-and-chips joint down by the harbor, where nobody will know you or her."

I got the address and directions on my phone. "Okay. Where should I pick you up for the ride to the airport?"

"Back at the condo. I'll Uber."

As I headed to where I had parked, Stan called out, "Don't do anything I wouldn't do."

"That, my friend, is *all* I intend to do!"

***

Even outside, I could catch the delicious scents of frying seafood. The restaurant turned out not to be a sleazy dive at all, but rather a good, solid proletarian hole-in-the-wall. The maritime decor—nets, glass floats, plaster swordfish, a poster of fancy sailor knots—had probably been moderately stylish around 1982.

Rosa Luckman occupied a gingham-covered table in the farthest corner, her back to the wall and facing the door. When she saw me come in, it was as if someone had punched her in the gut. She actually got halfway up to leave, but I managed to cross the small room and beckon her wordlessly to sit back down, which she did.

I sat across from her and didn't say anything for a minute or so as she stifled her tears and blew her nose. Meanwhile, I was trying to form my chaotic thoughts into some kind of careful, caring, sensible words. The woman's reality had hit me upside the head for the first time. I had been in her company only two times before—three if you counted the night I saw her clothes strewn across the condo floor and deduced her presence behind the closed bedroom door. This meeting was the first time Rosa Luckman as a unique, autonomous individual had become the entire focus of my attention, the whole reason for my being with her.

At first, I just tried to internalize her essence, to put myself in her shoes.

She wore a green knit dress with a high cowl neck against the autumn chill. At first glance, it appeared modest—until I noticed how it outlined every curve of her small-bosomed, well-toned body—a physique well above average for the age hinted at in her patrician features. Beneath this unremarkable surface roiled the hidden passions of a woman who, long ago, had started up a love affair with her sixteen-year-old student and then, decades later, taken up with the man he had become—both times at the risk of losing everything she had. But I hoped also to encounter her practical side, her genuine commitment to Luckman.

"Rosa, I'm sorry." That seemed the least terrible way to begin.

She had regained some measure of composure and acceptance, although the eyes showed her continuing hurt. "Why should you be sorry?" she said. "You're not the one who came back into my life with a lot of crazy talk and wild promises and hot sex."

"I know Stan somewhat," I replied. "We've been through a lot. And I think that whatever he said, he really meant at the time. But changing circumstances have a way of undoing things despite all our best intentions. His woman's coming back today. I have to leave soon to meet her at the airport."

"She must really be something. Because I am not exactly chopped liver."

I was gratified to hear her upholding her own worth. "No, I can see that, for sure. And yeah, Sandralene is a force of nature. And your husband—does he understand how lucky he is?"

Reminding her of her sacred marriage vows and all that guff did not seem a bad idea, and her reluctant sigh proved me right.

"Yes, of course," she said. "Ron practically worships me. He's told me many, many times how he couldn't live without me, how I made his life over, from drab to wonderful. But you know, sometimes that much worship gets hard to bear. It even gets old and cloying. Sometimes you want—well, you want a hell-bound train, and damn the safety and common sense and consequences."

"Well, you sure picked the right travel agent for that trip."

She gave a gravelly laugh. "Yeah, didn't I? If only Stan had managed to graduate, I'm sure his yearbook picture would have read, 'Voted most likely to fuck with your head.' I knew it had to end sooner or later, even if I did allow myself a moment now and then to imagine he'd chuck everything and we'd run off together. But that's not in the cards, I can see."

I reached over to touch her hand, and she grabbed mine and squeezed before letting go.

"Rosa, I hate to intrude practicality into this talk, but I have to know if you can keep it together whenever you and Stan come face-to-face again. We have a lot invested in this venture with your husband, and I'm sure you want it to succeed—for his sake if not necessarily for ours."

"Oh, of course. I'm an adult. I know how to lie and put up a good false front. Don't worry about any of that. I want my share of those millions as much as you or Ron do."

I got to my feet. "I hope I might salvage some of your good feelings toward Stan. He's not the worst."

Rosa stood and held my gaze with a passionate intensity I had seldom before seen.

"I will love that fucking sexy bastard as long as I live."

37

I was thinking I might just abandon my whole complicated life and get a job as a taxi driver specializing in the airport run. I had journeyed to and from this destination so often lately, I should have installed a meter in the Lexus. I practically knew the guys manning the booths at the short-term parking lot by name.

But such delusional dreams of escape and obscurity could not survive long under the pressures of what lay ahead for me. I knew that tomorrow's presentation was the make-or-break moment for our scam. Sure, if we failed to wow Derian Crespo and Pete Smalley, we could always start over with new clients, assuming Chantal and Les could roust some up for us. But if we failed to win over these first two—who might, I suddenly realized, spread bad news about us in the aftermath of a botch—then we weren't likely to lure in any others. Yes, I could adjust my pitch after any failure, but only by making relatively minor refinements. I had put everything I had into this presentation, and the product was what it was, and could not be glitzed up any further. So if we didn't get a bite tomorrow, we were probably staring disaster in the face. Not only would there be no life-changing riches for us, but Stan and I would be on the carpet again in front of Vin Santo, trying to arrange some kind of repayment plan for his loans that might conceivably end short of the year 2069 or else terminate with our ignominious deaths, whichever came first.

But while all these worries were running through my head, no such trepidations appeared to preoccupy my passenger. Stan was too excited at the return of his luscious supersize squeeze to be bothered with mere business matters. Not for the first time, I envied his ability both to focus on what mattered and to ignore the rest.

When I picked him up at our condo, he had simply said, "How'd it go?"

"It went okay. You are one lucky son of a bitch, you know. Not only because it looks like you got away clean with this breakup, but also because a woman like Rosa ever loved you in the first place."

Stan seemed genuinely chagrined, at least in some small measure. "I know, I know. What can I say? I never claimed to be some paragon of virtue. Thanks for handling it. I owe you one."

"Don't think I won't collect someday."

Now, as I merged onto the airport access road, this recent crisis was evidently all forgotten, disposed of, not to be dwelt upon. His was an attitude I wished I could cultivate.

"You think Sandy'll dig this perfume, Glen?"

Stan had brought along the bottle of fake Hermès perfume intended for her. "Sure, if she likes smelling the way some Chinese deputy factory manager figured Hermès ought to smell."

"Now you're just trying to piss me off. Besides, this stuff doesn't come from China. Gunther told me it's from India."

"Oh, well, then, it's sure to do the trick. It's the next best thing to building her the Taj Mahal."

Out of the car, Stan practically galloped into the reception area, even though Sandy's flight from Caboverde wasn't scheduled to arrive for another forty minutes. He had to have a drink at the schmaltzy franchised saloon to steady himself. Then, finally, Sandralene was coming through the exit, her face lit up with anticipation and joy.

Stan swept her up off the floor. With her right foot dangling a few inches above the carpet, she wrapped her mighty left leg halfway around his waist. They mashed their faces together with the force of particles colliding at CERN. I expected the sprinkler system to go off and the airport security guards to converge. Images from a college course on mythology swarmed unbidden into my mind's eye. The occasion demanded mythic associations: women turned into trees or waterfalls, men into stags, giant swans thrusting between parted thighs.

The clinch ended, and I got some of the fallout. Being hugged by Sandralene Parmalee was like being crushed in the embrace of the Greek earth goddess herself.

"Glen! It's *so* good to be back and see you again!"

But then she did something strange. She put me at arm's length and looked at me soberly, as if she had just encountered me on the wrong side of the ICU door.

"You're okay?"

"Of course I'm okay. Except for being a little keyed up about tomorrow."

She said nothing further, and Stan, putting his arm around her waist, said, "Let's get home."

Stan opened the rear door of the Lexus for Sandralene, then made as if to join her in the back seat.

"Oh, come on, you're not going to have me play chauffeur!"

"Just make like Kato and drive."

By the time I pulled into the condo parking lot, you could have bottled the pheromone fog in the car and sold it as a Viagra substitute. It was evident that whatever of the Rosa Luckman infidelity Sandralene might have been privy to had proved insufficient to crack the foundations of the Hasso-Parmalee entente.

Inside the apartment, I resigned myself to a long stint in the relatively cloistered confines of the laundry room.

* * *

The next morning, Stan and I mustered at the breakfast table before the clock showed 8:00 a.m. Sandy stayed abed. Stan was still in a pair of garishly striped pajamas. I had already shaved, showered, and donned my best suit.

"Let's hustle," I said. "Smalley and Crespo expect us to meet them at the factory at ten. Chantal and Les are escorting them. Do you think I should call Luckman? Nah, what am I thinking? He probably didn't even sleep last night, he's so excited. And anyhow, Caleb will make sure he gets there."

Stan rubbed his face, then downed about eight ounces of black coffee. "All right, all right," he groaned. "Let a guy get his head together first." And off he shambled like a lazy teenage woolly mammoth.

While Stan was in the shower and I was trying to divert myself with the Weather Channel, Sandralene emerged. Barefoot, clad in black leggings and an oversize sweatshirt featuring the logo of our local minor-league team, the Bandits, she looked preoccupied, even worried.

"You didn't hear from Nellie this morning yet?"

"No—not in about a day, in fact," I said, clicking off the TV. But I know she's really busy. Why?"

"When I was leaving, she promised me she would call you."

"Any special reason?"

Sandy sat down beside me on the couch. "Glen, I thought Nellie should tell you, which is why I haven't said anything yet. But it doesn't look like she's going to keep her promise to me, so I have to let you know. It's the only right thing to do."

I had no inkling of what Sandy was about to say, only that it probably wasn't good. "Let me know what?"

"Nellie is having an affair. That's why I came home early. I didn't like being part of it anymore. It made me feel sad and cheap and anxious, and unfair to you, so I left."

I tried to laugh it off. "An affair? Sure, with her importing company. I am kind of jealous of all the time she spends on it."

Resting her hand on my wrist, Sandy said, "No, Glen, it's more than that. She's screwing this guy there. Onésimo Dambara. You know him."

Now my brain was whirling like one of those playground roundabouts, the steel platters with rails that kids spin up to dizzying rates by sheer muscle power. And just like a kid who tries to stop or slow the disc's momentum, I could feel my mental muscles stretching as I tried to bring my chaotic thoughts to some steady state. Onésimo Dambara? Who the hell …

And then memory supplied a face and job title to go with the name.

Nellie was two-timing me with the manager of a third world pudding factory?

38

Sandralene did not respond to my disbelief with any words. She just nodded, continuing to look sad and serious as I staggered under the weight of this shocking news.

Part of me refused to believe that Nellie would stray from the implicitly monogamous relationship we had established since we first got together during the Nancarrow caper. But another, more pragmatic part knew that such an event could happen all too plausibly. Nellie was no plaster saint. She had needs, as I well knew, and was alone in a distant country—a place that, moreover, also provided familiar cultural touchstones that would have disarmed her traveler's wariness. And even when she had been home recently, I had been too immersed in this Luckman scam to lavish on her all the attention she needed and deserved. Mentally I cataloged all the times her enthusiastic stories about goings-on with Tartaruga Verde Importing had elicited from me only a grunt or a nod or a few blasé words of encouragement.

I hadn't even gone with her to the bank to offer support when she was applying for her line of credit! What a jerk I had been!

And yet, even this damning list of lover's slights seemed insufficient to propel her into someone else's arms. There had to be something else at the root of this astonishing development.

I regarded Sandy's gorgeous worried face, framed by the cascade of undulant black hair, with a probing look that must have hit home somehow, because she averted her eyes from mine.

"Sandy, what happened over there to make Nellie take up with this Dambara guy?"

"I don't know, exactly ..."

"C'mon, just tell me."

Sandy started to sniffle. "It's all my fault, Glen! I let her know what you and Stan are actually up to!"

To figure out what Sandy's confession meant, I had to play back all the lies I had told everyone recently.

"Nellie still thought Stan and I were working at a car transport job? And you told her what we were really up to?"

"It just came out. I thought she already knew!" she wailed, and then the tears began in earnest.

Nellie had never been part of the criminal milieu the way Stan, Sandy, and I were. An innocent kid from Nowheresville, with a respectable, conventional family, she had been just an unwitting pawn in the whole Nancarrow takedown. And in fact, when she discovered the true extent of our duplicity, she had deliberately but unthinkingly collapsed the whole structure around our ears in a near-fatal disaster. Afterward, it took many apologies, promises, and mea culpas for me to win back her trust. And I seemed to recall that somewhere in that outpouring of appeasement and self-abasement, I may have let slip a pledge to hew to the straight and narrow for the rest of my days.

And so, naturally, upon learning the awful and insulting truth that I had been lying to her for weeks, and that the reason for those lies was that Stan and I had embarked on another dicey voyage down the shoal-ridden coast of Scamolia, she had sought out comfort and consolation where she could find it. That I would have told her everything once we were filthy rich was not something she could know, and thus could not have come into play as exculpatory evidence of my loving good intentions.

I could just see her sorrowfully unburdening herself over drinks to that opportunistic cocksman Onésimo Dambara—a sympathetic fellow Caboverdean, handsome in his rough-hewn way but older even than I! She had confided in him strictly in the spirit of blowing off steam after work, and he, of course, twisted the occasion to his own loathsome horndog purposes. And then Nellie, in her stubborn and perhaps overly bighearted, simpatico way, would have maintained the relationship, not wanting to rudely cut Dambara off, and maybe even with a subliminal desire to repay me for my lies.

Sandy continued to sniffle, using the sleeve of Stan's sweatshirt as a handkerchief.

"Couldn't you have snapped her out of it, made her see how I was just doing what I thought best for everyone? You know I was only trying to spare her from worry and keep her from screwing the deal somehow with an excess of morals and such."

"I know all that, Glen. And I tried; I really did! But she was really angry and wouldn't listen!"

At this point, Stan emerged from the bathroom, clad in just a towel snugged around his waist.

"Hey, why are you making my woman cry?"

"Oh, put a sock in it," I said. "She's making herself cry."

I explained the whole deal, Stan nodding sagely as I talked.

"So that's why my poor baby sounded so freaky on the phone. She just can't stand to see anybody hurting. What a special gal she is!"

Stan walked over and planted a kiss atop Sandy's head. She turned her face upward to receive another on the lips. Having mollified Sandy, my partner turned his attention back to me. "Oh, well, you are truly boned now. Sorry, bro. Sometimes, things just shake out that way."

I stood up decisively, full of resolve. I was already up in the skies and halfway to Praia, Santiago, Cape Verde, mentally rehearsing my soothing speeches. "I have to go to her and make this right."

"What, now? On the day of the demo?"

I sat down again, my resolve temporarily shoved onto a stone-cold back burner. "Oh, shit no, of course not. But as soon as possible. Whatever happens today, good or bad, you are going to have to take over the reins, Stan, even if only for a little while. That's the favor you said you owed me, and I'm calling it in now."

"I can do that. I'm not entirely helpless without you, you know."

I got back up off the couch. I had to get my head back in the game, put aside all thoughts of my personal life. "All right, then, let's get our asses in gear. We've got to go sell a shitload of fake bomb sniffers for top dollar, or we might as well invest in two small plots out in Santo's marshes."

Stan trotted off to get dressed, and I had one last question for Sandralene.

"Sandy, sweetie, couldn't you have waited just a day longer to break this upsetting news to me. You knew how important today was, didn't you?"

"But, gee, Glen, I really couldn't! I almost told you a dozen times over the last week as it was! And when I left yesterday, Nellie said, 'You tell that *cabrão*'—did I say that right? I think it means 'bastard'—'you tell that *cabrão* he is not the only man who can make me happy.' And, gee, Glen, when a woman says that, well, you just know there's no time to lose!"

39

Arriving at the dreary entrance of the Luckman Enterprises factory with Stan in tow, I fully expected to make the worst pitch yet of a long scamming career. All the wealthy widows I had fleeced in my lawyer days, the tremendously convoluted snow job I had pulled on Nancarrow, my moving spiel to Vin Santo that had launched this whole precarious enterprise—none of those past victories inspired confidence any longer. I felt off my game. My head was whirling with thoughts of Nellie and how to win her back. Why did Sandy have to lay that load on me today of all days? I was convinced I would blow the whole gaff.

Stan, looking dapper in a decent suit, showed no hint of nerves, though I couldn't say whether this was due to his unflappable self-assurance or sheer blockheadedness. I, by contrast, anticipated only the worst.

The rental car driven by Les Qiao arrived as I was berating myself. (Chantal, weary of being at the mercy of Uber, insisted on this fresh expense.) Les climbed out first. The young guy was suitably spiffed up, wearing his luxury anorak over a loose gray knit pullover and some red-and-blue-checkered wool pants that only a brave or foolhardy fashion-defiant soul could carry off.

The rear doors of the car opened, disgorging Pete Smalley and Derian Crespo. Smalley resembled the prosperous manager of a cattle feedlot, while Crespo struck me as the guy who, though he doesn't actually kick the bound prisoner out of the airborne helicopter, gives the order to do so. But my attention was quickly riveted by Chantal Danssaert.

Beneath her unbuttoned Burberry, her unadorned red wool dress defined simple elegance. It featured a wide black placket from neck to halfway down the front, giving her the unsullied suggestion of Madeline the French schoolgirl. Opaque black hose suitable for the chill contoured her slim but shapely legs, flexed into sexy lines by spectator pumps with five-inch heels. Setting off the whole outfit, her green newsboy hat lent a charming Carnaby Street retro vibe, as if she had stepped out of a much kindlier, more fun-loving era.

As soon as I saw her, something clicked and turned over inside me. She seemed a goddess betokening success. It was not a matter of lust, but of epiphany. All my sweaty angst evaporated, my confidence flooded back, my focus on the task at hand narrowed to laser-like intensity, and I knew with uncanny certainty that I was going to pull off the smoothest con of my life. I couldn't explain the instant phase change, like the moment a molecule of water flips to ice, but the effect was undeniable.

I strode boldly and effusively over to the new arrivals and greeted them all heartily. Les was blithely cavalier as ever, not as if he were playing some video game, but rather as if he were simply watching someone else play it. Chantal accepted Euro-smooches on either cheek of her self-composed face. Pete Smalley radiated that grab-the-bull-by-the-balls zest he no doubt displayed in either boardroom or barroom. And Derian Crespo managed to convey the kind of politesse I imagined an Argentine knife fighter out of some gaucho romance would wear like a second skin.

Stan duplicated all my welcomes in his own inimitable Gulch-savvy manner, and I said, "I expect Professor Luckman and our plant manager, Mr. Stinchcombe, are waiting inside for us already. Shall we go in?"

* * *

Inside the factory, we arrowed straight to the conference room, where we found Caleb and Luckman. Both men looked trim and earnest, Caleb in his down-home manner and Luckman in his tweedy gravitas. I was relieved to find Luckman his usual self, with no evidence of any marital discord disturbing his professorial abstractedness. More introductions, then refreshments. The catered food that Chantal had arranged was superb. I was prepared to announce to the world that lobster breakfast tacos with scrambled eggs, goat cheese, and avocado cream would be my sole sustenance for the rest of my life. A steady infusion of mimosas did not detract from the delights of the food.

After this minifeast, we ran the promotional video. Its slick, bright surfaces seemed even more convincing to me than on the first viewing. When the lights came up, I said, "Let's take our factory tour now, if you would. And then Professor Luckman will put the LBAS through its paces for you."

All the workers seemed to my champagne-heightened vision

to be exemplary models of the intelligent profit-sharing employee: utterly committed to their work. I ran my spiel nonstop but without, I thought, any overbearingness, just humble pride, extolling Luckman's inventiveness, his long road to perfecting his invention, and the commitment of his financial backers. Caleb chimed in with nuts-and-bolts statistics. The random workers we stopped to question responded knowledgeably. I could feel with increasing certainty that both Smalley and Crespo were growing more and more impressed.

Our last stop was the area where the finished units were stored on high shelving—all thousand of them in their bumblebee colors. It made an imposing display.

Back in the conference room, Luckman eagerly went to the table that held the detectors—one functioning, one cutaway for inspection—and the explosive samples.

"Gentlemen," he said, "you are now going to witness a miracle of technology, unparalleled by any earlier versions of such sensors."

He went, reliably, first to his favorite ANFO sample and got the desired result. Then he managed to make the LBAS respond to the other samples, but only after some elaborate twiddling of various controls, which he neatly glossed over.

"Like any piece of sophisticated equipment, the operation of the LBAS requires a certain amount of technical expertise—skills that your users will rapidly acquire from their peers, whom we shall personally educate at no extra cost."

Luckman answered all the questions that Smalley and Crespo had, and I was able to contribute some convincing blather as well. Even Stan chimed in.

"Man, I just know that if I had been lucky enough to have

one of these gizmos when I was pulling my two tours in Kandahar, I woulda counted myself the luckiest GI in the field."

Of course, the closest Stan had ever come to serving in the military had been when he torched a building that housed an Army-surplus store.

Finally, the pitch was over. Having run out of things to say or do or show, the six of us on the Luckman Enterprises team stood back, awaiting the reaction of our potential buyers.

Smalley spoke first. "Well, y'all know I have to run this whole shebang by my compadres back at Steel Marquee. But I am pretty stoked about this device of yours, and I think there ain't much doubt but what we will commit to, oh, maybe five hundred units to start. That is, if you could come down a tad on the price. I think you quoted twenty K per in your prospectus, am I right?"

I got ready to bargain with Smalley when Crespo intervened.

"La Sombra Negra needs these lifesaving machines badly, señor, to thwart those brutes who would destroy our nation. And also, we would not care for any of our enemies to possess them. Therefore, I am prepared and authorized at this very moment to bargain for exclusivity. I have no need to speak with any superiors. And, of course, we would offer a suitable bonus for the privilege of being your sole client—at least for the first generation of machines, within a certain window of time."

"Bonus, huh?" Stan said. "And what might be the dimensions of that there sweetener?"

"La Sombra Negra will pay thirty thousand dollars apiece, and take delivery of the first thousand units as soon as our funds transfer into your accounts."

The numbers crunched themselves instantly in my brain. Thirty million dollars. Half to Santo, three million for our brokers, and four million each for Stan, Luckman, and me. And that was just for starters.

Smalley good-naturedly threw in the towel. "Too rich for us, hoss. Don't need to talk to management to know that. It's all yours, amigo."

He and Crespo shook hands, and Smalley wandered over to the remains of the buffet for a glass of champagne and a nosh.

Crespo regarded us with his somber, intelligent, merciless eyes. "There is just one condition to my offer, gentlemen."

"Yes?"

"There must be a field test, conducted in your city within the next few days. Our conditions, our location, our samples. *¿Está bien?*"

40

This time, I wasn't driving the airport run. Not wanting to leave my precious Lexus in their garage, I had bummed a ride from Stan and Sandy to catch my flight to Cape Verde. Stan's Uncle Sam Jeep, unlike any other member of its species, handled poorly in the icy slush that had come to our city's roads overnight. Or maybe it was just Stan's distracted driving and the Jeep's balding tires.

I sought to reassure both him and myself that everything would turn out fine, though privately I didn't expect that outcome with 100 percent certainty. But I couldn't be arsed to worry about it. We had made a solid sale to the El Salvador sucker—a bargain that would leave us all rich. There was just one last little seemingly impossible hurdle: getting the LBAS to perform as advertised under objective conditions beyond Luckman's sly control. And surely, if we had come this far on nothing more than a truckload of counterfeit semiconductors and a dream of fleecing the whole

wide world to line our pockets, we could somehow find the ingenuity and resourcefulness to take us the last mile.

But at the moment, I could only concentrate on what I had to
do to win back the affections of Nélida Firmino. Even the prospect
of all those millions of dollars that were rightfully mine but that
lay just beyond my immediate grasp failed to dominate my mind.
I was content to let the others wrestle with the problem, at least
for the next few days.

I emerged from my ruminations to ask Stan, "Are you sure
you can handle Crespo and his demands while I'm gone? I can't
imagine this mission of mine will take more than a couple of days,
and that's within the window he mandated for the testing."

"Yeah, yeah," said Stan. "Don't sweat it. I'll stall him somehow
if I hafta. And we'll come up with some workaround for that
lame-ass detector. Jeez, you'd think that brainiac Luckman coulda
made his frigging invention work perfect by now, all those years
he spent out in that damn garage of his, ignoring his wife."

His reference to Rosa Luckman in front of Sandy, oblique
though it was, startled me. I guess I hadn't really believed Stan
when he told me Sandy was okay with his tomcatting, but her
lack of visible agitation or ire seemed to validate his assertion.
Extraordinary, their relationship. It struck me as perhaps an object
lesson in how I had to approach Nellie. I realized I wasn't really so
upset that she had enjoyed—was enjoying—a fling with smarmy
pudding maven Onésimo Dambara as I was angry and worried
that she no longer loved me and wouldn't come back. And after
all, what, exactly, were my horrible sins? Just trying to secure a
nest egg for our future together, albeit through illicit means I had
solemnly forsworn in her presence. If loving Nellie and money
and criminal kicks was wrong, then I didn't want to be right.

Sandy suddenly turned around, interrupting my thoughts.

"And maybe the horse will learn to talk."

"What's that?"

"I thought everybody knew that story."

"I do know it. I just didn't know that you knew it."

"I am not a dummy, Glen. I know a lot. I knew I had to come home and wake you up, for starters."

"Please forgive me, Sandy. I am very grateful for all your wisdom."

"She's got a fuckton of brains," Stan offered. "And at least half of them are in her pants."

Sandy punched his right shoulder hard, causing him to swerve the car just as we were approaching the drop-off at my airline's terminal, nearly running down a security guard.

"Oh, great, get us all arrested for terrorism just when we most need to keep a low profile."

But there seemed to be no consequences to Stan's erratic driving, and soon I was climbing out of the Jeep and securing my single carry-on bag.

I shook Stan's hand and he said, "*Vaya con dios, amigo.*"

"Portuguese, Stan, *kriolu. Bai ku deus, amigu.*"

"Whatever."

"We'll be thinking of you, Glen. Good luck."

I turned to Sandy for one of her awesome pillowy anaconda hugs, but my experience was spoiled in midecstasy by the pinging of Stan's phone.

"It's a text from Chantal," he said. "She's got an idea on how to flimflam Crespo."

"Excellent! Work it all out. She should be plenty motivated since she and Les don't get their money unless we get ours."

As I entered the terminal, Stan and Sandy were already speeding away.

* * *

The flight on TAP Air Portugal was long, moderately relaxing, and generally uneventful. I watched a bad heist movie, read a book about the future of the Supreme Court that I had picked up on a whim at the airport, and caught up partially on all the sleep I had missed lately. I guess I got my eighteen hundred dollars' worth—or the first half of the open-ended ticket, anyway. If I returned with Nellie, or at least with the feeling that we were back on an even keel, I'd count the money well spent.

It was around two o'clock by the time I checked into the Hotel Pestana Trópico, where Nellie and I had spent that idyllic working vacation. The place seemed an improbable oasis compared to all the chaos of my life back home—an oasis at once familiar and strange after all that had happened in the intervening weeks. Also, being here alone felt weird.

The desk clerk, a colorfully dressed, handsome young fellow with impeccable manners, remembered me with a smile and volunteered the information that Nellie was not on the premises at the moment.

"I believe she was planning to visit her factory again today, *sinhór*. Her enterprise requires much attention. She is bringing great acclaim to our island, I believe. Soon, all of your country will know the virtues of our *doce de café*."

I chose not to shatter his dream of Caboverdean fame and glory via coffee-pudding export. "Can I get a car and driver to take me out there?"

"But of course!"

The car was an ancient barn-red Ford Ranger whose lacy undercarriage seemed more air than steel. Valdo, the driver, appeared to be about twice as old as his vehicle, which would put him in his sixties. His salt-and-pepper mustache was evidently his pride and joy, so fondly and regularly did he stroke it. I recalled that my rival, Dambara, had the same mannerism, and I vowed then and there never to grow any such brush. Valdo spoke little English, and my stock of *kriolu*, I suddenly realized, was made up largely of words I would have little occasion to use outside the bedroom. But the written address sufficed to get us on the road.

The daytime temps were still in the eighties on Santiago, and after the November chill back home, I relished the hot air blowing over me through the opened hand-crank windows. Once we got out of the city, exotic fragrances exuded from the lush vegetation. I took the Edenic ambience as a good omen.

Valdo understood he was to wait for me outside the factory. After all, I couldn't count on winning back Nellie immediately and riding home with her. The road back to our loving reunion might be a long one.

Inside the factory, I made a beeline for the manager's office. I figured that while Nellie might be elsewhere with Dambara— screwing their brains out in dappled sunlight atop a burlap sack full of coffee beans?—they would have to return to the office eventually.

Convinced of this situation, I opened the office door without knocking first.

Dambara and Nellie stood intimately abreast beside his desk. Their heads were lowered over something and in close enough proximity for a kiss.

I was inside the office and had the door shut just as they looked up. I wanted to say something nonchallenging and dignified and conciliatory, but all my good intentions flew out the window when I saw them, and I defaulted to wounded snark, even mixing all my hopefully pointed metaphors.

"Sorry to bust in like a third wheel on this cozy little tête-à-tête, but I thought I could introduce some sanity to this madhouse."

Dambara and Nellie both straightened from their studious pose, and I could see on the desktop a heap of green coffee beans blotched with disease. I recognized the beans and their troubling condition—a vital concern for pudding plant operations—from our previous time here.

Dambara regarded me with a certain stern and regal disregard. But Nellie's expression dominated my concern. With her hair pulled back, the youthful planes of her face stood out all the more vividly. Her look managed to mingle surprise, anger, contrition, defiance, and longing. I weighed all the factors together and judged the blend to be ever so slightly in my favor.

Dambara's English was accurate and pleasantly accented. "*Sinhór* McClinton, I would please like you to meet my wife."

My brain blanked out. Had Nellie *married* this gigolo? Sandy never hinted that things were that bad.

A polite cough caused me to turn around.

Seated in a tatty armchair that had been concealed behind the open door when I entered was a very large and merry woman, clad in sandals and a flowing dress of many bright colors. She seemed to be enjoying the situation immensely. She stood and held forth her plump hand.

"Graciela Dambara," she announced.

I shook her hand as a sleepwalker might.

Smiling most unsportingly at my confusion and comeuppance, Graciela's husband stepped to her side and put an arm as far around her equator as he could manage. "My wife and I could do with some refreshment at the factory canteen. Perhaps, the two of you will join us there after you make your hellos. I am sure you have much to say."

The Afro-Iberian lovebirds left, and I turned to Nellie.

Her arms were folded across the bosom I so fondly recalled, and any pro-Glen elements in her expression had been sent packing by the anti-Glen forces.

"You want to get yourself killed? Is that it? Or get me killed, too? So that we never have a happy old age together?"

I thought the old-age stuff was positive. "What? I'm gonna get killed by coming here to challenge Mr. Jello Pudding Pop?"

"Ay, *tolobásku*! Of course not. You see that Onésimo is not that kind of savage man—unlike some I could name! And he does not deserve to be made fun of. He is gentle and honest and was good to me when I felt hopeless. And he did not offer me his close friendship without causing some trouble to himself. It took plenty of persuasion and saying sorry for Graciela to accept him back, once she discovered our small encounters. In any case, such matters are all over now. You saw. And that is all I have to say about him."

I certainly wanted to say more about this selfless Good Samaritan who had so generously filled in for me in my absence, but I refrained. Using my silence, Nellie plunged ahead.

"No, I am talking about you and Stan getting mixed up with that Vin Santo *criminoso*."

I dared to take a step or two closer and was pleased that she did not back off. "Oh, honey, listen to me, please; it's not like that at all. Vin Santo is totally a businessman. And Stan and I are just his business partners. This is strictly a no-violence gig. The people involved are not like Nancarrow. I'm just doing a little snake-oil peddling. The buyer will never know he got rooked, and will go home happy. Suckers want to believe they are smart businessmen, and so even when the gadget fails a hundred times, they won't believe it. And if they do come after us, Santo will handle it. And you and I and Stan and Sandy become instant millionaires. It's better than winning the lottery. Just think what this kind of money will mean for our lives together. That happy old age you just mentioned. Don't you want to be free of worries about your business? We can do it, Nell, without any danger. You have to trust me on this. It's my field of expertise."

She seemed to waver a tad. "But all I can think about is those thugs from Nancarrow holding us all at gunpoint. It was the worst moment of my life. I don't want to find us there again."

"Not gonna happen."

"Then why did you lie to me about it? You must have felt there was some danger. How can I trust anything you say now?"

I got within holding distance. Nellie seemed to bend toward me involuntarily before reasserting her enforced remoteness.

"Dearest, I only kept you in the dark because I didn't want you to worry about anything. You're so busy and swept up in this wonderful enterprise of yours. It's demanded all your attention, and I didn't mind! I wasn't jealous, was I? I just wanted to place this gift in your lap. And I knew that you are a very moral and ethical person and might be a little disturbed by the unconventional approach Stan and I had to take in order to swing this deal. But I'm *not* a good person. I admit it! At least, not when it comes to making money. And so I did not want to burden you with my utterly disreputable choices. Choices, however, that would serve as a shortcut to never having to do anything bad ever again. I swear! You knew all that about me years ago, when my last little project first brought us together. And aren't you happy it did? Our whole relationship together stems from me being a—what did you call it?—a *criminoso*! So how can this new scam be bad?"

I could tell she was wavering, so I plunged ahead.

"We need each other. We *complement* each other. Good and bad, yin and yang, light and dark, north and south—man and woman."

I wrapped her up in my arms, and she didn't resist one iota but instead melted into me. Our lips together, tongues found each other. Her mouth tasted of all the exotic spices in the local food. I grabbed the waistband of her pants and yanked down, popping the one-button closure apart and divesting her of that encumbrance while she unzipped my fly. Coffee beans scattered.

Panting after our boisterous reunion, I realized that my vision of Nellie and Dambara banging on the burlap bags had been spot-on.

PART FIVE

41

Nellie did not come immediately home with me, but that was fine. Two steamy nights together in the Hotel Pestana Trópico had recemented our bonds. I even made an effort, during the daytime, to become fluent in the argot of coffee production and to conduct myself in a gentlemanly fashion around the unrepentant Dambara, whose smarmy face I refrained from punching only because his wife set such an example of forgiveness and nobility. Also, because Graciela proved to be an amazing cook who served us delicious lunches and dinners.

So, knowing that Nellie, her fling over, still had legitimate business to conduct on Santiago but would be home shortly after my return to the USA, I flew back happy.

And the fact that Nellie even seemed a tad intrigued by the scam, now that I had laid it all out on the table, was reassuring to me. I had had to describe all the players to her first because, of course, she had never met the Luckmans, Chantal and Les, or the buyer. But she was a fast study and good at envisioning people and their natures, so she quickly got up to speed.

"So, Glen, *nha omi malandru,* tell me one more time. Once you fake this last test some way for the *polsia* from El Salvador, they just pay you and go home and you never see them again, this is so?"

"That's about the size of it."

"They won't get mad when they find out the boxes are *inutil*?"

"The way we figure it, the detectors will register just enough positives back in El Salvador on a day-to-day basis to keep them happy. And after all, how will they even know most of the times that they *failed* to detect something? A car or a person blows up after you scanned it, it must be because the bomb was planted after your test. No, our tails are covered, especially since Luckman is the figurehead for everything."

Nellie looked concerned. "But this poor *profesoru* Luckman—he can handle any trouble?"

"Oh, sure. Plus, he'll be rich enough to hire the best lawyers if anything goes wrong, because he'll be swimming in dough, just like us. We don't have to worry about him. Besides, he's the guy who invented this flop. Let him stand behind it. All Stan and I are doing is helping him market it."

I felt a little guilty justifying all this aloud to Nellie, but she seemed to accept my rationale at face value, finding it not too reprehensible.

"I guess it's okay, then. So how can you fool this final *testi* that Crespo wants?"

"I don't know, exactly. Stan won't tell me over the phone. He says I need to come back first. So that's why I have to leave tomorrow."

"Then I guess we'd better get busy with some fresh loving *zup-zup!*"

* * *

Memory of that last bouncy bout did indeed linger to console me all the way back to the chilly clime where our final challenge awaited.

Stan showed up at the airport before 9:00 a.m. to meet my red-eye flight. It seemed to me I had been away much longer than four days.

"How's it going?"

"Okay, I guess. But things are shaking down fast. Crespo has the place for the test all picked out. I'm gonna drive you by it. He wants it to happen two days from today."

"Does that give us enough time for our workaround? What is it, anyhow?"

"I think we'll be set. But I can't say for sure. The person who's supposedly gonna save our asses comes into town today. Chantal knows her and arranged everything."

"Our ace in the hole is some gal?"

"And her partner."

I experienced nausea at the idea of driving to the condo and then to the airport once more. "I suppose we have to come back here to pick her up?"

"Nah, she lives close enough to drive herself, even though it took her a day. And besides, she couldn't bring her partner on the plane."

The faintest nebulous tickle of what Chantal had in mind teased at the periphery of my jet-lagged brain but failed to coalesce fully. "Okay, I can be patient," I said. "I like a mystery as much as the next guy. Let's go see the site of the test, though."

Halfway back to the city, I said, "Where's this gal going to stay?"

"It's actually her, her husband, and her partner. We booked them into the Hyatt, the room right next to Chantal and Les. Gotta be careful not to let Crespo run into them, natch. Oh, by the way, Smalley's gone home now that he's been outbid."

"I guess that's a wash on room expenses then. One out, one in."

"Just remember, dude, it's all penny ante when you're talking multimillions."

"I won't worry, so long as you don't find another bad investment and blow through your share."

"My angel investor days are done," he said. "I am strictly a self-serving devil from here on out."

I stayed quiet, thinking, until we were back within the city limits. Then I said, "How is everyone holding up? The Luckmans? Sandy? Crespo? Caleb?"

"The prof's a little down. It took him a while to admit his gadget is a piece a shit and that we'll have to cheat on the final test. Really seemed like kinda a big shock to his self-esteem. Chantal was sorta brutal with him. But I think he's finally coming round. Rosa has kept a low profile, which suits me just fine. Sandy's actually been helping Caleb at the factory while they gear up to slap together the second thousand units. That's another thirty million bucks there for us, remember. He says she's making his life a lot easier, and they work together like two kids building a fort. And Crespo—well, that bastard is an icicle inside a corpse buried at the North Pole. He don't give nothing away. I guess he's still on board with our wonder product, or he wouldn't be going to all this trouble to arrange his big test."

Stan had driven us to a section of the city that used to be known as Chocolateville. Long ago, several candy factories had clustered there. But that line of business had petered out long ago, though residents claimed they could smell the sweet-pungent ghosts of the factories for years afterward. A couple of the old brick mills had been repurposed into shops and condos, including one project helmed by our old nemesis Nancarrow. But the largest complex had burned down about three years ago and gone into some kind of legal limbo, leaving a four-acre parcel of undeveloped land, surrounded by a chain-link fence and lots of rusting KEEP OUT—PRIVATE PROPERTY signs.

Stan pulled to the curb at one corner of the lot, which was dotted with charred concrete foundations, heaps of debris, sinkholes dropping into water-logged basements, and the bare branches of lanky weed trees. It looked like the set for some young adult dystopian film. I could picture the kids dodging their pursuers through the ruins before they all get mercilessly exterminated.

"This is it," Stan said. "Somehow, Crespo pulled strings and got temporary access to the place through his local connections. He's going to seed the whole lot with hidden samples of explosives and then make us sniff 'em out under his supervision."

"There's only that one locked gate into the property?"

"Yup. And I assume that once he lays down his Easter eggs, he'll have the place guarded right up to the time we arrive."

"Shit! He's not making it easy for us, is he?"

"Where'd be the fun in that?"

Back at our condo, I got the travel fug off me with a shower, shave, and new outfit. Then we headed to the Hyatt, and the suite where Chantal and Les awaited us.

The pair maintained their usual disparate attitudes, Les all stylishly disheveled unconcern, Chantal all tightly wired competence.

Seeing this cryptic, composed woman for the first time since she triggered my small epiphany, I was not surprised to find that she still raised a kind of spooky mental and bodily resonance in me. It felt as if we were walking different ends of the same thrumming tightrope stretched across a gulf as wide as the Grand Canyon, and the survival of each of us depended on the actions of the other.

"Lina just texted me," Chantal told us. "You should know that Lina Llull is her full name. Ex-Ranger, Special Forces. I met her at a show some years back and have stayed in touch since. She and her husband are parking now in the garage. I don't know him. Eddie Greenfriars. I believe he has some military connection as well. She's coming straight to our room while her husband checks in and deals with their bags."

I had a Skyy vodka with tonic from the room's minibar while we waited. It would probably cost me thirty bucks on Chantal's bill, but I had given up caring. Stan joined me with a beer, but the others refused.

Waiting, I tried to picture what a badass woman US Army Ranger would look like. But when Chantal responded to a knock at the door, I realized just how far off the mark I had been.

Subtle indicators put the woman at my age, late thirties, but she looked no more like a clichéd warrior than did Taylor Swift. If you pictured a petite, pretty, perky young blonde who might pass for a clerk at a makeup counter, you'd have an image of Lina Llull. About the only discordant feature—she wore no coat, which I assumed her husband had carried upstairs for her—were her ripped biceps and calves. I suspected she could punch a guy through a wall or kick a mosquito out of the air.

Lina toted an elongated, semirigid fabric carrier, taupe in color and screened on both ends, about the size for a cat. She hoisted it to eye level and announced with a smile, "Folks, meet Algernon, the answer to all your troubles!"

42

I had to admit, once I recovered from my surprise, that Algernon was the cutest goddamn animal I had ever seen outside of a Pixar cartoon. And I was someone who generally thought that pictures of cats and dogs were the entropic sludge of the internet.

The African giant pouched rat comes big, up to eighteen inches long, and Algernon was a champion of his breed. A gorgeous tawny coat peppered with white and gray, perfect little pink hands and outsize ears, eyes not too alarmingly beady, and an elegant tapering face and rounded snout all contributed to his dashing good looks. An almost excessive cleanliness and not unpleasant odor didn't hurt his presentation, either. Not a marsupial, not even really a proper rat, he derived the "pouched" part of his name from his large cheek capacity. The fact that he wore the most darling tiny tartan harness was the final zinger in his winning looks. Even Stan fell in love, stroking Algy's fur and going "Aw-w-w" like a thirteen-year-old girl in a corral full of ponies.

I got to hold the well-behaved three-pound rat while Lina explained his origins and purpose.

"Algy and his pals are trained by a Tanzanian group called APOPO to sniff out explosives. They're also used to identify TB carriers by their spit samples. Not relevant to our purposes, but kinda neat. I got to work with Algy when I was on assignment in Niger a couple of years ago, and we really bonded. He was three years old then, and although his kind generally live to seven, he was almost ready to retire. I had just put in my twenty, and so was I. So we left the service together. He hasn't done much professional work since then, but he's still sharp and healthy. Perfect for what Chantal said you had in mind."

"He can really sniff out bombs?"

"Try him."

I passed Algy back to Lina, and she clipped a lead to his harness and set him down on the floor. She said something in what I assumed must be Swahili, and Algy scurried across the room to Chantal's purse. Lina rewarded him with a little treat.

"Do you still have that chunk of C-four in your bag?" I asked.

"Yes. And also something else you need to see."

Chantal opened her purse and took out a sugar packet that looked as if it had lain outside in all kinds of nasty weather. She set it on a table, and Algy immediately leaped up to nuzzle it, whiskers waggling.

"Open it."

I tore the packet open cautiously and spilled out the familiar ANFO particles into my palm.

"We have fifty of these all made up, all containing the only explosive that Luckman's gadget can reliably detect. They're not all sugar packets, but other likely trash as well. Candy wrappers, fast-food wrappers, seemingly used condoms, hypodermics. Perfectly plausible urban discards. The night before the test, Lina and Algy will enter Crespo's test site and find all his samples. They will plant one or two of the disguised ANFO items within a few inches of each sample. The next day, we will conduct the trial under Crespo's supervision. And we will find every single one of his seeded caches, because each one will have an ANFO trigger beside it."

I had to admire Chantal's devious ingenuity. "That is absolutely brilliant," I said. "But I do foresee one major hang-up. How are we going to get past any guards?"

"This is where you play a part. You must visit Vin Santo and request that he arrange a distraction."

"A distraction? Like what?"

"Santo has contacts with MS-Thirteen. I assume those gangsters would like to know where they could find a few unsuspecting Sombra Negra operatives and have their revenge."

"You want to stage a *firefight* as cover for Lina sneaking in?"

"More or less—the exact level of violence can be optimized."

Lina seemed unperturbed. "Gee, just like field conditions in Africa! I'm going to feel right at home. But I might have to up my fee a little if there's live fire. Let's call it seventy-five thousand now."

Stan, who had earlier lectured me about being too miserly, got a bit testy—I think, mostly on matters of principle.

"Seventy-five K! For a night's work? Why can't we hire some local off-duty cop and his trained mutt for a couple of thousand?"

Chantal said, "Number one, stealth. Lina and Algy know their infiltration tactics and are less conspicuous than some fat flatfoot and his barking German shepherd. Number two, reliability and confidentiality. Do you really want some drunken city cop bragging about what he did, and it gets back to Crespo?"

Stan was already nodding. "All right, I see your point. Algy and Lina for the win."

Lina said, "I'm going to need a helper. I can't manage Algy and a satchel full of ANFO props as well."

Les chimed in. "Count me and Chantal out. Not what we signed on for. You're lucky we came up with this idea to save your ass."

I looked to Stan, and Stan looked to me. He beat me to the punch.

"I got this trick knee, and my night vision is going, and I make a pretty goddamn big target."

How did I find myself so often in situations not of my choosing, where I had to accept dangerous, dirty jobs that were absolutely crucial to the success of our schemes? Much as I wanted to blame cruel fate, I suspected that somehow I was usually the one responsible for such karmic cock-ups. Maybe if I hewed to the straight and narrow, I wouldn't find myself in such fixes so often. In other words, forget about it.

"Okay, I guess that leaves me," I said. "But I want everyone to know that if I catch a stray round or fall down a pit and break my neck, I am going to come back and haunt every last one of you till your own miserable dying days."

"It's a deal," said Stan.

A knock sounded on the connecting door between rooms. Eddie Greenfriars—Lina's husband, I assumed.

Chantal went to the door and unlocked it, swinging it wide and stepping back.

I got a quick impression of Greenfriars as a kind of amiable jock, a bit older than his wife: short hair, trim physique, open-faced good looks. Spotting Chantal, he beamed a huge smile and moved to hug her. She, in turn, registered utter shock, her expression shattering into fragments of alarm—the only time I had ever seen her lose her cool.

"Cherry! Cherry Goldschlager! Goddamn, you have grown some for sure!"

43

Chantal stiffened in the friendly and familiar embrace of Eddie Greenfriars, not returning his hug. She had pivoted slightly away from him in alarm as he came through the door, making it easy for me to observe her face. Her features, normally as unrevealing as Amarillo Slim's, now displayed her racing train of thought so clearly I could almost narrate it. *Deny or affirm? Fight or flight? Bluff or fold?* In a second, she had obviously settled on the former stances. She slithered not too rudely out of his grasp and said to Lina, "Your husband thinks he knows me. I'm flattered, of course. But I'm afraid I can't say the same."

Greenfriars looked innocently perplexed, even hurt. "Aw, c'mon, Cherry, I realize it was a long time ago, but you must remember me. I worked for your dad at Raytheon, at the Waltham office. Sy Goldschlager. He brought you into the office practically every weekend, starting when you were ten years old. How you dug all the military stuff! You got so you could talk to the engineers like you were one of them. Not surprising to see you in this line of work now."

"This is all a very charming history. But I am afraid my parents in Ghent would be very hurt if I were to disown them so unkindly."

Stan, who had been absorbing the drama with a keen and perceptive eye, now stepped forward with an outthrust hand.

"Eddie, I'm Stan. Stan Hasso. The one and only—not another guy like me on the whole fucking planet. But it is true most of us got doubles. Take my buddy Glen here. Everyone says he looks just like Steve Buscemi. I put him as more of a Don Knotts."

Greenfriars laughed heartily. "He doesn't look like either one of those dorks."

"Thanks for the affirmation, Eddie. This is the kind of treatment you get when you partner with a bad amateur comedian who looks like the Hulk."

Greenfriars turned back to Chantal, who was now her old model of self-possession. "Awfully sorry, Miz—"

"Danssaert. Chantal Danssaert." She put out her slender hand.

With the focus on Chantal and Greenfriars, I hadn't paid much attention to Les' reactions until now. So I was surprised to spot him grinning broadly at his partner's consternation and subsequent recovery.

Greenfriars scratched the back of his neck. "Well, Chantal, you sure as hell look like the little girl I knew, all grown up. But maybe my memories are fuzzy. Too much mescal. Hey, sweetie, did Algy strut his stuff yet for these guys?"

"He aced it, dear. He wasn't bothered at all by the long drive."

From here, the conversation moved easily and without any lingering awkwardness to a recap of our plans, for the sake of

Greenfriars. He nodded attentively throughout, then said, "I can get Lina and Glen through that cheap old fence faster than a thirsty tart tonguing out a Jell-O shot. And I'll leave it looking like no one ever snuck in."

With everything falling into order, I felt more sanguine about passing Crespo's test two days hence. Our infiltration tomorrow night could not come soon enough for me. But there was a lot to do before then.

Suddenly, I felt really beat, not having slept well on the plane. But I knew I couldn't falter now. I looked at my phone and saw that it was nearly lunchtime.

"Why don't you four go out to eat," I suggested, "and try to think of any details we may have overlooked. Meanwhile, Stan and I will visit our trail boss."

I was halfway out the door and a few feet into the hotel corridor, with Stan already punching the elevator button ahead of me, when Chantal caught up with me. She pitched her voice low.

"Could I see you tonight sometime? Alone?"

"Of course. I'll call."

Riding down in the elevator, Stan whistled cheerily and tune-lessly until I was forced to say something.

"You're happy I'm riding shotgun for Lina and the rat instead of you? Is that it?"

"Not at all. Just trying to picture what's gonna happen when you visit Cherry Goldschlager tonight."

"You think Greenfriars nailed her real identity?"

"C'mon, could there be any doubt? I never really bought that ultra-ultra accent and hokey backstory anyhow. But I hadda shut him down. We're counting on Miss Cherry-Chantal to help us put everything over on Crespo, and we can't have her waving her arms around with her nerves all shot to pieces. Not that I figure she woulda stayed spooked too long, even without me stepping in. She is one cool cucumber. She'd have to be, to carry off a fake identity for so long and get as far as she has. But whether she sucked her mama's tit in the USA or Europe, she seems to know her stuff. So I was happy to smooth things out for her."

Back in the car, I said, "Can we stop for a hamburger before we see Santo? I feel kind of low-energy."

"A burger? As in Mickey D's? And you claim you got good taste. No sir, I got just the cure for you, boy."

Stan delivered us to a funky place called Rudy Spline's BBQ. The warm, savory smells when we opened the door made me quake at the knees. One whale-size pulled-pork sandwich and a mountain of collard greens later, I felt ready to arm-wrestle Army Ranger Lina Llull to at least a draw.

* * *

Vin Santo received us with a mix of annoyance and curiosity. "I never had no partners before who needed so much goddamn hand-holding," he grumped. "What the hell is it now?"

I explained everything to the tubby mobster as he drew down the level of his ever-present soda. I had never yet seen a fresh Big Gulp delivered here, and was beginning to suspect that he had a pony keg of the stuff concealed in his desk. I concluded my speech with our scheme of having the Mara Salvatrucha boys attack the guards around the test site—not necessarily in a *totally* fatal manner, but just enough to lure them away for a while. We didn't want Crespo's attention the next day to wander from closing the sale to further thinning the ranks of MS-13.

Santo said nothing for what seemed an eternity, and I mentally prepared myself for a verbal reaming. So I was taken aback when he said, "Your timely suggestion, my friends, is like being handed the head of my enemy on a silver platter. I been trying to think of how I could make nice with the MS-Thirteen boys after Crespo cut a swath through them, and this is perfect. Consider it done."

We departed after receiving a barely discernible congenial quirking of lips from the two guardian goons at the door—the equivalent of a whoop and a high five from anyone else.

"Where to now?" Stan said.

"I want to see Luckman and impress on him that his performance day after tomorrow has to be flawless."

We headed to the factory, where we found Caleb, Sandralene, and the professor in the office. Sandy and Caleb sat side by side at a long table, going over some printouts together. She had one lower leg pressed lightly against his. I looked to Stan to see if he noticed or cared, but he seemed untroubled by any innocent intimacy between the childhood sweethearts.

"Sandy! Johnny Reb! Look who I brung home."

Caleb stood, and Sandy jumped up and hugged me, then pushed me to arm's length, her hands still on my shoulders, and demanded, "Well?"

"It's all cool with Nell," I said, "thanks to both your caring intervention and my innate irresistibility."

She squealed, which for Sandy amounted not to an adolescent's shrill warble but to something more like a lioness' exultant red-fanged chuffing cry upon bringing down a gazelle.

"I knew you two could make up nice! I'm so happy, Glen."

Caleb shook my hand solemnly. "Congratulations, Glen. It's

always nice to see lovers reunite." His voice held a note of melancholy, though.

I turned then to Luckman, who had not joined in welcoming me back. He had been sitting apart from the others, evidently studying the cutaway LBAS demo model. He continued to peer solemnly into its guts like a wizard trying to unriddle some chicken entrails, and with about as much success. He looked haggard, with uncombed hair, two-day beard, rumpled shirt—worn down by the demands put on him and his dream device, its failures, and the compensatory cheating required.

"Ronald, it's good to see you again," I said. "I hope you're ready to impress our buyer day after tomorrow. You've got to do us all proud."

"'Vanity of vanities; all is vanity. What profit hath a man of all his labor which he taketh under the sun?'"

This was not exactly the rah-rah attitude I had been hoping for and that would glide us to success. I pondered how to buck him up.

Caleb came over to Luckman, leaned down, and whispered in his ear. The professor sighed, seemed to shake himself temporarily out of his fugue, then reasserted at least a pale shadow of the enthusiasm he had shown us that day we first saw his device.

"Glen, I intend to do my best to get through this trial without disgrace," he said. "I just wish it were not necessary to fudge matters so. If you were to trust me on fine-tuning the LBAS—"

Stan interrupted. "No way, José! You just set it for that ANFO stuff and follow the plan."

"All right, all right. But, Glen, I did have one more item of concern. These Sombra Negra people—are you sure they're on the up-and-up? I've been reading a few disconcerting things about them online. You know I won't stand for my invention to be perverted."

"Oh, sure, they're good people. Don't you worry about that. Listen, why don't you go home to Rosa and rest up for at least a day? No more work for a while. Take it easy."

Luckman wearily stood. "Rosa, yes, that's a good idea. Although she's been a little impatient with me lately. Says I can't get out of my own way. I suppose she's right. She always is."

Caleb and Sandy walked Stan and me out to the car. None of us had anything useful to say regarding Luckman's unsettling decline.

"When ya coming home tonight, babe?"

"Caleb and I have to work a little late, Stan. You know how it is."

"Sure, sure, it's all so's we win, and win big. I get it. I'll see ya when I see ya, then. But in the meantime ..."

Stan and Sandy went into a passionate clinch that reminded me of Bigfoot sexing up an Amazon. Caleb and I each found imaginary things elsewhere that required our attention.

Driving away, Stan said, "Jesus, I couldn't get by for one second without that woman. I'm glad you and Nellie hooked up again. Meant to tell you that before now."

"Thanks. Let me see the time ... almost four. Let's head back to the condo so I can get a little rest before tonight."

* * *

I never passed out so swiftly or experienced such a deep, almost sedated sleep. When my alarm went off at 9:00 p.m., I had to reassemble my personality from pieces scattered across several distant dimensions. But I felt like a million bucks—or five million, actually, given our impending score.

Out in the living room, Stan, in a frowsy tracksuit, was slumped like a lazy leopard on the couch and eating ice cream from the carton. The TV was tuned to *Ice Road Truckers.*

"What a great life these guys got. Didn't you kinda like when you and me was hauling freight, Glen? Things were simpler, that's for sure."

"Yeah," I said. "It's good to know we have job options if we fail. Yukon Territory, here we come."

"Say hi to Cherry Goldschlager for me if you see her."

* * *

I had texted Chantal I was coming, so I was not surprised when the door to her and Les' suite opened swiftly to my knock.

Les was not present. Maybe in the other room? Sent away on some errand? No matter, Chantal's presence filled this space. Her expensive scent beckoned me in, and this time her traditional Euro greeting of parallel kisses made firm contact with my cheeks and not with the air over my shoulders.

She wore what I would call harem pants, although they sported a subtler cut. Lilac georgette crepe with an elastic waist. Her pale-rose silk pullover blouse stopped short to display her navel. Her feet were bare.

I tried to joke, although my voice sounded a little squeaky at first.

"Did you emerge like smoke from a bottle, or what?"

Chantal's laughter was effervescent and delightful. "That is the nicest thing anyone has said to me lately, including Les."

"Speaking of, where is he?"

"Oh, around. Here, sit down. I've ordered us some real drinks from room service."

I took up a spot on the couch, and Chantal sat about a foot away. A frosted pitcher disbursed margaritas as strong as my desire to help her out of what few clothes she wore.

She sipped her drink, then said, "I was worried you would be put off or lose trust in me because of that silly incident earlier today. You know, when Lina's husband thought he recognized me. How utterly ridiculous that was!"

"Well, really, Chantal, I don't care about your past. It's only your performance now that matters. And you haven't let us down. Your plan to defuse Crespo's test—just brilliant, really. We are in your debt."

She sidled closer. "How I hoped that would be your reaction! It would have been so inconvenient and, yes, disturbing to me if you had given any credence to the bizarre notion of my being some gawky suburban girl who had sought to remake herself into a cosmopolitan creature. Who would ever do such a thing? It would smack of desperation, I think."

"Oh, I agree completely. Better to be whatever we're born to be, I say."

"Well, perhaps I wouldn't go so far as to say in *all* cases. But for me, I'm very happy with what I am and what I have, and I would hate to see it put in jeopardy. I have found that reputation is everything in life. So, again, you have my deepest gratitude for your faith in me."

When she leaned forward to proffer a small kiss emblematic of that gratitude, there was still time and resistance enough for me to apply the brakes. But when she laid her hand on my thigh as she had that night in the car, I was a goner.

She toppled backward on the wide, long couch, pulling me onto her. The silk blouse whisked away, my shirt unbuttoned itself, and the harem pants slithered to the carpet.

And then, in my carnal fog, I sensed someone beside us.

Boyish Les Qiao stood watching with his typical wry expression. Without speaking a word, he pulled his dress shirt off over his head.

I wanted Chantal, sure, but maybe not *this* badly.

I'm not sure what I expected to see, but it wouldn't have been a too-small sports bra tight enough to press into Les' narrow sides and chest.

Off went the bra to reveal the loveliest pair of middling-size natural breasts.

"Oh, it feels like heaven to get that off!" Les said, rubbing the red marks where the bra had dug in. I wondered how I could ever have thought that voice was male. It appeared that, this time anyway, Les was indeed more.

44

Les hadn't even bothered to change her name—just abbreviated it from "Leslie." She had begun dressing like a boy in middle school. Her unadorned explanation was that she just found male clothes more comfortable and authentic-feeling, reflective of her inner spirit. No deductions about sexual preference were to be drawn. In college, however, where she and Chantal met—which college and how never came up—she had come out as bisexual. She and Chantal became lovers, although Chantal likewise refused to define her mutable appetites by the usual labels. And as I could now attest, she was not averse to male attentions of the carnal sort. In fact, I felt as if I had done a three-way with the Mata Hari and Catherine the Great.

I recalled Chantal telling me that her relationship with Les was "complicated." Always the queen of cool understatement, that gal.

When they had entered the high-powered arena of arms

brokerage, they found that having a male partner gave Chantal a shield of acceptance and a level of buyer confidence that two women without a man would probably not have received. And it was hardly a challenge, after so many years' practice, for Les to continue presenting to the world the identity that made her most at ease.

Les had once had a bad experience with a guy who resembled Crespo in many details; hence her rare unease at the prospect of sharing the back seat with Crespo on the ride from the airport. But her resiliency and spunk were more than sufficient to meet him in professional situations with other people around.

After our invigorating romp, I felt, for one poignant moment, a surge of guilt at this flagrant though unplanned infidelity to Nellie. But then I recalled the suave Latin leer of Onésimo Dambara and told myself I was just evening out the balance sheet. Chantal and Les would soon be out of my life, and Nellie and I would resume our solid monogamous relationship on a fresh footing as soon as she got home.

* * *

I woke up around 8:00 a.m., alone in the suite. It was the morning before the evening that Lina, Algernon, and I were to infiltrate the testing grounds and plant our fool's gold, and I was feeling as ready for such strenuous, dangerous activity as a one-armed climber staring up the face of El Capitan.

I picked up my scattered clothes, dressed, and headed down to the hotel garage, where I had left the Lexus.

All the way to the condo, I could smell Chantal's perfume on me. I was just glad Les didn't wear men's cologne, which would clash.

Stan was having breakfast alone: a plate of microwaved burritos and a twenty-five-ounce can of Foster's.

"Where's Sandy?" I said. "Off to work already?"

"I guess you could say that. She never came home."

"What do you mean?"

"She called and said she wasn't gonna be home last night, simple as that. Which is more than you bothered to do. Jeez, you think I don't care if my roomie is safe or not? I was practically outta my head with worry! I called every hospital in the area."

I actually believed Stan for one whole second, until he broke into a shit-eating grin.

"I probably *should* be in traction in the hospital by now after what I went through."

"Oh, poor baby. Tell Papa all about it."

Suddenly famished, I sat down, grabbed one of Stan's burritos, and bit off half. After washing it down with some of his beer, I laid out the whole scenario for him without going into undue detail.

Stan whistled with sincere appreciation. "What a brilliant pair of deceitful horny bitches! My hat's off to them. And you, too, Glen boy! You continue to surprise me with your resourcefulness. But you know you're supposed to call your partner for backup when you're outnumbered in a dangerous situation like that."

"I was overstimulated and confused."

"Okay, I'll let ya off this time. But please keep that rule in mind for any such future occasions."

"There aren't going to be any repeats. I took a bribe to keep quiet about Chantal and Les. It was a one-time payment, which I intend to honor. Besides, Nellie's going to be home soon." I paused, trying to phrase my next question delicately. "Uh, it doesn't bother you that Sandralene was somewhere else last night?"

"Haven't we been all over this territory before? Me and her got an understanding which is more or less elastic—up to a point. Besides, I knew Caleb would treat her right."

Stan had spoken the name I hesitated to utter.

"Just a few weeks ago, you were jealous as all hell of his attentions to Sandy."

"That was before I knew she would come back to me and everything would be just like it always was. And also before that big doofus saved my fucking neck from taking a plunge off the roof of Lura's place. I figure those two things changed the whole situation. Never let it be said that Stan Hasso is a guy who can't learn new stuff and change his mind. And besides, I feel sorry for old Johnny Reb. He's been lusting after Sandy in his polite hayseed style since they were kids, and that is a hell of a lot of years of blue balls to inflict on any poor guy—especially when the prize dangling under his nose is a girl like Sandralene. It's good she can help him finally take the edge off."

I dispatched the burrito and felt a wave of fatigue. Maybe finishing Stan's beer hadn't been the best idea.

"I'm going to bed," I said. "Wake me around three."

Stan got me up on schedule, and I imagined I felt rather peppy. A cold shower, followed by coffee and more food, helped solidify that delusion.

"Let's stop at the factory before we go the hotel," I said. "I want to see if Caleb's heard anything from Luckman."

We left the house, with me carrying a bundle of clothes for tonight's mission.

At Luckman Enterprises, we found Caleb and Sandy busy accepting a delivery of parts, so we didn't interrupt. Caleb was reading off the stenciled contents of the crates while Sandy checked off the corresponding items on the bill of lading. Their public professional attitude to each other seemed basically unchanged from yesterday—an amiable coworkers' companionship. But every now and then, Caleb would let a look of helpless smitten adoration stray Sandy's way.

When they had finished, Stan and I came forward. Caleb shook Stan's hand with unashamed manly candor, and Sandy gave Stan a moderate kiss. Yesterday's melancholy air had evaporated from the Southerner's affect, and although he wasn't actually smiling, he seemed to be radiating happiness from the inside. I imagined he was restraining himself from bouncing around like Tigger.

"Heard from Luckman?" I asked.

"I did. He and Rosa were going to the movies and supper tonight."

"Good, good. How'd he sound?"

Caleb looked a little less upbeat. "Not too chipper, but hanging in there."

"We'll have to settle for that," I said. "Okay, Stan and I are off to Chantal's. Wish us luck."

I got a solid back-thumping from Caleb, and a full-body clinch from Sandy, which, had I not been temporarily depleted, would have activated all my gonadal circuitry and hydraulics.

At the hotel, Chantal's room held all four of our coconspirators—five, counting Algernon.

Chantal and Les greeted us with meticulous adherence to the old baseline business formality we had established from day one. My estimation of the quid pro quo had been accurate. Stan actually managed to refrain from any off-color innuendo.

Eddie and Lina were dressed ninja-style, all in black, and soon so was I—not quite so professionally as they, but in a good enough approximation: sweats, toque, gloves, soft-soled but rugged shoes.

Lina handed me a stick of shadow-black war paint. "We'll use this on our faces, but not quite yet. It's only five o'clock, and we won't go in until oh-one-hundred hours, at the exact time Vin Santo has arranged the diversion. Meanwhile, we can have some supper sent up. No alcohol, though. Gotta be sharp, and you don't want to have to pee in the middle of the op."

"Where's Algernon?" I asked.

Lina un-Velcroed a special oversize pocket on her pants, and the giant rat peeked out. "The star of the show is chilling in his dressing room."

Sandwiches came. We killed time playing cards. I lost a hundred bucks or so. I think Algernon was peeking out of his pocket and reading my hands, then relaying the info to his owner. At one point, Les threw down her cards in disgust. Stan could not resist saying, "Man up, Les, man up!"

At midnight, the four of us left the hotel by the fire staircase. In the car, we painted our faces, slouched down, and let Stan drive.

45

Eddie Greenfriars handed me the pair of night-vision binoculars he had brought along so I could enjoy an eerie false-color view of the fenced-off lot where tomorrow's test was to take place. Military vets had the neatest toys, I was learning, and for the first time I began to see some of the allure of that vocation.

We were hiding nearly two blocks away, standing just inside the mouth of the alley that Stan had selected as the place to stash the getaway car. (We were using Chantal and Les' rental, its plates smeared with mud. There was no sense in taking a chance that someone would spot and later remember Stan's one-of-a-kind Jeep or my slightly less distinctive Lexus.) The time was five minutes to one in the morning, and the four of us were alone in the cold November streets of this mixed residential and retail district, which still had a slightly louche and off-putting reputation since half its older buildings were still underoccupied.

Though the lot's back fence was ungated, Crespo's men

patrolled it nonetheless. We had counted six, walking alertly up and down the four-acre domain. I felt a little queasy thinking of the measures they might take if they encountered intruders on the property.

Lina had Algernon's thin but strong lead looped around her wrist, although the rat was still in her cargo pocket. For the thousandth time, I patted the shoulder bag that contained the ANFO props. I sent up a silent prayer, to whatever deity might be listening, that I could maneuver through the obstacle course and plant them successfully. I received no immediate assurance back.

Crespo had promised to limit his planted samples to thirty, for we had bargained with him that if we could not justify the device with thirty attempts, ten or twenty more would do neither party any good, and he had agreed with that logic. I had fifty samples so I could double up at some sites. Also, I was to scatter one or two lures apart from Crespo's seeds. These would produce what would appear to Crespo as false positives in the LBAS. Similarly, I was to leave a couple of Crespo's samples unattended. Going undetected by Luckman's deficient machine, these omissions would register as failures also on the part of the LBAS. These "flaws" together should produce about an 80 to 90 percent success rate, thus making the device's powers more realistic than would a perfect score. Or so Chantal had reasoned, and we concurred.

Eddie rolled the tool he was in charge of—an aluminum floor jack with its long levering handle—back and forth on its wheels, across the span of a few inches. The lightweight device had been well oiled for silent operation, and was rated for two tons of lift— far more than needed to hoist a section of the chain-link fence. Eddie's unconscious nervous actions were making me jumpy, but I said nothing.

Inside the car, behind the wheel, Stan sat looking as if he hadn't a care in the world. I could have sworn he was daydreaming, probably about getting home to Sandralene.

Lina consulted her phone for the time. "Get ready ..."

Right on schedule, the MS-13 boys arrived. It was nice to see that the killers had good work habits and could follow instructions.

The first sign of their D-day assault was a simultaneous burst of gunfire and expletives. I heard a lot of "*cabrons*" and "*chingadas*" and "*hijoeputas*." "*¡Mara Salvatrucha siempre!*" seemed the most popular battle cry. Crespo's guys began to return both bullets and team smack talk.

Instantly, Lina and Eddie were off running, hunkered over, with me close behind. Eddie pushed the floor jack in front of him like a hockey player sweeping his puck down the ice.

The gangsters had instructions not to massacre the Sombra Negra watchers, which they might easily have accomplished, but rather just to draw them away from the site. We didn't want the whole place cordoned off tomorrow with yellow police tape. And in fact, we counted on any responding cops to follow the hurly-burly down whatever distant blocks it might traverse, and never peg the test site as the origin of the disturbance.

Suddenly, we were at the fence, and I was pleased to see I could still breathe almost normally, though my heart was pounding like a jackhammer.

Eddie shoved the plate of the jack under the fence and began pumping like crazy. The fence groaned and lifted, and in a few seconds, there was a gap big enough for Lina and me to belly-crawl through.

Lina had estimated that we would need ten to twenty minutes of unimpeded access to track down all the samples, depending on how far apart they were scattered. Algernon could operate that fast.

Eddie stayed by the jack, lying flat and awaiting our return and exfil. (I was really digging the military-speak. It helped me imagine I would come out of this alive.)

Once inside the chaos of the ruins, I wished I had night-vision goggles that worked as well as the binoculars. But those had been deemed expensive and bulky, and worse than useless for an untrained civilian such as I. So we had to work with the available ambient light. Distant streetlamps illuminated bits and pieces of the obstacle-strewn terrain, but they made more shadows than they dispelled.

It felt weird to be operating as a team without talking. But, of course, we couldn't risk alerting any remaining guards.

Lina tapped my shoulder in the agreed-upon signal. At the end of his taut leash, Algernon had found his first score. Sweaty-palmed under my gloves, I fumbled with the pinch clasps of the messenger bag and got it open. Reaching inside, I came up with an ANFO-treated candy-bar wrapper. I traced the lead to where the giant rat quivered in obediently suppressed excitement, his nose pushed into a jumble of bricks. I couldn't see whatever Crespo had planted, but I had to assume it was there. I stuffed the candy wrapper into the crevice.

A whispered short burst of Swahili, and Algernon and Lina were on the move again.

I continued to hear distant exchanges of gunfire and profanities. Probably no more than ninety seconds had passed since the ruckus kicked off, but it seemed like ages to me. So far, no good citizen had alerted the cops—or, if someone had, the men in blue were slow to respond.

Algernon's next foray took us close to the front gate. I could see one silhouetted guard stationed there. But he was straining forward, as if eager to join his comrades, and all his attention was directed outward, not into the empty lot. But if he should turn ...

Better not to think about that.

This time, I could see Crespo's sample: a small metal box about the size of an Altoids tin. I partnered the box with a flattened Styrofoam cup rich with ANFO.

After that, the rest of the operation blurred into a mad, timeless scramble across weedy potholes and unstable tumuli, which kept me too busy to freak out. I began to feel a spooky mental rapport, not with Lina but with the rat, as if Algernon and I were some kind of unified symbiotic organism. It almost seemed that I could anticipate where he was going to stop, a few seconds in advance of his actual discoveries. I would slap down the new ANFO trigger, and we'd be off in a flash.

Once, I took a bad step into a hole and got that sickening premonition that I had really jacked up my ankle. But although my foot came out of the hole a little sore, the necessity of continued movement seemed to restore it to full though aching use.

I remembered to skip a couple of saltings and place a couple of false positives, as planned.

I sure hoped Lina was keeping count of how many samples we had hit, because I had lost all sense of number. Our calm frenzy of motions seemed to form one continuous blur of insane activity, racing through a cold labyrinth of debris that smelled like decaying lumber, leaf mold, and stagnant puddles. All I knew was that when I reached into the satchel now, it was practically empty.

The noise of police sirens suddenly entered my consciousness, although I suspected they had been wailing for a while.

I also heard some aggrieved and angry voices approaching, not exchanging smack talk, but doing a play-by-play recap of the evening in Spanish.

Lina gave me the double tap in the small of my back that meant we had to book it. She scooped up Algernon and got him safely stowed in her big pocket.

I had lost all sense of direction in the darkened wilderness, but Lina hadn't—Ranger training to the fore! I stuck to her like a shadow.

Eddie popped up from his prone position and got ready to jack down the fence, and I finally began to feel I could indulge in a little optimism.

Lina and I got through the gap, and Eddie started to lower away.

Then the MS-13 gangbangers, in an otherwise laudable demonstration of hireling initiative, couldn't resist staging one more vindictive assault. They began firing in the direction of the Sombra Negra dudes, who, though still some hundred yards off, were reconvening on the property. Of course, the vigilantes began firing back.

No one saw us, I think. We weren't a target, but that made no difference to the errant bullets that I felt whizzing by.

Suddenly, Eddie clutched his leg and went down, with only the smallest repressed sounds of pain. I moved to aid him, but Lina shoved me toward the jack, then went to her husband's side. She whipped out the tactical one-handed field tourniquet she had shown me back at the hotel—with some black-humored japes about its uses—and tended to his leg. I got the fence down and the jack retracted.

Then a car screeched up alongside us. I prepared to be arrested or executed.

Stan had the jack stashed in the trunk and the trunk lid closed, in about three seconds. Then, he picked up Eddie as if he were a duffel of dirty laundry and flung him onto the back seat. Lina and I scrambled into the car, her in back, me up front. Stan vaulted into the driver's seat, and we were off.

No chasing bullets, no pursuers, no evidence whatever that we had even been spotted by Crespo's allies, much less connected with the disturbance.

Stan said, "Saw everything through the binocs. Thoughtcha could use a hand. Ya think Vin Santo knows a reliable doc for bullet wounds who doesn't keep such good records?"

46

The morning following our guerrilla foray, the day of field trials for Luckman's gadget, I awoke feeling my overtaxed legs and rolled ankle and abused lower back. Yet I also felt unnaturally confident, with a sense that the successful end of our scam was in sight. We had gotten away without botching the Great Midnight Pouched Rat Bomb-Sniffing Caper. And Vin Santo's surprisingly competent and professional off-the-books surgeon—a young woman, no less—had stitched up and antibioticized an out-of-danger Eddie Greenfriars quickly enough that we all were back home by 3:30 a.m. So if our nerves permitted, we could get a good five or six hours' sleep and still have time to prepare for our two o'clock meet with Crespo at the site.

Now rested, with the low-angled sunlight of 9:10 a.m. pouring into the condo as I lay in bed contemplating a hearty breakfast, I recalled another reason to feel chipper: Nellie was coming home roughly thirty-six hours from now.

When I entered the dining area, I found Sandralene and Stan already dressed. Sandy was serving Stan a stack of pancakes as high as a spindle of fifty CDs. There was a tangled heap of bacon on a platter, as well.

"Any for me?"

"Sure, Glen. Stan, give him some of yours and I'll pour some more on the griddle."

"Cripes, the sacrifices I make for this guy! It's not enough I pulled his nuts out of the fire last night; now I gotta go hungry for him!"

"You'll live healthier with a few less carbs."

"But will I be any happier? Happiness is another factor in good health."

Stan's phone rang just as I had finished my hotcakes and was draining my coffee cup. But the timing of the call proved the only pleasant aspect of the interruption.

Stan listened for a few seconds, said, "Okay, we'll be right there," and clicked off.

I could already feel my sunshiny attitude melting like Madame Tussaud's livelihood in a firestorm.

"What's up?"

"That was Rosa. Luckman's drunk outta his gourd."

"Oh, Jesus, no," I groaned. He's the only one who can work that snake-oil Geiger counter of his. What are we going to do?"

"Well, obviously we gotta get him sober enough to perform. I got something that could maybe help."

Stan went into his bedroom. Sandy was already donning her coat.

"I'll come, too," she said. "Maybe I can give Rosa some support."

Stan returned and said, "Let's go. Luckman's gotta be totally functional by two or we are screwed, blued, and tattooed. No way Crespo will postpone this test. Last night's brawl will jump into his head, and he'll figure we're trying to pull a fast one—and that wouldn't bode well for our economic or physical health."

On the way to Luckman's in Stan's Jeep, I said, "What could've made him do this?"

"How do I know? He's been whining for days about how all this cheating doesn't honor him or his crappy gadget. Also, he ain't too crazy about Crespo's pedigree, what he knows of it."

I hesitated, looked at Sandy, then said, "You don't think he found out about you and Rosa, do you?"

"Nah, no chance. She ain't gonna blow her share of his millions, and I sure as hell didn't confess."

"I just worry about what he'd do if he ever did find out."

Stan showed some irritation. "You can quit worrying. After today, we don't even need the nutty professor no more. Caleb's got the factory running like a Swiss watch. We crank out the other four thousand units without Luckman's help, Crespo buys 'em, and we pocket the money and split."

"You really think Crespo wants another four thousand detectors?"

"Chantal does. She figures La Sombra Negra plans to set themselves up as unauthorized resellers for all of Central America and peddle the gadgets for more than they paid us. Crespo thinks he's pulling a fast one on us. Let him. The easiest con is the guy who thinks he's conning you."

The Luckmans' shabby suburban home looked bland and quiet, belying any tensions behind its closed door and curtained windows. I regarded the attached garage and tried to recall the thrill I had felt when I first realized how Luckman's gadget could parlay our silicon chips into a fortune. That day, just a few weeks ago, seemed like another geologic era.

Before we could ring the bell, Rosa Luckman had the front door open. Although she stood solid, putting up a brave front, she looked like hell, all her patrician charm and looks having been scraped down to the bone.

"Come in, come in," she said. "I'm so glad you're here. I've been up all night with him. I didn't call sooner, because I thought I could talk him down, and I knew you were busy. But I haven't done any good. Maybe I've even made things worse. He hates himself and everything he's done."

Rosa suddenly seemed to collapse in on herself and quietly began to sob. Sandy swooped her up like a mother hen, saying, "You need some coffee, sweetie. Get me to the kitchen."

The two women marched off. Stan and I found Luckman in his study.

The guy was a real animal, all right. Not only had he worked his way through the whole bottle of port he had opened when he signed the contract, but he had killed a pint of blackberry brandy as well.

Slumped in a recliner, his clothing nasty with flecks of vomit, he looked up blearily when we came in, and seemed to recognize us.

"Mr.—Mr. Hasso. Mr. Glen. You're just in time to say goodbye. I am done with all this. All this big bad mess I have caused. 'We have walked in lasciviousness, lust, excess of wine, revelings, banquetings, and abominable idolatries. And now we shall pay the price. And the wages of sin is death!'"

Stan got his hands under Luckman's armpits and hoisted

him up like a rag doll. "Goodbye, nothing! You are in this till the end, Pops. And you won't regret it, believe me, when you and the missus are rolling in greenbacks. You don't wanna let her down now, do you? So suck it up! You are going to have a cold shower and some hot coffee. But first, down a couple of these."

Stan propped Luckman up on the edge of his desk while he took out a prescription bottle from his pocket and spilled out two pills.

"Get me a glass of tonic over there, will ya?"

I poured sparkling water from the bar into a tumbler and handed it to Luckman, who took the glass and studied it as if it were the Hope Diamond.

"Take these pills, Prof. They're just a little harmless pick-me-up."

"Don' wanna. Can't make me."

Stan's benign expression and voice assumed the menacing tone of an unhappy mama bear. "You'll swallow the pills, Pops, or you'll swallow some teeth. Which is it gonna be?"

Like most academics confronted with the threat of actual violence, Luckman caved faster than a home-ec-class soufflé. He swallowed the pills and guzzled the water.

"Okay, good man. Now, let's get you under Niagara Falls."

The three of us went to the bathroom upstairs. Stan and I managed to strip Luckman and get him in the stall. Stan turned the cold water on full force, and Luckman bellowed his distress. Stan kept him nailed in place even though he, too, was getting soaked. Luckman's wet, fish-belly-pale middle-aged body wasn't particularly flabby or gross, but he still evoked a drowned corpse cast up on some alien shore.

By the time Stan relented, Luckman seemed perceptibly more

alert and sensible. We wrapped him in towels and escorted him to the bedroom, where a framed picture of Rosa occupied the nightstand.

"What were those pills?" I said.

"Just some Adderall—fairly lightweight stuff, but it'll kick booze in the ass."

Rummaging through closet and bureau, we put together a set of clothes for Luckman, then moved to dress him. But he motioned us off with growing indications of sobriety. A sheepish look further confirmed his gradual return from his alcohol-infused funk.

"I have dressed myself for many years now," he said. "I think I can continue a while longer. May I have some privacy, please?"

We left Luckman alone and went downstairs to the kitchen, where Sandy and Rosa were conferring quietly, their heads close together. Rosa supported her bowed head with one hand planted against her brow, while Sandralene had an arm draped over Rosa's shoulder. They both looked up when we came in.

"He's gonna be fine," Stan said. "Get a big mug of java ready however he likes it."

By the time Rosa had the coffee ready, Luckman himself manifested. His guilty expression seemed to affirm that he would be repenting and paying for this shameful fall from self-control and duty until his dying day.

"I am very grateful to you gentlemen for your help. And, Rosa, dear, well, you know how I feel. I owe you so much. But I promise you all, as the Lord is my shepherd and witness, I will live up to the demands of the day."

"Fucking A, Prof. Your come-to-Jesus moment was a bitch, but that's all behind you now."

"Amen," I said, but no one else chimed in.

47

Standing outside the locked gate of the test site, waiting for Crespo and company, the five of us shuffled about in a vain attempt to stay warm. Despite the sun, the temperatures today hadn't gotten much above freezing. I recalled previous Thanksgivings when we had snow on the ground. The holiday was only five days away, and I wondered what we'd be doing and feeling and experiencing then. Jubilation and relief and togetherness? Anxiety and despair and separation? All we could do was forge ahead and hope for the best.

Chantal and Les stood close together for warmth, Chantal regal as ever, Les somewhat wry and goofy, like a kid on a field trip. Stan seemed impervious to the chill, despite wearing only an unzipped leather jacket. Luckman, with the garish detector slung over one shoulder of his stadium coat, was too wrapped up in his interior life even to notice the conditions.

"I believe this is their car coming," said Chantal.

I saw a big blood-red Nissan Armada SUV, almost military grade in its heft, approaching down the block.

Chantal added in an off-the-cuff fashion, "Oh, by the way, Lina and Eddie are on their way home already. But before they left, they informed me that they need a hundred and fifty K now, not seventy-five. That wound is going to incapacitate him for a while."

Again with the death of a thousand fiscal cuts. I said, "I thought the seventy-five-K fee included the bonus for facing live fire."

"Yes, for facing it, but not for actually receiving it."

Stan said, "Just let it go, pard. Not worth the hassle."

The Nissan pulled to the curb, and Crespo got out on the passenger side up front. The driver and one other fellow emerged. Looking like undertakers, they all wore black cloth coats that came down almost to the knee, underneath which could be concealed anything from a shotgun to a small shoulder-fired missile. I wondered whether these two had been on duty last night and, if so, just how mad they might still be at the MS-13 assault, and what they would do if they knew we had rigged it. The three of them together—no-nonsense dudes wrapped tight as the inside of a golf ball, somehow managed to resemble both the conquistadores who had invaded El Salvador, and the righteous Mayan warriors who had defied them.

Crespo's eyes might as well have been two polished hematites for all the emotion they conveyed. He shook hands all around, though his comrades didn't bother. I assumed from the formal cordiality that we had not been rumbled.

"You will please excuse Señores Mejía and Alvarado from any attempts at small talk. Their English is not too good. But their eyesight and powers of discrimination are acute, so I rely heavily on them. Let us begin."

The driver unfastened the padlock on the gate, and we entered the field of rubble. It looked a lot less spooky by day. I had a hard time even believing it was the same field of postapocalyptic nightmares I had traversed with such fear only twelve hours ago.

Luckman unslung the LBAS and activated it. His expression was neutral, maybe a tad on the determined side. He fiddled with the controls, then said, "Ready."

Here was the moment of truth, after weeks of scheming and striving, with all our fortunes riding on it.

Luckman exhibited just the right blend of scientific inventor's confidence and newbie businessman's desire to impress. He even kept up a running monologue, explaining what he was doing to fine-tune the detector. It might have been all bullshit, but it sure sounded convincing. Crespo shadowed Luckman diligently while his henchmen made certain the rest of us were not somehow kibitzing.

Luckman arrowed straight to every place I had salted the ANFO. He found the unidentifiable strays that did not correspond to Crespo's samples and hence looked like false positives. And he was unable to discover those items I hadn't tagged. And so, in just a little longer time than Lina and I had spent taking Algernon on his little walk, Luckman finished the trial, with the LBAS shining like an explosives-detecting beacon of wonderfulness.

Crespo and his brothers-in-arms had betrayed no sentiments about the performance while it was underway. But once we all were back out on the street with the gate locked again, they huddled near their car for an animated conversation more in keeping with the passionate Latino temperament I had anticipated.

Crespo returned to our little knot of quiet observers—just the four of us, for Luckman had gone to sit in Chantal's car, where he could be seen, blank-faced and unobtrusively sipping at intervals from a travel mug of coffee, which I was pretty sure had been stiffened with some of whatever cloying booze he still had back at his house. The promise of that reward had been part of his motivation.

Crespo nodded back at his compatriots, both of whom were busy on their phones. "Señor Mejía is arranging for the pickup of the thousand units, using our own trucks. We will not ship them and have them subject to customs, but rather transport them overland ourselves, along less obtrusive routes. Señor Alvarado is okaying the funds transfer. You should find the money available by the time you reach the factory. I thank you, gentlemen, for helping to maintain the security and stability of my beloved country."

And just like that, we were thirty million dollars in the black.

* * *

Vin Santo himself greeted us at the front door of his club, still closed at this unhedonic hour of four in the afternoon. I almost keeled over at the sight of the rotund crime lord up and about— in the daylight, no less! I had never seen him outside his inner sanctum before, and during most of those visits he had been seated. For all I knew, he might have been like Professor Xavier, directing his operations by sheer telepathy from a wheelchair.

Santo threw his arms around me. It was like being embraced by a bag of suet. He bestowed the same greeting on Stan, who rolled his eyes heavenward and hugged back tentatively, as if he had been tasked with making love to a manatee.

"My favorite boys! Thirty million in the bag. Numbers on the screen don't lie, and I have seen it with my own eyes. Enter, enter! I got a big spread laid out for us."

Santo had a few cronies at hand, as well as his bodyguards, but there was enough food and drink for twice the number present. I nibbled on some shrimp and had a little champagne, not wanting to get too stuffed or too wasted. Stan, however, indulged like the doughty trencherman he was.

Santo took a spreadsheet printout from a flunky and corralled Stan and me into a quiet corner.

"Here's the breakdown. Expenses to date, including the initial cost of the chips: two million. The share for the Danssaert chick and her pal, three million. My half of the remaining twenty-five—well, let's just round up and call it fifteen million, okay? That leaves ten million as a three-way split for you boys and the professor. Not too bad, huh? And this is only the first batch of gadgets, with four times as many sales down the road!"

The champagne interfered with my math a little, but I eventually worked out that Stan and I would net over thirteen million apiece, once all five thousand units were sold. Not quite the astronomical figure we had first imagined, but not too shabby at all.

"Vin," said Stan, "we are in your debt."

"Pally, you ain't gonna be in nobody's debt ever again!"

48

The restaurant was called Morabeza, and we had rented a private room for the official celebration of the recent success engineered by Luckman Enterprises and its millionaire high-roller executives. But the evening included a second theme as well: Morabeza was a Caboverdean establishment, stocking many of Nellie's imports. As a good customer, they were helping her get Tartaruga Verde Importing onto a solid footing, and so she felt it only fitting to patronize them in return, steering diners there whenever she could. Her practical logrolling had not met with any resistance from the rest of us, since the place was lively and popular and had a great reputation for making delicious exotic dishes.

Two days had passed since we aced the sale, giving Nellie time to return from Cape Verde and get her head together. (Our Stateside reunion had been just as ecstatic as our reconciliation in the islands, and all was back on an even keel.)

We were a largish party: Chantal and Les, Stan and Sandralene,

Rosa and Ronald Luckman, Caleb (stag), and Nellie and me. It would have been cool to have Lina and Eddie present, too. I had wanted Nellie to meet Algernon, a vital player in this caper, whom I had grown very fond of during our shared trial by combat. But as Chantal had informed me, the two vets had eagerly hit the road once their covert ops were over. A check for their fee of one hundred fifty thousand, drawn on our overstuffed bank account, had followed them home. And by now, with our money almost in hand, I no longer regretted the doubled expense. The thirty million still sat in the Luckman Enterprises account, ultimately controlled by Vin Santo, but our shares would soon be dispersed to our individual banks.

Santo had politely declined our invitation to party down.

"Your hospitality is extremely gratifying to my tender sensibilities, Glen," he had said. "This is truly the kind of bighearted relationship which makes the type of work we do so much more than mere bash-and-grab. But I do not like to become the public face of any enterprise what could someday draw the attentions of our legally constituted authorities. And besides—no diss to your sweet little coochie—that Portagee food don't sit too well in the Santo gut. I always get the trots from it. Now, if you had picked out a nice Italian spot …"

So it was just the nine of us who assembled at seven o'clock in Morabeza's colorful back room decorated with island motifs, both natural and cultural. At the edge of the room to respect our privacy, a young guitarist with the beatific look of a beachcomber saint sat on a tall stool, already tuning up. When he began to play, visions of tropical nights and lazy surf filled the room.

The women were all dressed to stun. (I excluded Les from this lovely contingent since, while undeniably well-attired, she still maintained her male drag, and only Stan and I, apart from her lover, knew the truth.) Chantal wore heels and a floor-length gray chiffon dress whose gauzy see-through top was rendered seductively modest by filigree and beading. Nellie sported a supple cotton earth-tone dress, patterned like some mythical hybrid of snakeskin and giraffe hide, that fitted her like a second skin, its low-cut spaghetti-strap top showing off her splendid bosom while its short flaring skirt did justice to her gorgeous legs, which were laced up with the straps of her sandals. Sandralene loomed taller than ever in high black Louboutin boots and a violet cashmere sweater dress whose fabric lovingly caressed every voluptuous curve and plane. Even Rosa Luckman, who generally came off as severe, had managed to look at once festive and elegant in a nicely tailored pantsuit that mimicked a tuxedo.

As for us men—and here I include Les—well, I guess we looked as good as males ever do next to beautiful women. But I couldn't really pay much attention, not even to the riveting sight of Stan's glossy palm-leaf-print silk evening jacket.

Luckman, I was relieved to see, had pulled himself together, although he still had a fragile air, as if one more straw added to his burden would send him into a neurasthenic collapse.

The space could have hosted a party five times our number, and at first I worried that we all might feel a bit like BBs rattling around in an empty bucket. But we staked out a big round linen-covered table in the brightly lit area next to the bar, where an employee was mixing up *ponche*. This sweet cocktail improbably blended high-octane native *grogue*, a kind of home-brewed rum, with crushed ice, molasses, lime, and condensed milk. The resulting drink packed all the kick of Babe the Blue Ox. After the first one, our little sphere of warmth and light and nascent conviviality began to expand into a whole universe of delight. And by the time each of us had downed a second cocktail, the walls of the larger room receded into meaningless infinity and we were minor deities inhabiting an Afro-Latino themed Olympus. All the cares and concerns and fears connected with the recent caper seemed to evaporate. We were in the winner's circle, and nothing and no one could touch us.

The head chef of Morabeza, a handsome middle-aged fellow with the dignified presence of a symphony conductor, actually came out to greet Nellie warmly and inform us of the menu. We were going to start with several appetizers, including goat cheese with papaya jam, *camarão em vinha de alhos* (shrimp in wine and garlic), and brochettes of fried eel. Then we'd move on to *muamba*, a chicken stew accompanied by a manioc glop known as *funji*. Then would come *chamuças*—stuffed savory pastries— and *cachupa,* the essential hominy stew I knew well from Nellie's home cooking. Also included: half a dozen other mouthwatering dishes, all to be topped off with the famous coffee pudding and a mango mousse.

The appetizers had a lot of work to do to sop up the alcohol, which had an unfair head start, and in this they were only margin- ally successful. And the drinks kept coming.

Naturally, the dinner conversation turned mostly on the success of our venture. In deference to the more sensitive and innocent members of our party—Caleb and Luckman, mainly— we instinctively deemphasized the more illicit aspects of the production. And, of course, the conversation moved down other avenues, too, relieving us of the need to dissemble.

I asked Chantal where she and Les were headed next.

"Oh, perhaps Europe. Maybe Asia. The Defense and Security

Conference in Bangkok is always profitable for us. Really, wherever our fancy takes us and money is to be had. Our fee from this affair will set us up nicely for some time, so there is no urgency to earn more."

Luckman chose this moment to interpolate in somber tones, "'For the love of money is a root of all kinds of evil, for which some have strayed from the faith in their greediness, and pierced themselves through with many sorrows.'"

Stan slapped the savant heartily on the back. "Prof, you slay me. It's always easier to say money's shit when you got plenty yourself. And you and the missus sure do now. So get useta it!"

I turned then to Caleb with an impulsive urge. "You're getting a bonus, too, you know. We couldn't have done this without you. How does seventy-five sound?"

Caleb had been mostly mooning over Sandy till now, but I had his attention. "Seventy-five hundred?"

Stan seconded my previously undiscussed gesture of gratitude with gusto. "Jeez, Stinchcombe, don't you West Virginia yokels know how to dream big? Seventy-five *thousand*!"

"That—that is almighty fine of you, Stan. You, too, Glen. I can set up my business right smart once I get back home."

Course after course arrived, borne by efficient, smiling servers. The *ponche* flowed like spring melt, and I began to lose track of the fine details. I seemed to recall that at one point, Chantal was sitting on Les' lap and they were drinking from each other's glass with arms intertwined. Stan and Sandy were feeding each other messy morsels with their fingers. Luckman and Caleb were holding a spirited discussion on the more bizarre aspects of the Book of Revelation. In an odd pairing, Nellie and Rosa were talking about having kids. And I found myself trying to instruct the guitarist on how to play Prince's "When Doves Cry," despite there being no common language between us.

Our little bubble of light and activity occupied a much larger realm of shadows, since the rest of the room's lights had been turned down. At the back of the hall were the restrooms, two doors behind a decorative freestanding wall that afforded some privacy. I had visited the gents' several times already.

I looked up hazily from seeing how high I could stack empty clamshells. Sandy was holding Caleb's hand and whispering in his ear. Luckman and Nellie were chatting about Cape Verde's geologic origins—or rather, Luckman was lecturing while she listened politely. Chantal and Les were smooching like teenagers. I leaned over to break them up with some appropriate witticism, and Les grabbed me by the neck and smashed her lips over mine. Seeing me apparently French-kissing a delicately handsome Asian boy, Nellie faltered in her attentions to Luckman but showed admirable urbanity in deciding to ignore the whole thing.

After the kiss, I noticed that Stan and Rosa were nowhere to be seen.

Luckman stood up. "Excuse me, Miss Firmino, I have to visit the double-you-cee."

Some instinct made me jump up to follow him. "Hang on, Ron, I'll leave a trail of bread crumbs so we can find our way back."

The walk across the darkened room seemed to take forever, as if we were crossing some vast and danger-fraught expanse. Eventually, we turned the corner of the partition.

I have to give Stan credit. He wasn't canoodling; he had stuck by his vow to break it off with Rosa. He stood frowning with his arms folded across his chest, keeping Rosa at a distance. But his chaste stance could not offset the impact of Rosa's tear-stained face and sotto voce pleas.

"What do you want from me?" she moaned. "What do I have to do? I can't stand being with him anymore! Take me with you; take me away from him. I don't care if you have Sandy, too. I can share you. I just need to get away! Please, Stan, I'm begging you!"

Luckman didn't collapse physically, but things snapped almost audibly inside him. He seemed frozen in place for an eternity before he spun about and marched off. I didn't try to stop him. What could I have said or done to negate what he had just seen and heard?

Watching her husband's broken retreat, Rosa grunted as if she had been kicked in the stomach, then rushed into the ladies' room to retch.

Stan was genuinely shocked, I could tell. His voice faltered as he tried to minimize the catastrophe.

"This is bad juju, sure. But everyone'll bounce back. You'll see."

"Maybe," I said. "Maybe not."

49

Uncle Ralph's cramped, too-warm house was filled with delicious smells of turkey, stuffing, vegetables, and pies. With three chefs—Sandy, Nellie, and Ralph's irrepressible squeeze, Suzy Lam, the Asian Ethel Merman—whipping up an array of recipes both traditional and exotic, I looked forward to eating myself comatose. After the past couple of nerve-straining days, I could use the all the ritual hearthside comfort and simple-carb overload I could get.

After Luckman had walked robotically out of Morabeza, the remaining partyers' attentions had turned to consoling Rosa. The women had rushed into the john in a show of female solidarity, while we four men (including the rogue double-agent Les) dithered guiltily around the table, our mellow buzz rapidly evanescing. Stan had the grace to look hangdog and sheepish. I didn't have the heart or desire to guilt-trip him. Sure, in the best of all possible worlds, he wouldn't have gone sniffing around

Luckman's wife. But she had rushed into his arms uncoerced and was equally guilty of the infidelity. Then, when he had seen fit to break it off—selfishly or nobly or from a mix of both motives—Rosa had not followed a similar mature and stoic path. So no, I couldn't blame Stan for this mess. Not entirely.

Eventually, the women emerged from their powder room in group-counseling mode. Rosa Luckman had regained some composure but still looked demon haunted.

Nellie said, "Glen, we need to get Rosa home. She is sure Ron took the car."

"Okay, of course. Just let me settle the bill." I turned to the others and said, "Sorry to break this up early, friends, but I think you can see why."

In truth, no one felt like continuing the festivities, and we all were ready to call it a night.

Caleb had his own car. Les and Chantal had already turned in their rental to the agency. They were flying out the next day and would get a cab to the airport. Stan said, "I'll get Ell and Cee back to the hotel. C'mon, Sandy."

Nellie walked Rosa out the door to my car. The restaurant's officious owner, perhaps alerted by the bartender to the disturbance, was hovering discreetly by the exit, formal but sympathetic. I gave him my credit card and added a 30 percent tip when the check came.

Out in the chilly parking lot, the arms brokers and Stan stood beside his ridiculous Jeep, with Sandy seated up front. Rosa and Nellie were in the Lexus already, for I had given Nellie the fob to warm it up. I went over to Stan.

"I fear this is goodbye, Glen," said Chantal. "Maybe we'll work together again someday. Thank you for everything." She gave me a kiss that would have scorched the scaly lips of a crocodile, and Les followed with a similar one. Stan snickered.

I staggered over to the Lexus, drunk on kisses and *ponche*. Luckman's old Pontiac was indeed gone from the lot.

We took Rosa home and got her settled. On the way back to the condo, Nellie said, "*Ai, kantu tristi!* We got to do something for that poor woman."

"Maybe we can patch it up between her and Luckman somehow. But right now, it doesn't look good."

Stan and Sandralene had already gotten home.

"How was Rosa?" Stan asked.

"About as serene and cheerful as you might expect."

"Aw, Christ, Glen, lay off. I feel like shit already, okay?"

"Sorry. Sorry."

* * *

For the next two days, we tried to track down Luckman. We couldn't really go to the police, for there was no cause. And we were likewise reluctant to involve the always-questionable resources of Vin Santo. The less Vin knew about any screwups, the happier he'd be and the safer we'd be. Conveniently, we had shut down the factory on the Friday before Thanksgiving, giving all the grateful workers a full week off with pay, so we were at least free of any headaches involved in keeping the assembly line going. But even that bit of breathing room was not enough for us to find the absent professor with our amateur detective skills. So by Wednesday night, still worried about Luckman's condition more than about what he might do, insulated as we were by the all but impenetrable walls of holding companies, we gave up, turning our thoughts to the holiday.

And now the holiday was upon us. All the invitees were assembled except for Rosa, who had reassured us by phone this morning that she really did feel with it enough to drive herself and would show up by noon. It might be a bit awkward to have Stan's two women together, but we all felt we owed it to the deserted wife. I figured Stan was experienced enough to handle any scenes if a deflated and grieving Rosa were even so inclined.

The weather outside was splendid, bracing but sunny—a day made for parades and high school football games. On the garish oversize couch that Suzy Lam had installed a couple of years ago sat Uncle Ralph, Caleb, and Stan, looking like the Pep Boys and bathed in a downpouring of sunshine, drinking beers and watching the concluding segments of the Macy's parade. Lura was lying down in her bedroom, having a last-minute nap. Rosa was due to pull up any minute, with dinner to be served in about an hour.

But by twelve thirty, she had not shown.

Nor by one.

Stan looked apprehensive. I had been trying to tamp down the same feeling in myself. Sandy came out of the kitchen, wearing an apron and drying her hands on a dish towel.

"I think you should call her."

"Good idea."

The call went straight to voice mail.

Stan said, "Maybe she went down for a nap and overslept, or something. Let's go get her."

Now Nellie and Suzy were out in the living room as well. "What about the food?" I said.

Suzy Lam berated me. "You big-time koo-koo or what, nephew? Food not important; girl is! Just go!"

Caleb wanted to come, too, so the three of us set out in my car.

The drive out to the burbs where the Luckmans lived seemed like one of those nightmares in which the dreamer travels an endless road that never delivers him to the desired familiar place but instead substitutes one peril after another for the usual landmarks. If the traffic hadn't been negligible, I would have caused half a dozen accidents on the way. But eventually, we got there.

The front door was slightly ajar. We rushed in.

Rosa Luckman was dead—she had to be, lying unmoving on the carpet with what seemed a quart of blood pooled by her head, her face pale as skim milk.

Stan and Caleb moved swiftly to pick her up.

"What're you doing!" I gasped. "Don't disturb the body! The police—"

"Hey, Mr. CSI, she ain't fucking dead! She's just out. Reb, go find me a wet cloth. And some booze."

Stan tenderly bathed the ugly wound on Rosa's skull with the warm rag, then used whiskey to sterilize it. I nervously chafed her bare calves for lack of anything better to do, until Stan yelled at me to stop.

Rosa groaned and stirred, but didn't come around.

Caleb said, "I think she needs an ambulance. She's got a concussion."

Stan got up. "Guess so. I was hoping she'd wake up first and tell us what happened."

"Luckman?" I ventured.

"More'n likely."

The ambulance raced up in less than seven minutes. The EMTs had Rosa well in hand and loaded on the stretcher in jig time.

As they were wheeling her out, she did finally come around. Her not-quite-focused eyes found Stan, and she limply raised one arm.

"Wait ... please ..."

The EMTs weren't happy, but Stan had gotten a hand on the gurney to halt it. He bent his head tenderly to Rosa's lips, and she spoke so softly I couldn't hear. When she was finished, the ambulance crew took her away.

Stan's eyes smoldered, and his lips were tightly compressed. "Luckman, all right. He came back, but just for a gun. Ignored Rosa till she tried to stop him; then he slugged her."

I pictured Luckman tracking all of us down to Uncle Ralph's, showing up and blasting away. "Did she have any idea where he was headed?"

"Oh, yeah, he told her. Back to the factory, where he's been holed up since the night he took off."

50

I pulled into the parking lot adjacent to Luckman Enterprises—a shabby weed-dotted expanse of cracked asphalt and rusting stretches of fence interrupted by vandal-torn gaps. Luckman's faded blue Pontiac of ancient vintage was slewed across three spots.

None of us had been to the factory since last Friday, almost a week ago, when we had shut things down and given the staff their pay and bonuses and said, "Happy Holiday!" And in our search for the missing inventor, it had never occurred to us that he would return to such an obvious, risky place where anyone might spot him. We had pictured him blowing town in disgust at all of us, or maybe holing up in some anonymous motel under an assumed name to drink horrible liqueurs and nurse his psychic wounds. Or taking a dive off a convenient bridge into the bay. But in retrospect, we should have known that he would go to ground with the thing he loved most in the world: his detector.

Loved most behind Rosa, or before?

I got out of the car, and the others followed. The day was still beautiful, but now, transformed by the savage attack on Rosa, it possessed an air of numinous menace, like a bejeweled fish with venomous spines.

I took out my phone. "We need to tell someone where we are, in case anything happens. I'm calling Nellie."

Stan laid a hand on my arm to stop me. "No offense, dude, but your gal is too excitable. Let me tell Sandy instead."

I hadn't really been relishing informing Nellie that we had tracked down a distraught and deadly Luckman and were about to beard him in his lair, so I gave in easily. "Okay. But tell her to break the news calmly to everyone else."

Stan pulled out his phone and had a succinct conversation with Sandralene. Putting the phone away, he said, "Okay, let's go have a look at his car. Maybe we got lucky and he left the gun inside."

Luckman hadn't locked the Pontiac. No gun was visible inside. I opened the rear door because I had seen something else: a spill of white granules on the tatty fabric of the seat. From the car gushed forth a pungent, pissy odor.

"That's fertilizer," said Caleb.

"You don't think ..."

Stan said, "Oh, that's exactly what I think. Bastard's mixing up some more bomb stuff with something crazy in mind. We gotta get in there and stop him!"

"He's got a gun."

"I ain't scared of no damn university egghead with a gun or without. If he was gonna shoot us, he woulda tried something by now. Staked out the condo or like that, caught us when we pulled into our slot, all unsuspecting like."

I said, "He might react differently if we look like we're threatening him or trying to interfere."

Caleb said, "I'll go in first. Ron and I are friends. He certainly won't shoot me. You two hang back. Especially you, Stan. After that scene with you and Rosa in the restaurant, I'm pretty sure he hates your guts."

Stan clapped Caleb on the shoulder. "Takes balls, Reb. We appreciate it. But you know, this really ain't your circus, so you shouldn't be the one sweeping up the shit."

Caleb smiled grimly. "That's where you're wrong, Stan. I'm neck deep. You folks invited me into this deal, and I accepted. And what would Sandra and Nellie say if I didn't do my best to keep you guys safe?"

"All right, then. Let's do it."

I dug out my keys to the factory, and we approached the front door. But I didn't need them, because it was unlocked.

Caleb entered first. No lights were on in the entrance hall, but we could see a glow from under the office door.

Additional spilled fertilizer grains led to the office, as if in confirmation of Luckman's hiding spot. I could almost picture him toting the leaky bag—one heavy bag after another, in fact, until he had all he needed. And the place was filled with the motorway smell of diesel fuel, another component of the ANFO. On Friday, we had lowered the heat in the factory to fifty degrees for the week off, and the building was cold as an Eskimo's tomb.

Caleb flipped on the hall lights as a token of an honest, straightforward approach and called out, "Ron! It's me, Caleb! I'm coming in!"

Stan and I kept a few yards back as Caleb advanced to the office door. He opened it, but the slice of office thus revealed showed us nothing of note. Caleb stepped through the door. I waited, nerves taut as a bowstring, but no gunshot came—only conversation in low, calm tones.

In a minute or two, Caleb returned to the door. "You can come in now," he said. "Ron promised me he won't do anything bad."

Stan and I stepped tentatively into the office. My eyes went first to Luckman. The professor was half seated on a desk edge, the foot of his extended leg braced on the floor, the other bent leg dangling. He wore the same suit he had on at the dinner party, but it now resembled castoffs long inhabited by a homeless person. He had discarded his tie somewhere along the way. His stubbled, puffy face did not seem especially maniacal, but his eyes possessed a frozen determination.

In one lax hand he held a revolver that looked to be at least sixty-five-years old. But I had no doubt it could make just as big a hole as a brand-new one.

I tried to picture Luckman impulsively smacking Rosa with the gun and strained to see some evidence of it on the weapon, as if visible blood would prove to me that this nightmare was real.

I quickly sized up the rest of the room. Debris from several fast-food meals littered the conference table. Two padded chairs, pushed together, formed an improvised bed. The entire place was a mess: carpet tracked with dirt and oil, furniture shoved aside to open up a space in the middle of the room.

And in that open space sat the most anomalous thing: a fifty-five-gallon industrial drum, with electrical wires issuing from the lid. I saw now that the wires ran from the drum to Luckman's perch. As if tracking my gaze and obligingly responding to my curiosity, Luckman stood to reveal what his body had hidden: a cobbled-together box with its detonator switch.

The inventor's voice sounded defiantly proud. "Five hundred pounds of ANFO, gentlemen. The booster charge consists of all the other explosives we had lying about. It took me days to make it, even with my experience. I wish it could have been more, but it should suffice."

Caleb said, "Don't think about that now, Ron. It's all in the past. After all, you promised me."

Luckman massaged his brow with his free left hand. "Did I promise you something just now? I can't really recall what I said. I imagine I just wanted you to think me harmless, so that these other two would enter. Once you told me they were waiting outside in the hall, I knew, my prayers had been answered. The Lord has tried me, just as he tried Job and Abraham. But he is not without mercy. 'Thou preparest a table before me in the presence of mine enemies: thou anointest my head with oil; my cup runneth over.'"

Stan had plainly heard enough of this mad talk, and he took a step toward Luckman, though with hands sensibly raised as if to placate and lull the guy. Stan started to speak, but Luckman swung the revolver up with surprising speed, and his grip did not tremble. Despite the cold, I could feel myself sweating from my every pore.

"Just stay right where you are, Mr. Hasso—Stan, that is. I may still call you Stan, may I not, despite our little falling out the other night? After all, we are practically family, ever since you started fucking my wife."

Stan had stopped, and even retreated a step. Amazingly, though, his voice didn't quaver. "Listen, Luckman, that wasn't totally my idea. I'm sorry for what I did, but Rosa was more'n willing. What went down with me and your wife was ultimately all about what you had with her, which was going to pot before I ever showed up."

"Perhaps it was. But you didn't help, Mr. Hasso. Oh, no, you did not help at all. You took away my jewel. 'Who can find a virtuous woman? For her price is far above rubies. The heart of her husband doth safely trust in her, so that he shall have no need of spoil.' And yet, 'A virtuous woman is a crown to her husband: but she that maketh ashamed is as rottenness in his bones.'"

I felt I had to say something, anything, just to get Luckman's thoughts moving along other lines. "Ronald, listen to me, won't you, please? It's true that this affair was a very sad and unfortunate incident for everyone involved. You're hurting; Rosa's hurting—especially after your treatment of her today. And believe it or not, even Stan is hurting. But it's over now. You can pick up the pieces. Especially with all the money at your disposal. You and Rosa can do anything, go anywhere. You can perfect your machine—"

Luckman shouted, "Shut up! Just shut up! Why did you have to mention what I did! I hit my wife! I hit my Rosa! I don't know what came over me. I haven't slept, you know. I'm sure that's it. Just not enough sleep."

Luckman closed his eyes for a moment, and I could tell we all were calculating the odds on jumping him. But he snapped to attention again, with the gun steady in his hand and pointed at us.

"Have you seen her? Is she …?"

Caleb said, "She's okay, Ron. We had an ambulance take her to the hospital."

"Oh, thank you, Lord! My soul is not utterly blackened." Luckman turned his attention back to me. "You! Glen McClinton, with all your talk of money and wealth, profits and deals! You're almost worse than your vile, randy bull of a partner. He is a creature of foul lusts, yes. But you are wily Satan himself! You seduced me! You got me to sell my invention to the devil!"

"Oh, come on, now. La Sombra Negra—"

"They are pure evil! I learned all about them at last, once I had time and the scales fell from my eyes. They kill indiscriminately. They are as bad as the evil men they fight. And now they have exclusive possession of my machine! How could you do this to me? The name of Luckman will be forever tainted. Unless …"

Caleb said quietly, "Unless what, Ron?"

"Unless I end it all here. Shut this place down in the only effective way. What else is left for me? You two have stolen every-thing else: my woman, my invention, my reputation."

Luckman picked up the detonator box with his left hand and gazed lovingly at it. His thumb hovered over the button. I felt my stomach clench. Cold sweat trickled down my spine, yet my knees felt like warm candle wax.

"Ron," Caleb said, "the Lord frowns on a man killing himself."

"Not always. What of Ahithophel? 'And when Ahithophel saw that his counsel was not followed, he saddled his ass, and arose, and gat him home to his house, to his city, and put his household in order, and hanged himself, and died, and was buried in the sepulchre of his father.' And don't forget Saul. 'Therefore Saul took a sword, and fell upon it.'"

Even under the probable threat of imminent death, all this pious preaching and milksop dithering caught in Stan's craw.

"We having frigging Sunday School lessons now?" he said. "Christ Almighty, just blow us the fuck up and spare us the damn sermon! I said I'm sorry, and I can't do nothing else."

Luckman regarded Stan with some reluctant admiration.

"Mr. Hasso, you are not a coward, I give you that much. And so I will honor your request."

I got ready to hurl myself at Luckman. Better to die doing something than to do nothing at all.

Then Caleb spoke. His voice was calm and strong, resonant with faith.

"You quoted Psalms, Ron. Only you forgot some important parts."

Caleb's voice assumed magisterial dimensions.

"'The Lord is my shepherd; I shall not want. He maketh me to lie down in green pastures: he leadeth me beside the still waters. He restoreth my soul: he leadeth me in the paths of righteousness for his name's sake. Yea, though I walk through the valley of the shadow of death, I will fear no evil: for thou art with me; thy rod and thy staff they comfort me. Thou preparest a table before me in the presence of mine enemies: thou anointest my head with oil; my cup runneth over. Surely goodness and mercy shall follow me all the days of my life: and I will dwell in the house of the Lord for ever.'"

When Caleb stopped speaking, the silence manifested the solidity of a mountain. I felt a timeless moment of forever—which ceased with Caleb's next utterance.

"Now, Ron, hearing those words, do what you feel you must."

Luckman's face contorted. "To dwell in the house of the Lord forever. That was all I really wanted."

Caleb stepped toward Luckman, arms spread wide to embrace him. At the same time, he turned his head to us and mouthed, *Go!*

Stan, however, moved to join Caleb in his advance. Frightened, Luckman snapped off a round that went wide of any target, but the immense report of the gun stopped us all.

"Ron, don't fight me. Show the Lord's mercy on these men. On yourself. Turn the other cheek."

Luckman started to weep. But he did not release the gun or the box.

Caleb's voice was strangled, imperative. "Get out of here! Ron and I need to talk."

Stan and I both hesitated. Then Stan said, "Talk him down, Reb. We'll be right outside."

As we moved slowly toward the office door, Caleb closed the gap with Luckman, who allowed himself to be enfolded in the big man's embrace.

Outside, the sunlight and open air were the sweetest gifts ever bestowed on a mortal. Stan and I crossed to the far side of the street, then retreated some distance farther.

Stan's jeep barreled around a corner, Sandralene at the wheel, Nellie beside her. It screeched to a stop, and the women jumped out. We hugged, and I recounted everything.

With her fierce and ardent yet impassive determination, Sandy said, "I'm going in there to help Caleb. I know I can."

"No, no, honey," Stan said. "Believe me, Luckman won't listen to no one but Johnny Reb. We just have to wait it out."

There was movement at the factory door. Caleb and Luckman appeared in the entrance, arms around each other's waist. Caleb looked joyous, Luckman ashamed and repentant. I was reminded of those arcadian pictures in the literature from the Jehovah's Witnesses, depicting a postcivilized paradise on Earth, with children petting tigers and lions.

And then the bomb went off.

EPILOGUE

Uncle Ralph's cramped, too-warm house was filled with delicious smells: turkey, vegetables, pies. A big bowl of *doce de café* took pride of place on the side table of desserts.

Sitting at the dining-room table, waiting for Uncle Ralph to bring the turkey from the kitchen, I had a moment of mind-blanking déjà vu, a feeling that I would yet be compelled to live all over again the mortal crisis at the factory, experience endlessly all the dread and fear. But then the eerie sensation passed, and here I was, in the present.

Two weeks had gone by since the explosion at Luckman Enterprises. I had stopped picking splinters out of my hair after the first three days. The five-hundred-pound bomb alone would not have been enough to destroy the building utterly. Even with seven thousand pounds, Timothy McVeigh had inflicted only partial damage to the building in Oklahoma City. But the old wood-raftered building had gone up like a pile of straw. The leftover diesel fuel that Luckman had stored (and spilled) further stoked the conflagration.

Stan, Nellie, Sandy, and I had been hurled to the pavement. The tremendous noise seemed almost more potent than the force of the blast. When we picked ourselves up, the building's facade was already wreathed in smoke and flames.

Sandralene made a heartbreaking sound I would have said she was incapable of. It was a helpless whimpering squeal. But only that one animal cry, that one failure of her core of strength, that one eruption of despair and grief came out of her. Then she pulled herself together and had the presence of mind to call 911.

By the time the first fire trucks arrived, the factory was an unquenchable inferno.

Caleb and Luckman were simply gone. The finished inventory of LBAS units, for which La Sombra Negra would have paid us good money, was gone. (Luckily, Crespo had taken possession of the first thousand, which were already on their way to El Salvador.) All the remaining counterfeit chips that could have made additional profitable units were gone. And, of course, Luckman's expertise, such as it was, and his schematics for the LBAS were gone as well.

And in the parking lot, even my Lexus was gone, a separate pyre in tribute to Luckman's insane and ultimately accidental auto-da-fé.

Man, I really did like that car.

Luckman's lack of inventorly skill had extended even to his bomb making—although, to be fair, the materials he was working with were notoriously unstable.

We never did recover a single shred of either body. It seemed fitting somehow, as if they both had been transubstantiated heavenward, like the resurrected Jesus when he finally left his apostles. And Caleb's relatives proved to be as impossible to find as his mortal remains. Even Mama Lura's familiarity with the genealogy of Hedgesville failed us.

The police, of course, had swiftly followed the firefighters, and certain lines of questioning began to feel particularly sticky. Which is, fortunately, where Vin Santo stepped in.

But at a cost.

The final meeting that Stan and I endured with the mob boss, just a couple of days ago, had none of the bonhomie and good cheer of our previous encounters. We entered not knowing whether we would emerge in the same condition.

Behind his desk, Santo regarded us with the expression of a father who has seen his favorite son arrested for screwing a dog on the courthouse steps—and an underage dog at that. When he drank from his Big Gulp, he managed to invest the act with all the tragic gravitas of Lee surrendering his sword to Grant at Appomattox. The two goons at the door radiated a chill just above zero degrees Kelvin.

"Boys, boys, boys. Tell me what you think I should do with the two of you. What would your impulses be if you were me?"

Stan said, "Maybe you wanna congratulate us on getting outta that fucking catastrophe alive."

Santo's smile was crocodilian. "That is not my first instinct, no. I had in mind something more like arranging a one-way trip to the bogs. They tell me that once a stiff is planted deep into that muck, you can dig him up a hundred years later and he's still recognizable, even if he does look like Clint Eastwood at ninety."

"Vin," I said, "are you forgetting that we were responsible for raking in thirty million dollars? Even if we were not able to realize one hundred percent of the potential profits from those fake Intel chips, we still brought you more than you would have gotten by just dumping them raw on the market."

"Right, right, how could I forget? Thirty million, you say? Like that amount went straight into my pocket! Maybe you got some notion of what your little escapade has cost me?"

"Vin, we know there were some collateral expenses—"

"Your idea of 'collateral expenses' is very amusing to me. Let me run them down. Out of that thirty million, it has taken me six to satisfy Rosa Luckman. She is now a very contented widow and averse to pursuing any further damages. Or so her high-priced mouthpiece assures me, in writing. Then there was the landlord of your temporary place of business, who was naturally kinda disconcerted to find himself the owner of a pile of steaming ashes instead of a dated though still quite serviceable light-industrial building. He needed three million to restore his happiness—a distinctly outrageous number given current real estate values in that district, but he had me over the proverbial barrel. Or, at least, his insurance company did. Those bastards are the worst criminals I have ever met. Next, I came face-to-face with the various outstretched hands among our police and politician friends—hands that we needed to grease if we intended to make this whole affair go away. I will not tell you the actual numbers involved, because it reflects poorly on the public spirit of our civil servants and elected officials. But to make a long story short, my own share, which, you recall, was going to be about fifteen million, has been reduced to eight. This is not the kind of adjustment I generally favor."

I couldn't believe Stan's next words.

"What's left for us?"

Santo's jaw dropped. "You really think I am going to share my woefully reduced take with the *authors* of that reduction?"

Stan persisted. "Glen and I were due three million apiece. But since Danssaert and Qiao got to split three mil, we'll settle for that."

"Why don't you try for a clawback from them? I expect you would get nothing but rude laughter."

"Oh, no, they earned it. And so did we. Sure, there was a major fuckup at the end—out of which we all came clean—but we held up our side of the bargain, and you need to hold up yours. Or do you want the whole city to know that Vin Santo welshes on his deals?"

Santo took another swig of his soda while considering Stan's words.

"There's always the bogs."

"Oh, forget that shit! You know we can be useful to you in the future. Why throw away a good thing?"

"*Humph!* A 'good thing.'" More suckling at the straw. Then he said, "I am gifting you each, out of the sheer goodness of my heart, six hundred thousand apiece. Just because I like you both and realize that you are not entirely to blame. And because maybe there is something to what you say about being of future use to me."

Once I had resumed breathing, I said, "We appreciate all your hard work, Vin, and we'll take the money with thanks."

"Go now, and never darken my doorstep again—until you got another scam that is a thousand times more foolproof, which I could maybe decide to back."

Back outside in Stan's Jeep—the star-spangled roof was dented in where the explosion lobbed a brick missile onto it—I said, "We could've done a lot worse."

"I don't know. Sometimes, the thought of lying down in the marshes for a long, restful nap doesn't seem so bad."

The women brushed off the bad financial news as if it didn't even matter. Which, I kept telling myself, it really didn't, even as I continued wistfully counting and recounting all the imaginary money I would never see.

And so here we all were, seated around the table, its surface crowded with steaming dishes, having our belated Thanksgiving with, I must admit, some things to be genuinely thankful for.

I found myself taking in with fresh appreciation the vivid living presence of all the people around the table, gathered here to celebrate one of the best holidays, to make a new tradition, despite all the troubles and challenges they had faced and surmounted. Stan and I finding our mad, greedy scheme gone kerflooey. Nellie striving to make the most of her heritage and become independent. Sandralene coping with her mother's old age. Ralph and Suzy taking Mama Lura into their home. No one had quit striving in the face of setbacks and selfish missteps. Lovers had betrayed each other, yielding to the demands of the flesh and wild, impulsive affections. But somehow, after getting bumped out of their orbits, the various sets of twinned planets had returned to the central luminary of love. I wondered what would have happened had I not gone to Cape Verde to get Nellie back. Where would I be sitting today? Thankfully, I didn't have to face that alternate, doubtless sadder reality. Imperfect as they—as we—all were, unbreakable bonds had been forged that drew us together today. I knew I didn't really deserve any of these good outcomes, but I sure as hell wasn't about to turn them down.

Uncle Ralph, Suzy Lam, Stan, Nellie, Mama Lura, and I looked up when Sandy emerged from the kitchen, carrying a perfectly cooked golden bird on its platter. She brought it to the head of the table, where an empty chair stood with a black sash draped across its back.

Sandralene set the platter down and looked at us all with a solemn and compelling gaze.

"I knew Caleb Stinchcombe since we were three years old," she said. "He was a very good man. He has earned a minute of silence from us, at the very least."

Mama Lura began to sniffle, and I felt my own eyes well up. That poor unfortunate bastard Caleb had made us his family, and now we would have to keep his memory alive.

I looked to Stan. I don't believe I had ever seen him actually appear reverential before. But I suspected that his feelings were more for the awesome magnificence of his woman than for the departed soul of his erstwhile rival.

The minute of silence ended, and Sandy picked up the carving knife and fork.

"Who wants what? And don't be shy!"